UNTIL THE DEBT IS PAID

ALEXANDER HARTUNG
UNTIL THE DEBT IS PAID

TRANSLATED BY
STEVE ANDERSON

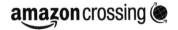

Text copyright © 2013 Alexander Hartung
Translation copyright © 2014 by Steve Anderson

Previously published as *Bis alle Schuld beglichen* by the author in Germany. Translated from German by Steve Anderson.

Published by AmazonCrossing, Seattle

www.apub.com

Amazon, the Amazon logo, and AmazonCrossing are trademarks of Amazon.com, Inc., or its affiliates.

ISBN-13: 9781477826072
ISBN-10: 1477826076

Cover design by Marc Cohen

Library of Congress Control Number: 2014909557

Printed in the United States of America

For my son, Philipp.
I didn't know what happiness was until
I got to hold you in my arms the first time.

Prologue

Pain jolted George out of unconsciousness. He glanced down at his lower leg and whimpered at the sight of his own shattered, exposed bone. A dark, sticky pool of blood had collected beneath him. His cheek pressed against the cold tiles of his living-room floor.

He had arrived home that night in the usual way, hanging his overcoat on the rack before going into the living room to pour himself a scotch. All he'd wanted was a strong drink and the sports channel's late-night show, nothing more.

The last thing he remembered was reaching for a glass. Then nothing. Until now.

George turned his head and looked at the clock on the bookshelf. Just before midnight. He had been passed out for an hour. Disoriented, he tried to make sense of the situation. Perhaps he'd managed to slip and fall on his leg in this horrible way. Or perhaps someone had robbed him? His eyes darted to the huge flat-screen, still in its spot, and the two valuable paintings on the opposite wall. None of it made sense. But one thing was certain: he needed help.

He patted his suit pants for his cell phone and noticed its absence. He always kept it in his right pocket. Maybe he'd lost it as he'd fallen. Or had he left it up on the counter? He shut his eyes and cursed. Today was not his day.

Then he heard music. Soft, barely audible strings accompanied by a baritone's sad song. George turned his head to look at the stereo. White pillar candles had been placed on the speakers. They lit the room with a hazy glow and gave off a subtle vanilla scent.

George gathered the fabric of his pant leg in one hand and tried to move his broken leg. The pain brought tears to his eyes, but he managed to turn onto his back.

The house was dark except for the living room. He could have sworn that he'd turned on the lights in the hallway.

"Hello?" he shouted into the darkness.

It was silent. For a moment more.

Then the sound of heavy boots began to echo off the tiles. Slowly at first, then faster. A moment later, a figure loomed over him, wearing black pants, a leather jacket, and a stocking mask.

"What the hell . . ." George began. Then the figure lunged and brought down a hammer with brute force onto his arm. Bones cracked with a loud crunch.

George screamed. The pain almost robbed him of his senses. Stars danced before his eyes. He bit his lower lip and felt blood flowing into his mouth.

When he dared open his eyes again, he was alone. He cursed the vast, manicured grounds around his house. The walls surrounding his elegant garden stopped sound from traveling beyond them. No one would hear him screaming. And the cleaning woman wouldn't be coming until early the next morning.

The steps sounded again. A moment later, George saw military boots shining in the hazy candlelight. He began to cry.

"Please," he begged, raising his good arm over his head in defense. "I'll give you everything I have. Money, my little stash of gold, the car. I have a numbered account in Switzerland. There's a hundred thousand euros in it."

The figure didn't move. George lowered his arm and stared at the boots.

At that moment, he knew that he was going to die. His attacker only wanted to see him suffer before beating in his skull. With his shattered arm and broken leg, he had no chance of defending himself. His only hope was the alarm button near the entry.

It was the type of system that banks and businesses installed. After a colleague's home had been violently broken into, he'd equipped his place with the alarm as protection. If there were ever trouble, a push of the button was all it would take to immediately inform the police of an intruder. There were two spots in the house where he could trigger the alarm. One in the bedroom. The other in the hallway.

George pictured the button in the hallway. To anyone else's eyes it would look inconspicuous, almost like a light switch. He estimated it would take three big steps to get there. The intruder stood next to him, to the right. The path was to his left and clear. If his leg weren't broken he might make it, but the pain was unbearable. Moving quickly was out of the question.

"What did I do?" George said, hoping to distract the intruder by talking. He pulled himself to a sitting position. "If I've given too harsh of a verdict, I'll help you get out of it. I'll talk to the state prosecutor or your parole officer. I have connections in politics. I'll make this right again."

The figure still did not move.

George shifted his weight onto his healthy leg. His eyes went to the alarm button. Two leaps, on one leg. Then he could let himself fall forward on the third leap and trigger the alarm. Ignore the pain. Keep going. No matter what happens. Just one chance.

George heaved himself up. Excruciating pain tore through his right side. He cried out in distress but hopped forward, flailing with his good arm to keep his balance. He mustered all his strength and landed a second leap, although the shock of impact made him gasp. One more.

And then the hammer came down on his good leg. His knee broke with a loud crack. George fell to the floor and his head hit the tiles. His shrieking became an inhuman squeal.

The figure lowered its masked face until they were separated by only a few inches.

"How does it feel?" the figure said softly. "Lying helpless on the floor while getting all beat up? Is that fun?"

George squinted, surprised. He knew the voice. For a moment, memories blocked out his pain. Could it be? After all these years?

He opened his mouth. "Is it really you?" he wanted to ask, but the hammer came cracking down on his forehead. Then he slid into darkness, never again to waken.

Chapter 1

Jan instantly regretted opening his eyes. His skull throbbed, and his lips were sticky. His mouth was dry, and the glare of the morning light stung his eyes. He lay naked in a large bed. A thin linen sheet covered his legs. Betty's head lay on his chest, her arms wrapped around a pillow. He wished he were still sleeping. Then he wouldn't be worrying about the bitter taste in his mouth or that horrible, thudding pain in his head.

As he lay there feeling miserable, the intoxicatingly fresh smell of Betty's hair filled his nostrils. He gazed at her delicate nose and the gentle curve of her lips. From the first moment, he had fallen for the easy way her grown-up cleverness paired with her little-girl smile. Even asleep she was smiling.

Betty's doorbell rang and sent flashes of pain through Jan's skull. He turned to her alarm clock, which read 9:23 a.m. It was before ten on a Saturday morning in Berlin, a city where weekend carousing was normally respected. Who was dragging him out of bed at a time like this?

Jan gently nudged Betty's head to the side, and she rolled over sleepily, clutching the pillow more tightly. He sat up and put his feet on the cold tiles, but he had trouble trying to stand. The room spun around him, making him brace himself on the nightstand. He grabbed his pants from a chair. Standing on one leg while trying to put them on proved to be a struggle.

"Damn cocktails," he muttered, shaking his head. The second ring made him groan.

"I'm coming already!" he shouted. He dared a brief look in the mirror on his way to the door. The reflection did not help his mood: tired eyes, hair askew, bulging spare tire around his middle from too much good living. He unlocked the door and yanked it open. Someone this pushy better have a real good reason.

"Pat?" Jan asked in surprise. "What are you doing here?"

His fellow officer Patrick Stein stood in the hallway in a dark suit, with two uniformed cops behind him. He was the last person Jan would've expected. Patrick's hair was combed to the side with pomade, and his dark, tailored suit featured an old-fashioned pocket square. His look reminded Jan of the Berlin Comedian Harmonists, the all-male singing group that did tunes from the 1930s and was so inexplicably popular.

Pat had joined Jan's homicide squad a few years back. They worked well enough together, but it was obvious they didn't especially like each other. Jan thought Patrick was a smug busybody, and Patrick in turn viewed Jan as an undisciplined thug more suited to a SWAT team than a police investigation. Plus, he didn't like being called Pat.

"We have a new murder case," Patrick told him. Jan could have sworn he sensed a little schadenfreude showing through Patrick's normally contained expression as he raked his gaze over Jan's disheveled state.

"And we got nine homicide squads on the force," Jan grumbled. "Couldn't an on-call team fill in? It's Saturday morning. Can't you leave a guy in peace with his girl?"

"It's Sunday morning," Patrick noted, smiling. "Perhaps you should lay off the alcohol?" His amusement was real this time.

"What?" Jan groaned.

So what had he been doing yesterday? He and Betty had gone to Newton Bar on Friday and gotten drunk on raspberry coladas. There were none better in Berlin. He remembered calling for a taxi and staggering up the stairs to Betty's apartment. He had his share of mental lapses, but he had never lost a whole day.

"Why didn't you guys call me on my cell?"

"It's off."

"So how did you find me?"

"We put out a search on your car."

"You're shitting me, right?" Jan flared up. "What case would make you guys come looking for me? This has got to be a joke."

"Do I look like I'd be making jokes?"

"Hmm," Jan muttered. "You have a point." Patrick had the same pinched face and tense attitude as usual. Thinking back, Jan could not remember his colleague ever making a joke. Probably even ironed his underwear.

"I'll get dressed real quick and come in to the office. When's the team meeting?"

"Had it an hour ago. Everyone assigned to the homicide squad is on the case. I'm only here because your car was spotted at the scene of the crime, yesterday."

"My car?" Jan was dumbfounded.

Patrick nodded.

Jan rubbed his temple. If they gave trophies for the shittiest morning, he'd be winning in all categories today.

"Who the hell was murdered? And where? And what does my car have to do with it? It's been parked out front since Friday morning."

"Can't say."

"There a hidden camera around here somewhere?"

"As you yourself noted, I don't really do jokes."

Jan's brain was slowly waking up. "So, if there was a search put out for my car and you can't tell me anything, that means . . ."

"That you are one of the suspects."

Jan leaned on the doorframe. The throbbing pain in his head had teamed up with a horrible twisting in his stomach.

"Officers will take you down to the station. Herr Bergman wants a few words with you."

Jan raised his hands. "Okay, guys. I know you're not supposed to let me out of your sight, but please wait here a second. I'm leaving the door open, grabbing my cell, and getting dressed."

The uniformed cops hesitated. Then Patrick gave a slight nod.

"Thanks." Jan hurried inside. He pulled on his shirt. It smelled of smoke and sweat, but he had nothing else to put on. He sat on the bed and slipped into his Bikkembergs.

A sigh sounded from under Betty's blonde mane of hair.

"Jan?" she said wearily. "What is it? Who you talking to?"

"Nothing, honey," he said, playing it down. "Just an urgent case. I have to go, but I'll call you tonight and tell you all about it."

"Don't go yet," she said, laying her head on his arm. Feeling the warmth of her cheek, he was tempted just to lie back down again. He wanted to watch her fall back asleep, gaze at her chest as it swelled, and adore her beauty. It made his body ache to resist the urge, but he had to sort out this allegation and investigate what his car had to do with it. He caressed her back, kissed her on the forehead, and pulled himself away from her.

"Till tonight," he whispered. Then he grabbed his cell and stood.

Patrick and the two uniformed cops were waiting at the door. The pain in Jan's head had not gotten any better, but the weariness had gone away. He was a suspect in a murder case. It couldn't get any worse than that.

•   •

Jan got some coffee from the machine and added four packets of fake sugar. He took a big gulp and pulled a face in disgust. What was so hard about making coffee that didn't taste like metal and peat moss? He tossed most of it down the drain and set the cup in the dishwasher. He couldn't remember the Criminal Investigations Division offices ever having been so quiet. His colleagues in the newly created homicide squad—Team Judge—were still at the crime scene, while the on-call guys were doing time in their offices. Jan pulled down a glass, filled it with water, and took a swig. The strange taste in his mouth remained. He still felt wiped out, as if he'd slept only a couple of hours. He had no memory of the previous day—everything from dawn to dusk had been erased. If only he could catch up on his sleep. Then he'd be his good old self again.

His stomach made a desperate noise. He'd give a month's salary for a decent breakfast.

"Jan." His boss's voice echoed down the hallway. That one word told Jan the man's mood. He turned around and looked into the scowling face of Klaus Bergman. He was chief of detectives, had a law degree, and usually wore the surly expression of a man who had no use for laughter. His tense, lined face looked even more indignant than usual. As always, he wore a dark suit, laced-up wingtips, and a blue tie a bit loose at the neck. His dark hair was in messy tufts, as if he hadn't gotten enough time for his morning grooming ritual. A rare spectacle, Jan thought, given his boss's meticulous habits.

"Interrogation room," Bergman barked at him. Jan fought an urge to salute and followed. He hated the interrogation room. It

9

had no windows and only one table, with four chairs that had seen better days. The air conditioning squeaked, and that glaring fluorescent lighting made his eyes water. Bergman plunked his notebook on the table and pulled a golden fountain pen from his jacket as Jan sat down across from him. It was an odd feeling to be on the other side. He was supposed to be the one doing the questioning.

"I'm in no mood right now for creating a nice vibe, making a connection with the person questioned, or any of that bullshit," Bergman began. "I have the video camera off, so if you don't tell me everything—"

Jan cut him off. "Why in the hell am I here?"

"What did Stein tell you?"

"Only that my vehicle was spotted at the crime scene and I'm a suspect."

"Where were you yesterday evening?"

"I don't know."

"What's that supposed to mean?"

"It means that I don't know," Jan replied, irritated now.

"This is starting off real well," Bergman grumbled.

"What's the gist of it?"

"George Holoch was discovered dead this morning. Cleaning woman found him."

"George Holoch the judge?"

"The same judge who ruled against you for assault on duty and screwed your chances of advancing a pay grade."

"I haven't even seen him for over two years."

"So why did they identify your car at his house?"

"My car?"

"Holoch's neighbor called the police because your BMW was blocking his driveway and he was barely able to get into his garage. When the tow truck got there around midnight, the car was gone

10

again. Which brings me back to my first question: Where were you yesterday evening?"

Jan, weary, rubbed his face. "I don't know. Friday night I went to my girlfriend's in Charlottenburg. Then we went to Newton Bar and drank to her passing her medical exams. I do know we took a taxi home. The next thing I remember was this morning."

"You had a mental blackout lasting thirty-six hours? What the hell were you taking?"

"I wasn't taking anything," Jan replied. "Okay, I may have one too many sometimes, but I'm clean otherwise."

"You seen yourself in the mirror? Look me in the eyes and tell me that again."

"Damn it." Jan pounded on the table. "What am I supposed to do now?"

"Homicide squad is still at Holoch's house. They found blood. Probably from the murderer. We'll get a DNA sample from you, then compare it with what we found. That way we'll keep you out of the woods. Once the crime scene is secure, KT will examine your car."

KT was the *Kompetenzzentrum Kriminaltechnik.* The department's crime-scene investigators. Real clever people who knew their way around securing evidence, analyzing DNA, and investigating ballistics, among other things. If someone else had used his car, they would find out.

Bergman stood and opened the door. "Ricky," he shouted into the hallway and slammed the door shut again. He wrote something in his notebook without sitting back down. A moment later Richard Matiak entered the room. One of the best crime-scene tech guys in KT. His graying hair and beard made him look ten years older than he really was. For no apparent reason he always wore a white lab coat, giving him that mad-scientist look. He had an IQ of 150 but no friends apart from his computer. Today, as usual, he had his briefcase with him, which he cherished like his only child. The big silver block probably didn't even leave his side while he was sleeping.

"DNA profile, full blood work," Bergman ordered.

"Why blood work?" Jan asked. "Isn't it enough that—"

"I'm done discussing it," Bergman interrupted. "If you can't remember anything, we'll have to know what got you there."

Jan sighed. He was no wimp, but he hated having a syringe stuck in his arm and the thought of blood leaving his body in a tube. Having blood taken always made him shudder.

Richard smiled and unwrapped a syringe. Jan looked away, trying to act detached as the blood drew out into the tube. Richard pulled out the needle and stuck a little teddy-bear Band-Aid on Jan's arm.

"Should I analyze the shirt too?" Richard asked.

Bergman raised his head. "Why the shirt?"

"For blood traces." Richard pointed at a sleeve. Jan had pulled on his blue shirt in a hurry. He hadn't noticed the spot, but now he saw it too. Blood. No doubt about it.

"Jan," Bergman said, shutting his eyes a moment. He was obviously struggling to control himself. "I hope for your sake that's just the result of some jostling around in the pub."

Jan pulled off his shirt and stuffed it into the sterile plastic bag Richard had conjured up from his case.

"I want to see something by this evening, Ricky," Bergman said.

The crime-scene tech nodded, packed up his stuff, and left.

Jan shivered. He had on only pants and a pair of sneakers. He didn't want to think about that weird taste in his mouth, which was still there. Something that not even metallic vending-machine coffee could wash away? This had to be the nastiest hangover of his life.

"Go into my office and get my overcoat," Bergman ordered without lifting his head. "It better not pick up that smell you have.

The thing is made of cashmere, so be careful. Then take a taxi home, shower, and get dressed. Be back here in an hour. If you are even one minute late, I'll call Special Ops and have you picked up by armored car. You do know that I'm supposed to be keeping you here."

Jan stood up. "Thanks, boss."

He rushed into Bergman's office. The area rug and leather chair in the corner gave the room a distinguished air. Papers lay in stacks on the desk. Bergman seemed to always be working on ten cases at a time, and yet it all looked so orderly. He spotted the overcoat on a stand behind the door. It was at least a size too big for Jan, but he pulled it on. He paused at his reflection in the office's plate-glass window and swore. He looked like a vagrant. He left the station, sulking, and headed for the nearest taxi stand. An hour was not much time, but he was looking forward to a change of clothes. Then, he would find out what his car had been doing at the crime scene.

•   •

Jan hurried up the stairs to his apartment. On the second floor, he ran into Father Anberger. The priest was retired now and just went by Hinrich, but he'd retained his priestly dignity, so to Jan, he was still Father.

"Good morning, Father Anberger." He liked the old man. Hinrich was balding and combed his gray hair from right to left, covering the bare spots. His kindly smile showed through his full white beard. His black trousers were neatly ironed, as usual, and his dark shirt was decked out with a white collar. He always started off on a stroll through his former parish around this time of day, his fellow citizens' well-being remaining dear to his heart. Church, it

13

wasn't Jan's deal. Father Anberger was the only reason he was still a member.

Jan's time on the homicide squad had turned him hard-nosed and cynical. Sometimes he couldn't believe what humans were capable of. Yet Father Anberger, with his naive belief in good, had always been able to convince Jan that evil received just punishment in the end.

Jan felt awkward standing before his neighbor in his clearly disheveled state, but he didn't sense any condemnation in the priest's eyes. Hinrich took people as they were.

"Good morning, Herr Tommen." His warm voice greeted Jan. "Must we go to work today already?"

"Good never rests," Jan said, keeping it light.

Hinrich rewarded the joke with a polite laugh.

"We have a new case, unfortunately," Jan continued. "You'll read about it tomorrow in the papers, but right now I have to go get changed." And get off this scratchy overcoat, he thought to himself.

"Then I wish you much success hunting the criminals," Father Anberger said and continued on his way.

Jan hurried into his apartment. He'd pulled off the overcoat before the door even shut. He set it on a chair and started scratching himself all over. Either the overcoat was from the crappiest cashmere in the world, or his boss was using itching powder to clean it.

Happy to be rid of the thing, Jan opened the fridge, drank a big gulp of milk, and stuffed the last of a dark-chocolate bar in his mouth. He sighed with satisfaction. His impatient stomach calmed, and his knees stopped shaking. He drank down more milk and grabbed his cell from his pants pocket. He tapped the Favorites icon, turning to the kitchen window. This hazy Sunday was perfect for staying in bed. But instead he was a suspect in a murder case and wracking his brain as to what he'd been doing for the last thirty-six hours. He wondered if he should ask Betty about it—but then he'd have to tell her he was suspected of a murder. She was such a sensitive soul and took everything to heart. He didn't want to upset her. Besides, the DNA test would clear him, and the car thing would get resolved. He'd be back at her place that evening. Then all would be good again.

After the third ring, she picked up.

"Jan?" Her voice sounded sleepy. "Is that you?"

"Yeah, Aphro," he said tenderly. Aphro was short for Aphrodite. He'd given her the nickname because of her wonderfully long hair and her passion for Greek mythology. Her living room looked like a bad Greek restaurant: there were little statues everywhere that she'd brought back from vacations. She devoured so many books on the subject that Jan sometimes wondered if maybe a degree in history would have been a better choice for her than medicine.

"I just wanted to say, we have a new case. I'm going to have to work today."

"How come murderers always kill on weekends? It couldn't wait till Monday?"

Jan laughed. "I wish it was that way. It could have been such a nice weekend."

"It was a nice weekend," she whispered suggestively.

Jan's resolve was waning. The thought of Betty lolling around in bed, waiting for him, made his pulse quicken. For a second he was tempted to ride the subway back to her place.

She sighed. "Where are you now?"

"I went home to change. I have to leave again right away. I don't think our cozy little dinner is going to happen."

"Too bad," she said seductively. Jan gritted his teeth. He had to hang up now, otherwise he'd decide to head over there immediately. And his career in homicide would be done. He wouldn't even be allowed to write parking tickets.

"I have to go. Love you, Aphro."

"Same to you." And she hung up.

Jan pulled off his shoes and pants. He rushed into the bathroom, turned on a cold shower, and stepped in. He let the water run over his head, almost yelping as the cold forced the anxiety from his body. He waited a moment before turning up the temperature. By the time warm water started coming through the shower jets, he was beginning to think clearly again. Later, he'd get Betty to tell him what they'd done on Saturday—he'd find a way to ask without bringing up his memory lapse. But what mattered first was finding out more about the dead judge. It was a shitty feeling, being a murder suspect.

• •

Jan was back at the station promptly an hour later. Knowing Bergman, being late would have brought serious consequences. In Jan's absence, the homicide squad had requisitioned the largest conference room for the investigation. Laptops were set up, whiteboards scribbled on, and the first crime-scene photos printed out and scattered across the big table. Jan knew he wasn't allowed to go inside—he wasn't even supposed to be near the room—but he risked a quick glance at the images anyway.

The judge had been finished off in a nasty way. He was lying on his back on the tiled floor of a living room. His mouth was open, as if in one last cry of pain. His bones had been beaten to pulp. On his forehead was a large laceration, which looked to be the cause of death. From there, blood had run down his face, gathering into a gooey puddle at his chin. It was clear this had been no easy death.

"Jan," Bergman's voice thundered down the corridor.

Jan stopped looking and dashed into Bergman's office. "Your coat," Jan said and placed it over the back of a chair. "Thanks a lot."

Bergman's eyes scrutinized the fabric. "KT hasn't reported in yet, but as long as I don't have those DNA results, you won't be leaving the station. Not even to buy yourself a kebab. Sit yourself down, do some work or surf the Internet, but don't go snooping around. I want this to go off without a hitch. Once the blood work clears you, you can move freely again."

Jan nodded. Bergman was a short-tempered boss who constantly criticized and harassed Jan and everyone else in the office. He sometimes took out his frustrations by flinging things against the walls in his office. He always showed up when he wasn't needed. He'd never praised Jan, although he'd threatened him with death by strangulation more than once. In short, he could be a nightmare. But when push came to shove, Bergman was actually as protective as a mother wolf. He loved every one of his people, even though he'd never admit it, and shielded them from overzealous judges, lawyers, and journalists. It was a relief to know that Bergman trusted him without reservation.

"Thanks for believing me. It's good to—"

"Don't go all sentimental on me," Bergman interrupted. "I just have too much to do—otherwise I'd be all over your ass. So get your butt out of here and make yourself invisible."

Jan went out grinning. There were some things you could simply rely on.

On the way to his desk, it was all he could do not to head into the squad room and read the interim report. Still, he didn't want to make things difficult for his fellow detectives or endanger the case, so he sat down at his desk and started up the computer. He smiled at the sight of his new screensaver, a stormy landscape photo featuring a mint condition Harley-Davidson. Jan clicked open the sports page and read the weekend's results. He squinted at the tiny font used for the soccer scores and almost reached for his glasses, but resisted. They made him look five years older.

After he got caught up on the Bundesliga standings, he opened his e-mail. Access to Google Mail, GMX, and Web.de were blocked on the office computers, but his hacker buddy Max had told him how to get around the ban using an anonymizer. Jan had no idea what that was, but it was easy to use, and it worked. He loved being able to check his private e-mail whenever he wanted. Smiling, he wrote a message to Aphrodite1988. Betty had set up the account just for him.

As he did so, he yawned wide. Sunday afternoon. There was no time more lazy. Normally if he wasn't sleeping, he'd be hanging around Betty's or watching a DVD. He sent the e-mail and closed the program. Tired again, he laid his arms on the desktop, lowered his head, and closed his eyes. A moment later, he was fast asleep.

• •

Klaus Bergman clicked through the crime-scene photos. Whoever murdered George Holoch must have really hated the judge. The autopsy wasn't complete, but it was looking like hardly one single bone in the corpse had been left intact. According to the initial forensics exam, many of the blows had been administered postmortem. So the murderer had beaten Judge Holoch to death and then run riot on his corpse.

The phone rang. Bergman lifted the receiver without looking from the screen. "Bergman," he barked. He listened to the report.

"Is that certain?" he asked. "Did you verify?"

The caller confirmed it.

"All right." Bergman hung up. He exhaled long and loud. Irate, he flung the phone from the desk. He shot up and kicked the chair, which clattered and crashed against the bookshelf. "Goddamn it!" he roared and stormed out of his office.

Jan's head shot up with a start as Bergman's fist reverberated on his desk.

"Wake up!" his boss shouted.

Jan took in the sight of Bergman standing before him, his hands planted on his sides. The man's mood had clearly not improved.

"The results finally in?" Jan asked drowsily.

"Yes."

"Can I go back home now?"

Bergman removed his glasses and leveled a gaze at Jan that mixed rage and disappointment. The man was wrestling for self-control. Jan had never seen him this way.

"Your DNA is consistent with the blood at the crime scene."

Jan's heart cramped tight. The breakfast in his gut tried to find its way back up.

"Did you get the results verified?"

"Twice," Bergman replied. "That's not the only thing. The blood spot on your shirt is the victim's."

Bergman sat down and plunked his notebook on the table. "The state prosecutor has needed less to put people behind bars for life. I suggest you start explaining."

"I don't know what happened!" Jan bellowed in frustration.

"Don't give me that bullshit," Bergman shot back just as loud.

"You have to believe me," Jan said. He could understand Bergman's anger. The man had picked him out of the detective force for the homicide squad. He'd always helped Jan when he'd fucked up before. But now evidence showed Jan was a murderer. What choice did Bergman have? He'd have to throw Jan in prison.

"You know I drink one too many now and then, but I've never blacked out."

Bergman opened his notebook. "We tested your blood for controlled substances. Besides alcohol, large amounts of MDMA turned up."

Jan cursed under his breath. MDMA. Methylenedioxy-something-or-other. What the hell had happened to him yesterday? He didn't take hard drugs. He'd seen enough people ruined by the shit. He never would have gotten drunk enough to want to swallow ecstasy.

"Maybe someone put something in my drink."

"Sure. And on top of that, he took your blood and spread it around the crime scene. After that, he took the victim's blood, went back into the bar, and squirted that onto your shirt, all while he was parking your car over at Holoch's neighbor's."

"We have to call my girlfriend," Jan pleaded. "I spent the whole weekend at her place."

"And what good would that do us?"

"She can tell me what I was doing yesterday evening."

"I don't think you're getting it, Jan. Even if your girlfriend herself swears on her life that you were at her place the whole day yesterday, it changes nothing. The evidence is conclusive."

Jan buried his face in his hands. He hadn't committed the act. He didn't like the judge, but even loaded and high he would never be driven to murder someone. Never.

"Just for one minute? She'll fill in this blank I got in my head."

"Jan," Bergman said slowly, as if explaining to a four-year-old. "Your girlfriend is a witness. I let you talk to her, the state prosecutor will give me hell. I can't." He rubbed at his eyes. "You know that."

"There has to be something I can do."

"You can help me a lot by remembering Saturday."

"I've been trying all day long. I'm guessing the ecstasy's to blame."

"I'm no doctor, but you'll have to come up with a better answer than that for the state prosecutor."

A gloomy silence arose. The sort of stillness that happens when two people know a painful reality is bearing down but don't want talk about it out loud.

"What happens now?" Jan said.

Bergman raised his head, looking frustrated, as if he'd had enough of all the questions.

"You guys will have to take me into custody," Jan said, beating Bergman to it.

Bergman nodded.

"I didn't murder the judge. On all that's holy."

"I would like to believe you. Really."

"Someone wants to pin it on me."

"Who?"

"I don't know," Jan said. "But I'm no murderer. If my blood's at the crime scene, it only means someone's trying to drag me into this."

"Jan," Bergman said, sounding gentler for once. "I promise you, we're putting all our weight behind working this case and looking for any evidence that will clear you. But you're right. I can't let you go home. You have to remain in custody, at least for now. Later, I'll talk to the state prosecutor and try to get you free until the trial. If you agree to stay put."

Bergman paged through his notes. "You have a ton of vacation time. I'll try to keep this news contained. I'll only let people in on the DNA evidence who absolutely have to know. I'll stall any disciplinary action as long as I can. This could all be cleared up in a few days. Please, Jan, don't screw this up. Rein in that temper of yours, talk to no one, and do not tamper with the case."

Jan closed his eyes. "All right. Promise."

Bergman relaxed a bit and shut his notebook. "You'll have to turn in your badge and your duty weapon to me for the moment."

Jan nodded grimly and handed them over.

Bergman swept the items into his desk drawer. "I'll call Stein. He'll take you to Moabit. The guards know the score. None of the prisoners will know you're a detective."

"Give me five minutes, to hit the restroom. This whole deal is getting to my stomach and I got no desire to use a jail can."

"Stein," Bergman yelled into the hallway. A second later, Jan's fellow detective came into the room.

"Hi again, Pat," Jan said, trying to keep his expression neutral. He couldn't help but think that the guy might derive some minor pleasure out of bringing him to jail.

"Escort him to the restroom and keep him from doing anything stupid. Then take him over to Moabit."

"Thanks," Jan said, standing. Patrick followed one step behind him all the way down the hall and into the bathroom. Jan opened the stall door, locked it shut, dropped his pants, and sat down on the toilet.

"Won't take long," he shouted. He drew his cell from his pocket and switched the setting to silent. He'd quietly text his friend Chandu. His African friend was in the Berlin underworld. But ever since Jan had saved his ass in a shootout, Chandu was indebted to Jan. Chandu would do anything for him, and today Jan needed a favor like never before.

Jan's fingers flew across the keys, and he fired off the text before standing to flush. Hopefully, Patrick wouldn't put cuffs on him next, because now it was time, Jan knew, for doing something stupid.

Chapter 2

Jan tried to look defeated as he left the building with Patrick, but all his senses were keyed up. His eyes darted around, and he eyed his colleague's every step.

He was hoping Chandu had gotten his text and had headed out right away. By hitting the toilet and asking to drink one more coffee, Jan had been able to gain twenty minutes. More would have been suspect. Jan was stronger than Patrick, but he wanted to avoid a brawl.

The street had a lot of traffic for a Sunday. A large SUV rolled slowly by them. The woman at the wheel could barely handle her big vehicle. She kept jerking her head around as if scared she was going to hit something. Following behind that was a black Mercedes sports car with blacked-out windows, chrome wheels, an aggressive rear spoiler, and headlights shaped like demonic eyes. The muscular arm of a black man was propped up in the driver's-side window, with thumb and little finger splayed out. Hang loose, the Hawaiian surfer salute. The car slowed down, and Jan watched as the passenger door was pushed open a crack. From the corner of his eye, Jan glanced at Patrick, who was just then pulling his ringing cell phone from his pocket. Jan thanked the God of Mobile Phones, waiting till the Mercedes was even with him.

Most problems in Jan's life were caused by his impulsive reactions. As early as kindergarten he'd been getting in trouble for it. The chickens had really come home to roost, though, when George Holoch had ruled against him for assault in that one unforgettable court hearing. And still he couldn't kick the habit of acting rashly. Because what he had planned now would put everything he'd done in the past to shame.

"I'm going to regret this," he muttered, grabbing Patrick by the collar of his coat and pulling him down backward. Jan's colleague screamed, fell on his butt, and dropped his cell phone. Jan sprinted away. He ran to the Mercedes, ripped open the door, jumped into the passenger seat.

"Having a good Sunday, Jan?" the driver joked.

Before Jan could manage a greeting, Chandu stomped on the gas. Jan clawed at the middle console of the Mercedes as the engine's sudden acceleration nearly tossed him from his seat.

• •

The telephone flew off the desk again. "Am I surrounded only by amateurs?" Bergman roared. "What's so hard about delivering a suspect to Moabit?"

"He had help," Patrick declared, as if that justified it.

"From who?"

"An unknown driver in a black Mercedes."

"You get the plate?"

Patrick nodded.

"So why are you still standing here? Put out a search and get Jan back here."

Patrick hurried to get out of the room.

Bergman suppressed a scream. He wasn't just dealing with a judge beaten to death anymore; now one of his own men was the prime suspect. And instead of sitting in custody, that man was on the run. And Bergman was going to have to explain why he hadn't ordered handcuffs for Jan. He didn't even want to think about the stories in the media. The police chief and the mayor were really going to lose it.

He found his desk again and sat down. He had known Jan for so long. The man was a good detective. A little quick-tempered and undiplomatic, sure, but he'd had a future in the homicide squad.

"Goddamn idiot," Bergman muttered, picking up the telephone. He'd have to let a few people know about this, and it wasn't going to be fun. How could he have been fooled like that?

If he had looked into the hallway at that very moment, he would have seen Patrick Stein there, grinning, a cup of coffee in one hand as he set out to launch the manhunt.

•   •

"What kind of trouble you get yourself in now?" Chandu asked. He wore big sunglasses and a grin. Two distinctive tribal tattoos were inked on his forehead. Broad shoulders and bodybuilder muscles showed under his blue shirt. At nearly six foot six, Chandu made an impressive figure, one well known in the Berlin underworld. He mainly worked as a bouncer and a debt collector. Not illegal in itself, though most of his customers were on wanted lists. But Chandu didn't talk about his jobs much, and Jan was grateful for it. That way he didn't run into conflicts with work and could enjoy his time with his crazy friend.

"I'm suspected of killing someone," Jan told him, trying to get comfortable in the seat.

Chandu let out a whistle. "So you thought it was a good idea to hightail it?"

"What was I supposed to do?" Jan argued. "They were taking me into custody."

"Suspected isn't the right word, then," Chandu said.

Jan scowled. "True. The evidence against me is watertight."

"So? You do it?"

"Of course not," Jan shot back. "Someone wants to pin it on me, though. And the way he did it points to some real good planning."

Chandu sped through a curve. Once again, Jan had trouble staying in the seat.

"Where we going, anyway?"

"You can lay low at my place." He tossed Jan a key. "My apartment on Oranienburger. You know the one. I'll let you off on the corner. Keep your head down so no one sees you."

"And you do what?"

"I have to lose this car. They got to be searching for us in it now."

"Shame," Jan said and ran his fingers along the dash. "Nice ride."

"It's . . . borrowed," Chandu replied. "I'll park it in the Spree."

Chandu slowed down. He put out a hand.

"What do you want?" Jan said.

"Your SIM card?"

"What's it to you?"

Chandu looked as if Jan had just told him the earth was flat.

"Any amateur detective can track you down with that. Give it here. I'll stick it in an old phone, turn it on, chuck it on a freight train. That's sure to get us a few hours."

Jan pulled his cell phone from his pocket and tried to pry out the little chip, but his hands were shaking too much.

"Easy now, Jan," his friend said. "We'll get there."

While Chandu held the steering wheel with his left little finger, he took the phone in his right hand and extracted the SIM card.

Jan pounded on the dash. He wasn't the type to cry, but being suspected of murder had really hit him hard. He was slowly becoming aware of the consequences. He couldn't go back home anymore, had to shut off his phone, and couldn't call any friends. Betty's apartment would be staked out. He couldn't even write a simple e-mail. Detectives would question all his friends and relatives. By this evening, they would all know that he was wanted for murder.

Jan wiped at his face. "You have to yank your card too."

"How come mine?" Chandu said.

"Detectives will trace my text to you. I take it your phone's not in your name."

"Of course not."

"I didn't mention your name in my text. The trace will lead nowhere, as long as you get rid of that SIM card."

"You got it all thought out," Chandu said, grinning.

He braked with a jerk and rolled to the curb.

"I restocked the beer. Make yourself cozy. Flip through the sports channels, but don't go looking outside. I have to go take care of a few things. I'll be back soon. I'll get us new SIM cards, then you can make calls again. You can tell me all about it later tonight."

Jan gave Chandu a friendly punch on the shoulder. "Thanks, my friend."

"Nothing to thank."

Jan climbed out, closed the door, and crossed the street. The Mercedes drove on, tires squealing. Jan fought an urge to run. He didn't want to draw any attention. It was all he could do not to look around, keeping an eye out for police cars. It seemed like an eternity before he reached the building's dim inner courtyard. The walls were covered with graffiti. It stank of urine and mold. No point checking mailboxes here. The stairway steps were worn down and lopsided. The elevator was kaput. A perfect hideout.

.   .

Once Jan got the heavy steel door closed behind him, the contrast with the stairway could not have been greater. Chandu's apartment was impeccably furnished. A tart aroma of incense permeated the air. A designer leather couch was situated in front of a wide flat-screen on the wall. On the floor was a tan woven rug, making the room nice and homey.

The furnishings mixed Western lifestyle with African tradition. Chandu had fled Rwanda as a child, with his mother. He didn't like to talk about that period, but shelves lined with countless statues and masks expressed his longing for the old homeland.

Jan went into the spacious kitchen and grabbed a beer from the fridge. He drank it slowly, thinking about the first time he'd visited this place.

It had been just days after his first encounter with Chandu—when he'd saved the man's life. Back then, Jan had still been doing patrol. He'd gotten a call to deal with an altercation at a nightclub. As the bouncer, Chandu had already been sorting things out when Jan had pulled up. Just as he stepped out of his car, some nut job drew a piece. The guy's first bullet hit Chandu in the shoulder. He'd rolled away, but the shooter had gone after him. He'd stood over Chandu, barrel pointing at Chandu's head, grinning wide. It had been an easy job for Jan. He'd taken the man down with two shots.

The inquest had taken a long time. A man shot dead was no small deal, even when he'd had a blood-alcohol level of .12 and a ton of cocaine in his system. Thanks to Chandu's testimony, of course, they couldn't find any wrongdoing on Jan's part. Still, the episode cemented Jan's rep as a trigger-happy cop. It hounded him even now, years later.

After he was released from the hospital, Chandu had looked up Jan to say thanks. Jan had liked the big guy from the first moment on. So he had accepted Chandu's invitation to come down to his local bar and give banana wine a try. Over the years, the African had become his good friend.

Jan sat on the couch, picked up the remote, and found the sports channel. Over the last few hours, he had been trying so hard to remember yesterday—Saturday—but the effort had only given him a headache. Maybe a distraction would help. He took a sip of beer and put his feet up on the coffee table.

He lasted for about five minutes in that position. Then, unable to stop his mind and pulse from racing, he jumped up and went to Chandu's computer.

• •

For Andreas Emmert, it was the toughest assignment of his career. He and Jan had worked together often. Jan's grit, combined with that incurable obstinacy of his, had always inspired Andreas. The guy stuck with a case, no matter if it hit a dead end. Andreas had always worried, though, that Jan would end up in hot water. He lacked tact at times and never seemed to grasp that cops weren't supposed go around giving the bad guys a taste of their own medicine.

Despite his doubts, Andreas didn't believe Jan had murdered the judge. Sure, Holoch had ruled against Jan for assault on duty, but that was hardly worth murder.

He felt sleazy poking around Jan's apartment, taking books from his shelf and searching for hidden evidence. Years ago he'd celebrated New Year's here with Jan. The two of them had sat on the battered sofa and lined up empty beer bottles on this old wooden table. Now a crime-scene investigator was examining the table for traces of blood.

"You napping?" Patrick's voice jolted Andreas from his thoughts. "I want to finish today already."

"Take it easy," Andreas replied. "This is Jan's place. He deserves a little respect."

"Respect?" Patrick gave a derisive laugh. "Jan is a wanted murderer. Since when do we treat people like that with respect?"

"First off, Jan is only a murder suspect," Andreas countered. "And on top of that he's put five times more people in the pen than you have."

"I don't give a shit if he was a good cop," Patrick sneered. "The point is, he worked in Homicide. Once that news gets out, all of Berlin is going to laugh at us. 'Murder in the Homicide Squad' the headlines will read, or something like it. Perhaps you should give that some thought."

"I still don't believe that he was the one."

"How much evidence you need? We have his DNA and his fingerprints on the scene. We have motive and we have the victim's blood on his clothes."

Patrick turned away from Andreas. "Everyone, listen up." He waved the investigators over. "Along with securing evidence, take all photos in albums and on the computer. I want to know where every photo was taken. That way we'll build a profile of Jan's favorite spots. Perhaps we'll find an old vacation home or some favorite pub. I need the first results coming in by tomorrow morning, even if it takes the whole night." He clapped his hands together. "Now keep at it."

Andreas grabbed another book and paged through it, frustrated. He could barely concentrate on the job.

"Jan, you fucking idiot," he cursed, irate now. The evidence gave Jan no chance, and judging by the way Patrick Stein was talking, he had no interest in helping clear Jan's name. That meant Jan really had a problem.

. .

"You do know that it's a crappy idea," Chandu said and drank a sip of beer.

"You got a better one?" Jan said.

"Just so I get this straight. You want to sneak into your girl-friend's apartment even though your detective pals are staking it out?"

"I'll know the cops who are assigned. We'll go around them."

"They'll be watching the entrance. How you going to get in? Fly onto the roof?"

"There's a rear exit, goes out to the garbage cans. We'll reach the stairway through the basement."

"So this rear exit is open at night?" Chandu asked.

"No," Jan replied, sounding irritated. "But next to it there's a poorly secured window. I told the building owner about the danger, but he hasn't done a thing about it."

"And what do we do then? Knock on Betty's door as if nothing's gone down? It is clear to you that she's been questioned and knows you're wanted for murder?"

"Betty would never believe that I killed the judge."

"How long you known her?"

"Four months."

Chandu chuckled. "Long time for building up trust."

"The plan has holes," Jan admitted, "but I can't sit around here doing nothing. I didn't go on the lam and destroy my career for that."

"A stupid plan, but I'm in," Chandu said, raising his bottle in salute.

31

Jan smiled. His friend, he never let Jan down.

"You have a glass cutter or something we can use to get the window open nice and quiet?"

"Of course I do," Chandu replied, sounding offended. "I'll go put on something more suited for breaking in, then we can get going."

"This isn't an actual break-in, you know," Jan said.

"I know, I know." Chandu appeased him with a grin and went into the bedroom.

Jan tried to visualize all the spots where his colleagues would be staking out Betty's place. If officers were waiting for him inside the apartment, they were done for. And Chandu would end up in Moabit right alongside him.

•   •

It was 8:30 p.m. when Chandu parked the car on a side street and the two of them crept over to Betty's apartment building. The big guy wore dark pants and a black turtleneck sweater and looked well put together, more like he was going to a nice restaurant than getting ready to break and enter. Jan was still in the jeans and leather jacket he'd put on when he'd gone home to shower earlier. It hardly seemed possible it was still the same day he'd woken up in Betty's bed with no idea that he was about to be charged with murder.

Betty lived on a typical Kreuzberg block. A one-euro store occupied the street level. The white facade was faded out, the windows busy with advertisements. Plane trees, barely illuminated by streetlights, cast long shadows across the sidewalk.

Jan sneaked behind a tree and watched the street. Plenty of cars were parked along the curb. Nothing looked unusual at first, but then a lighter flashed inside an Opel.

Jan smiled. Luckily, not all his fellow cops had given up smoking.

"The stakeout crew is across the street, in a dark Opel."

"What now?"

"We have to get inside the building next door. From there, we'll get to the basement window of Betty's building through the shared courtyard."

"Is the entry open?"

Jan shook his head. "Doors are locked after eight, but it's an older lock. We can jimmy the door. Hopefully no officers will look in the rearview mirror right about then."

"Won't working on the door be too loud?"

"Until two, a bus comes through here every thirty minutes. See that traffic light in front of Betty's building? If we make the noise right when the bus brakes for the red, no one will hear. If the guys just keep focusing on that front door, we're in."

"That's a lot of ifs."

"Child's play, actually. Just a question of timing."

"When does the bus come?"

Jan looked at his watch. "In the next five minutes. Take the jimmy and get set behind that tree, in front of the building. I'll keep an eye on my guys."

Chandu opened up their bag, pulled out the jimmy. The little crowbar looked like a toy in his big hands. He casually crossed the street and leaned against a tree trunk. Then he took his cell phone out and tapped around on the screen. He kept the jimmy hidden behind his back.

It was surprisingly quiet. Few cars passed by. Across the street, an older man was taking his dog out. Otherwise, they were alone. Jan pressed up to a tree trunk, keeping his eyes on the stakeout car. He nervously tapped his foot on the pavement. What would Betty say? Would she believe him, that he had nothing to do with the murder, or would she slam the door in his face and call for the cops? Chandu had a point. Four months was not long. And yet he trusted her. She would never leave him high and dry.

The roar of a bus engine jarred Jan from his thoughts. Chandu put his phone away, held the jimmy ready, and made for the courtyard door. As the bus screeched to a stop at the light, the big man inserted the jimmy, jerked his arm, and popped the door open. Jan watched his fellow officers. All was calm. They hadn't noticed. Jan grabbed their bag and went over to the pried-open door, where Chandu waited with a broad grin, all cool, the jimmy resting on a shoulder.

"Some folks should spend a little more on security."

"Let's get in quick before someone notices the lock's busted."

A dark hallway led out to the courtyard. Mailboxes were crammed with heaps of ads. Jan was tiptoeing along when he heard footsteps coming from the courtyard. He signaled Chandu, and they pressed up against the wall. They'd stay concealed unless the person came their way. In the moonlight, Jan saw a slender figure wearing a cap. The person had a bag in hand and was hurrying away in the other direction. After the footsteps faded, Jan counted to five, gave Chandu another signal, and rushed through the courtyard to the basement of the neighboring building.

Chandu joined him moments later at the basement window. He stowed the jimmy in their bag and took out a little tool that reminded Jan of a potato peeler. It had a wooden grip and a metal attachment shaped like an *E*, with little wheels at the ends. Chandu placed a suction cup on the glass and used the tool to cut the glass where it met the window frame. The grating sound made Jan's teeth ache. But it didn't last long. Seconds later, Chandu pulled at the suction cup and removed the window easily. He stepped to one side and pointed at the opening with a smile.

Jan climbed through headfirst. Once inside, he opened up the basement door, which only had a latch locking it from the inside. Chandu followed him. They crept silently along the hallway, reaching the stairwell. The streetlights' glow through the windows lit their way up.

Jan closed his eyes and listened. It was calm in the stairway. He went up to the fourth floor. With every step, his anxiety grew. Yesterday he had been on the homicide squad, and now here he was breaking into his girlfriend's building because she was the only person who could save him from a murder charge.

Chandu set a hand on his shoulder. "It'll work out," the big guy said, his voice low. "Just find out what happened yesterday, and the worst shit's over. I'll wait here."

Jan nodded, leaving Chandu behind and continuing into the fourth-floor hallway. His hands were slick with sweat. Doubt plagued him. Should he have called beforehand? He paused, uncertain.

"Jan." His friend's voice snapped him out of it. Chandu was pointing to his nose. Jan smelled it too.

Gas. It was coming from the hallway, in front of him. Jan wanted to keep going, but the door to Betty's apartment exploded with a loud boom. The pressure threw Jan to the floor. He landed hard, and the impact sucked all the air from his lungs.

The hallway spun around him. Chandu was shouting something at him, but then the whistling in his ears smothered all sound. Jan wanted to stand up, but his limbs felt too heavy to move. Then all went black.

Chapter 3

Jan came to in a small storage room. He barely had the strength to open his eyes. It was tough to breathe. A taste of vomit stuck in his mouth. His throbbing head tormented him.

A streetlight filtering through the room's one dirty window revealed some of the surroundings. Old chairs and tables stood stacked in one corner. A tabletop grill leaned against a wall. The smell of smoke and scorched plastic was everywhere.

He lay on an old couch about as comfortable as a torture chair. He sat up, groaning.

"Welcome back." He heard Chandu's deep bass voice. Jan's friend was standing at the door, watching the hallway through the crack. Loud shouts from outside filtered into the room. Noise from the stairway was deafening now, as if a whole class of schoolkids were running up and down.

"How you doing?" Chandu asked him.

"Had better days," Jan said. He held his forehead and winced, feeling a wound over an eye.

"Can you remember anything?"

"Just the explosion that took me off my feet."

The racket got louder. A man shouted orders and a siren sounded.

"What in the fuck is going on here?"

Chandu shut the door. He sighed. "As you noticed, there was an explosion. Probably a gas leak. You were lucky. Two steps more and the debris would've put holes through you."

"Were there injured, dead?"

Chandu bit his lower lip. "Betty's apartment exploded."

"What?" Jan howled. "We got to get up there right away." He stood but had trouble keeping his balance. His legs gave way and stars danced before his eyes.

Chandu caught him and laid him back down.

"Just lie here," he insisted. "You took a real good one. That wound on your forehead, it wouldn't stop bleeding. A miracle you don't have any burns. That leather jacket of yours got the worst of it."

"What about Betty?" Jan demanded.

"I don't know. Right after it blew up, I got you down here to the basement. Then all hell broke loose. Lights went on all over, people screaming. Your cop friends stormed the place just as we got to the basement. They almost had us. I laid you here and went upstairs, saw all the mayhem. Betty's apartment was just rubble. Even parts of the outside wall were blown out. The place was in flames, and the hallway was all smoke."

He put a hand on Jan's shoulder. "I'm sorry."

Tears ran down Jan's cheeks. "It can't be." He tried to stand up again. "I can't just hide down here. I have to know what's going on."

Chandu pushed him back down to the couch. "Whatever happened, you can't help Betty right now. It's swarming with police up there. If you go out this door, they'll arrest you. Two ambulances are outside. If she's injured, she'll be well taken care of. We'll find out

37

which hospital she's in and visit her. But charging up there will only put you in the slammer."

"Betty," Jan whispered. His head fell back on the couch. Then he lost consciousness.

. .

When Jan came to again, sunshine was coming through the filthy window and illuminating the fine dust drifting idly around the room. For a moment, he thought it was still Sunday morning and he was lying next to Betty, but then the couch's stale odor brought him back to reality. The cold, hard facts struck him. His girlfriend might be dead, every police officer was his enemy, and he was a criminal on the lam.

It had only taken one day for the world that he'd known to vanish, replaced by a nightmare worse than anything he could ever have dreamed.

He turned his head and saw the massive figure of his friend sitting in a chair by the couch. At least there was one ray of hope in his shitty life.

"How you doing?"

Jan moaned. "I got a jackhammer in my head, my girlfriend's apartment blew up, and I'm wanted for murder. I'm doing splendid."

"If you can crack stupid jokes, your head wound can't be that bad."

Jan grumbled, scowling.

"You went eight hours unconscious," Chandu told him. "I was about to get you to a hospital, but too much was still going down. I wouldn't have gotten far carrying you, and besides you would've woken up handcuffed to a bed."

"Thanks for looking after me." Jan stood. His legs still wobbled under him, but the dizziness was gone. "What's going on outside?"

"Most of the police and firemen are gone. It's quieter inside the building, but there are still some investigators inside Betty's apartment."

Jan rubbed at his eyes. He felt weary and strung out. He could hardly believe he'd slept so long.

"What do we do?" Chandu said.

"We have to find out how Betty's doing. First we get out of here, then I'll call hospitals."

Jan peeked out the room's lone dirty window. A young blonde woman stood out in the courtyard, cigarette in hand. She looked annoyed, as if she'd imagined her Monday morning going much differently. She had a flawless face, long blonde hair flowing over her shoulders, and a posture that suggested a bold self-confidence. Her slim-cut jeans clung to a slender body made even more picture-perfect by stiletto heels. To Jan's eyes, shoes like that tended to look slutty on most women, but on her they actually looked elegant. Next to her lay a white plastic coverall, the type that evidence analysts wear at crime scenes.

Jan went pale. "My God," he muttered. Speechless, he headed for the door.

"What's wrong?" Chandu said. "Where are you going?"

Jan heard his friend talking to him, but the words didn't slow him down. He forgot all caution and went out into the courtyard.

When the woman saw him she raised her eyebrows in barely perceptible surprise. Then her face returned to its impenetrable mask of cool beauty. She tossed her half-smoked cigarette to the ground, stepping on it till extinguished. And Jan knew what had happened to Betty.

• •

"Hello, Zoe," Jan said, despondent.

"I always took you for an idiot," the woman began without saying hello, "but I never thought you'd fuck up this bad."

"Maybe it was a mistake to take off," Jan said in defense, "but it doesn't matter now. Just tell me what's happened to Betty. Then you can run me in."

Zoe's hard face turned a little softer. "There is only one reason why I get called. I'm a medical examiner."

Jan nodded. "Did she . . . ?" His voice broke.

Zoe shook her head. "She was in the kitchen when the gas line blew. She died instantly."

"Where is she now?"

"She was taken to the medical examiner's office. The identity has not been confirmed yet, because the body was fully burned."

Jan swallowed. "My little Betty," he muttered.

Zoe, looking embarrassed, turned her head away. Despite the many crime scenes she'd worked, she'd never had to tell someone the bad news about a loved one.

"Did she have anything we can use to identify her?" she said.

"A nose piercing." Jan wiped at his eyes. "I also bought her a Gucci necklace, with these two nameplates that look like military dog tags. Her name's on that."

"She did have a necklace on, but the force of the explosion drove the metal into her chest. I'll find it during the autopsy."

Zoe took out another cigarette. Gauloises. No filter. She fired it up with a silver windproof lighter and blew smoke into the air without taking her eyes off Jan.

"What do you want to do now?" she said.

"Go to the pen. What else is there?"

"Why did you run away?"

"The evidence against me, it's conclusive. But I didn't murder the judge. Someone wants to pin it on me, and if I'm in custody I can't find out who."

"You couldn't trust your fellow cops after all these years? Now, instead of looking for clues to clear you, they're busy with a manhunt to bring you in."

Jan hung his head, ashamed. "I've acted like an idiot. But when my DNA matched the crime scene, I just wanted to run."

Zoe sucked at her cigarette and exhaled loudly.

"Who's that walking mountain behind you?"

"That's Chandu. He helped me get away."

"You mean Chandu Bitangaro, the bouncer?"

"You know him?"

"I used to go to a club where he kept watch on things."

"Really? Which club?"

"You don't want to know. He's connected to heavyweights in the Berlin underworld, you do know that, right?"

"He's not as much of a criminal as everyone thinks. Lots about him is just made up, could never be proven."

"Hiding you probably won't improve his record."

"Listen here, Zoe." Jan pointed at her. "Call Bergman for me, have me picked up, whatever, but if you ever mention Chandu helping—"

Zoe blew smoke in his face. "Spare me the threats, Janni. Save it for kindergarten. And do not piss me off or I'll add a broken nose to that wound on your forehead."

Zoe's face had tensed up, just a bit. A person had to know her to recognize how dangerous the change was. Jan had no doubt she'd pop him one.

He changed the subject. "How do you really know so much about him?"

"My job in forensics, it gets a little boring. Not exactly *CSI: Las Vegas*. So when I get bored, I click around and check out how the latest investigations are going."

"But the files are password protected."

Zoe shrugged. "Not the old ones."

"Why don't you just apply for homicide squad?"

"I'm a scientist, Jan. I graduated with biology and medical degrees. I never wanted to go to the police academy."

"Doesn't matter," Jan sighed. "So, get out your cell phone and call Bergman. I'll wait at the door."

"Why would I do that?"

"There's a manhunt for me. You might not be a cop, but you're still working in the same club."

She shrugged. "You might be a bore with limited intelligence, Jan, but somehow you are a good detective. I'm sorry about your girlfriend. So, what I'll do is, I'll go finish another smoke before I tell Bergman that I saw you."

"Why would you do that?"

Zoe paused. "Most think I'm just this superficial bitch, but I am a good judge of people. My dad, he was a lying bastard who brought people more bad luck than Berlin has kebab joints. That alone was a school of hard knocks. So if you'd killed that judge, I'd be able to tell. Plus," she continued between drags, "I don't see you going about it so stupidly."

Jan wanted to thank her and held out his hand to shake, but Zoe stepped away.

"Don't go getting all sentimental," she declared. "I don't do emotional crap. I'm not completely selfless in doing this."

"Uh, okay," Jan stuttered. "But what—"

"First off, lend me Steroid Man there." She pointed at Chandu. "My neighbor gets all bent out of shape when I play music too loud in the morning. He needs someone who can talk to him in just the right way. Beyond that? It's my chance for a little variety, for a change."

Jan eyed her, confused. He managed little more than, "Uh, I . . ."

"You really are slow on the uptake, aren't you?" She rolled her eyes, taking a drag. "I give you time to get out of here. In return, you let me in on your own little investigation. Bergman would never let me work a homicide, and I've always wanted to."

"You're nuts," Jan blurted.

Zoe nodded. She took a pen, grabbed Jan's hand, and wrote a number on the underside of his wrist.

"Call me this evening. I'll tell you what the crime-scene guys found out."

And she giggled. For a moment, she looked like a little girl who'd just done something forbidden.

"Now take off," she said, lighting up another cigarette.

Jan, astonished, took a second to recover. Then he signaled Chandu, and they tiptoed out of the courtyard.

•   •

Jan lay on the couch, staring at the ceiling. After Chandu had driven him back to his place and bandaged up his wound, he'd tried to cheer Jan up. They'd watched recordings of ice hockey and American football, but their usual enthusiasm had never kicked in. At some point it had grown dark again, and Chandu had gone to bed. Jan had never felt so lonely. He was glad to be staying here, but his life was in ruins. He could not call anyone or write any e-mails. The days of comforting city strolls were past. He couldn't even show up in his local pub.

Betty was dead. He still could not grasp it. Two days ago, he'd awoken at her place, and later he'd talked with her on the phone.

Now she lay in Forensics on a cold metal autopsy table, burned beyond recognition. All her beauty was gone. He would never see her smile again, caress her pristine back, or hear her voice. Maybe it was a blessing he was no longer with Homicide—otherwise he would've stormed right into Forensics and demanded to see her corpse. He was spared that much, at least.

He took out his wallet and gazed at the photo behind the see-through plastic. It had been shot when they first met. They had gotten to know each other at the birthday party of a mutual friend and liked each other from the start. He and the friend, Rene, had gone to school together. While Jan was trying his luck with the police, Rene had started college. Business administration. His stock phrase was, "I got no idea what I'll do, but business sounds good enough." Rene knew Betty from another university bash, so she'd ended up at the party. It had been a typical Rene party. Loud-ass music, tons of cocktails, and nothing to eat but chips and frozen sushi.

Betty had been eyeing Jan all night. At one point he went over to her. Then she had showed him that radiantly beautiful smile of hers, and his heart was done for.

He didn't leave her side after that. Eventually Rene had staggered through the living room, shooting guests with his digital camera. Betty stood close and put her arm around Jan, and he'd toasted Rene with a beer bottle. He'd liked the photo so much he'd gotten a wallet-sized print to carry around. Whenever he looked at it, his memory of her first touch came right back—her warm skin, the scent of her hair, her gentle fingers.

They had seen each other again the next day. And the day after that, and after that. The recent months they'd had together had been such a happy time.

Jan laid the picture on his chest. The clock above Chandu's TV read 3:08 a.m. He closed his eyes and let his thoughts drift back to that evening. To that very moment in the photo, among all those laughing people and the loud music. He thought he felt Betty's hand on his shoulder and heard her voice. His mouth spread into a smile. And he fell asleep.

Chapter 4

The sound of a garbage truck woke Jan. He'd only slept three hours.

He wondered if he should even get up. What was the point in keeping at it? He was suspected of murder and would probably never get his badge back. His girlfriend was dead. All he had loved was destroyed. Blown away.

Chandu's revolver lay holstered on the table. It was a .45 caliber. Dirty Harry make. It would be so easy just to get away from it all. A single pull of his finger, a brief, sharp pain. Maybe a guy didn't really die but only sank into eternal sleep. A tempting thought. Asleep, he could dream. Of bygone bliss.

Eventually, he stood up. He got dressed. He checked out his strung-out face in the mirror. He had never looked so pathetic, not even after the wildest partying. He washed and used his wet hands to fix his unruly hair. Then he slipped into his shoes, put on a hat, and went out.

He loved this city. This was his place in the world, but today it looked old and filthy. Gray and lacking love. On the way to the subway, it started raining. Pretty lightly at first. He barely felt the drops. Then it got stronger, as if the sky wanted to wash all the filth of the earth into the sewers. He raised his head, took off his hat, and showed his face to the clouds. He shut his eyes, the rain blending with his tears. As he cried without restraint, some of the anguish drained from his heart.

Eventually the rain let up, and his tears dried as patches of blue sky emerged overhead. He ran his fingers through his wet hair, breathing in the fresh air. It seemed a lifetime since he had last felt so free. Released. And his thoughts of dying were swept away.

• •

It was 8:00 a.m. Jan knew Father Anberger's habits. The old man always woke up at the same time, prayed, got dressed, and took a stroll through the Tiergarten. His knees were a little worn out with age, but neither the aches in his legs nor bad weather kept him from his stroll. Always the same. No matter if it was a workday or a weekend.

Jan stood next to an overhanging oak and waited, scanning a newspaper he'd bought but not really comprehending the words. His entire focus was on his surroundings. He needed to keep his guard up and at all costs avoid being recognized by any on-duty cops. Even the guys from city services knew him. Berlin was a small town sometimes. You were always running into the wrong people at the wrong time.

When Jan spotted Father Anberger, he exhaled with relief. Not much was happening in the Tiergarten on this Tuesday morning. People were riding bikes on their way to work, and the rain had scared off the stroller set. It was too early for tourists. The perfect time to meet.

Father Anberger was walking a little stooped, so he didn't notice Jan until the younger man was right in front of him.

"Good morning, Herr Tommen." The priest sounded happy to see him. Nothing in his demeanor suggested that anything about their friendly relationship had changed. Maybe he hadn't heard yet? Jan wondered. On the walk over, he had thought about how to proceed with this conversation, and he had finally decided to just be direct.

"Good morning, Father Anberger." Jan had trouble looking him in the eye. "As you might have heard," he began, getting right to it, "I'm under suspicion of murder."

"Yes. Your colleagues came to my place. They questioned me."

"I didn't kill anyone," Jan told him.

"And I did not believe it," Father Anberger said with such conviction that Jan got a lump in his throat. The priest never lost his belief in the goodness of people. Jan swore to himself he'd start going back to church every Sunday, if he ever got out of this mess.

"Thank you," he said. "Someone is trying to pin the murder on me, and I need your help finding out who's actually guilty."

"I'd be glad to help. What should I do?"

Jan cleared his throat. The man's casual offer surprised him but also filled him with a sense of calm.

"Just grab a few things from my apartment, if possible. The building is being watched, but as my neighbor, you could get in my place without arousing suspicion. I need a few clothes, but most of all, I need you to check my desk drawer for something that looks like a plastic ice-cream cone. It's actually a USB flash drive, but I'm guessing my fellow cops overlooked it. What's on there might help me clear my name."

"If you give me your key, I'll fetch it from your apartment. Then we can meet here again tomorrow morning," Father Anberger suggested.

"That's too conspicuous," Jan said. "My fellow cops might find it a little strange if you leave for your regular stroll with a big bag. Let's meet at about one back here."

Jan took out a pen and scribbled some notes in the margin of the newspaper. "I'm writing out the important stuff to get."

After they were clear on everything, the priest waved good-bye and was off. Jan sent up a prayer of thanks to heaven and crossed himself.

.   .

Back in Chandu's apartment, Jan stared at his old cell phone, now equipped with its new SIM card. He didn't want to know where his friend got the thing, but he had to admit that holding the phone gave him a reassuring sense of normalcy. He took a deep breath and dialed Zoe's number. He had to know if the corpse was really Betty. He heard the digits being dialed. After the third ring, she picked up.

"Hello?"

"Zoe, it's Jan."

"Wait a sec," she said. He heard a door shut. "Okay, now we can talk."

"I don't want to get you into trouble, but I had to call. Are you done with the autopsy?"

"Yes. I just got back when a fax from the state prosecutor landed on my desk ordering it. My coworker Walter had to do most of the work, because we've had multiple cases coming in tonight."

She cleared her throat. "Are you sure you want to know the results?"

Jan closed his eyes. "Tell me."

A lighter clicked on. He heard Zoe exhaling.

"As a first step, we had to determine whether the explosion was the cause of death," Zoe began in a matter-of-fact tone. "There was soot inhalation, found in the trachea and lungs. The airway lining was completely covered in soot. Plus, we detected elevated carbon monoxide levels in the blood, which suggests fire was the cause of death. Unfortunately, parts of the ceiling had fallen on her, making the work difficult. The firefighters' water hoses didn't help matters."

She took another drag of her cigarette.

"Using your description, we eventually were able to identify her without resorting to dental impressions. The piercings matched the ones in current photos of her. Plus, we found the pendant you mentioned. Her name was on it. The last thing is, height and weight do fit the measurements of Bettina Windsten."

Jan wiped at his eyes. Now he had certainty. Somehow, he had been fooling himself into hoping that the dead body might not be his girlfriend's.

"Anything else?" he asked wearily.

She paused. "One little thing."

Jan felt a cold shiver. He figured Zoe had yet another horrid finding ready.

"In all the havoc, we found a farewell note. Lying in the bedroom, in a plastic sleeve."

"A farewell note?" Jan gasped. "You're telling me that Betty—"

"Committed suicide."

"That can't be." He bristled at the thought. "She was a happy woman. Her joy for life was contagious. The last thing she felt was depressed."

"Some people can hide it well."

"You didn't know her. She never would have killed herself."

"I haven't read the note, Jan, but I did read the report. The gas line had been tampered with. She was sitting on a chair in front of the gas stove holding a cup in her hand. That, along with the farewell letter—circumstances like that don't lie."

"Are you trying to tell me that any investigation into this has been dropped?"

"I'm afraid so, yes."

"Has everyone lost their minds?" Jan shouted. He threw the phone against the wall with a scream of despair, stomping on the pieces until they broke into jagged shards.

. .

Chandu strode into the room, frowning as he looked from his friend's grief-stricken face to the busted cell phone on the floor.

"They're saying Betty killed herself," Jan said, turning his gaze away from Chandu. "She tampered with the gas line and left a suicide note."

Chandu nodded. Now he understood. Jan had really liked the girl, maybe even loved her.

"It wasn't your fault," Chandu said, hoping to console his friend, but he could tell how empty his words sounded.

"I know she didn't commit suicide," Jan said, finally looking up at Chandu.

"Sometimes we don't know people as well as we believe," he said as gently as he could.

"I don't buy it," Jan said. "She had so many plans for the future. She wanted to go abroad after medical school. In all our time together, I never once saw her act depressed. I'm positive she didn't take her own life."

"So what happened?"

"Someone murdered her."

Chandu raised his eyebrows. "Why?"

"To shovel more dirt on my grave," Jan replied. "Betty was the only person who could have filled in the gaps in my memory. Now that she's gone, I'll never learn what I did on Saturday, not unless I have the luck to run into a friend who saw me or find footage of myself on a security camera. And let's face it, both are long shots. The fact is, the only person who can clear me is dead. The evidence is stacked against me. Whoever planned this, they must really hate me."

Jan turned back to the window. "The day before yesterday? I was still a happy guy. Now my girlfriend is dead. And my fellow cops are hunting me down. These are guys I've celebrated birthdays and weddings with, who've spent whole nights drinking with me in Berlin clubs. How can they believe I'm a murderer?"

"Politics."

"What does politics have to do with it?"

"George Holoch was a well-known judge. You're the obvious suspect. And the media needs their story."

"But it wasn't me."

"Doesn't matter. They just need to bring you in with the cameras rolling. After that, no one will care about the case anymore."

Jan nodded slowly. "I haven't been looking at the big picture. You're right."

"We have to find the real killer," Chandu said. "Then, we just might get Betty's murderer too." He rummaged around in his bag. He pulled out two IDs and two badges imprinted with the words "Criminal Police." He tossed one to Jan.

"Where did you get these?"

"Here and there," the big man replied, shrugging.

Jan held up the ID, inspecting the details. "The hologram's missing."

"I know. An ID like this won't pass intense scrutiny, but it was the best I could get on short notice."

Jan peered over his friend's shoulder to check out the other ID. The photo showed Chandu with a clean-cut hairstyle and a tie. "I guess I should call you Detective Sergeant Chandu Aswanika."

Chandu grinned. "Not bad, huh?"

"You do know that you're as well known by the police as the criminals in the Berlin underworld?"

"Well, this here is for the regular folks, in case we need to ask a few questions."

"So what do we do now?"

"We go hunting for a killer."

"Someone killed my girlfriend to take me out," Jan said, his jaw clenching as he thought about Betty's murder. "Whoever it is, I'm going to make them pay with their own blood."

He clipped the ID onto his pants pocket. "I'll get my jacket. There's someone we need to go see."

Chandu nodded with satisfaction. His old friend was back.

•　•

They stopped the car in front of a sprawling villa, and Jan got out to take a closer look at the spiked metal fence surrounding the property. Through the wrought-iron bars they could see neatly trimmed hedges and the details of the home, which had vast windows and a balcony fitted with columns.

"Looks spendy," Chandu remarked.

Jan rang the bell and waited. The door opened, and an older man stuck his head out. He was wearing a bathrobe. His thin hair stood up all over his head. He took in Chandu's towering stature and facial tattoos with a wary look.

"Harald Nieborg?" Jan asked.

"Who are you?"

"Berlin police," Jan said, flashing his badge. "We would like to ask you a few questions about the murder of George Holoch."

"Again?" Nieborg sighed. "I already told your colleagues everything."

"I know," Jan went on. "But we have a few follow-up questions. Seems our fellow officers were a little sloppy entering the data."

"Why am I paying all these taxes to this shithole city anyway if detectives don't even know their way around a computer?"

Jan ignored the remark. "Mind if we come in?"

"That's not possible right now." Nieborg hedged. "My, uh . . . cleaning woman is here and the floor, it's all wet."

Chandu crossed his big arms, giving the man a questioning look.

"We can do this at the door," Jan conceded. He pulled out his notebook.

"Did you know George Holoch well?"

"We belonged to the same golf club, did wine tastings regularly. He was a smart, cultured man."

"He have any enemies?"

"He was a judge by profession. Sure he had enemies."

"Did he mention anyone specifically in that respect?"

"No."

"Hmm," Jan said, making a note.

"When did you come home on the night of the murder?"

"About eleven p.m."

"And that's when you noticed the car in your driveway?"

"Couldn't miss it. I hardly got past it. I called the tow service and police, but they didn't get here until about twelve thirty."

"Then what?"

"By then the car was gone, and I had to explain it to them."

"Did you write the plate down?"

"Yes."

"And it was a dark-blue BMW M3?"

"Yes."

"Did you see the driver?"

"No. One second the car was taking up half my driveway. A few minutes later, it was gone."

"Huh," Jan said and noted something down.

"Are we done with this yet?" Nieborg asked, impatient now.

"You certainly don't want to leave your cleaning lady unattended," Chandu said, winking at him.

"One more thing. Then we'll leave you in peace."

Nieborg sighed.

Jan leaned forward. "See, there was a little accident securing evidence," he whispered. "A box got misplaced, unfortunately. So now a few crime-scene photos are missing, and the house key too. George Holoch didn't happen to give you a spare, did he? It would be pretty embarrassing for us to have to call the locksmith. If you could just lend us that extra key, we'll be on our way."

Jan did his best apologetic face.

Nieborg sniffed in contempt. "Wait here."

"Not bad," Chandu said, once the man had disappeared back inside the house. "How did you know?"

"I didn't. I was just hoping."

"So what if he hadn't had a spare key?"

"We would have called the locksmith. We wouldn't want to try and break in, not in a neighborhood like this, where people watch for prowlers and the houses are well secured. If someone spotted us creeping around, they'd call the police. With the key, we can walk in through the front door and avoid arousing the neighbors' suspicions."

"So why did you bother with those basic investigation questions? You knew all the answers already."

"Asking for the key right away would've been too conspicuous."

"Let's just hope he bought our little story. If your coworkers find out you came over here . . ."

"They won't—not right away, anyway. Questioning was done a while ago and now the crime scene is sealed off. Nobody will bother to come back here for some time."

Harald Nieborg returned. "Here's the key." He pressed it into Jan's hand. "Don't go losing it this time," he said before shutting the door.

"Asshole," Chandu muttered.

"Finally," Jan said, a look of satisfaction on his face. "Now let's take a good look at the judge's digs."

•   •

Jan, wearing gloves, ripped off the official Berlin Police paper seal that stretched across the front door and slid the key into the lock. Inside, he paused, staring at the spotless marble floor of the foyer as an odd fear crept over him. What if he remembered the house after all? What if the crime scene looked familiar? What if he really had driven over here that night, high on drugs?

"Jan," Chandu said, jolting him out of his reverie. "What are you waiting for? Let's keep moving."

"Yeah," Jan said. He turned and shut the front door behind them. He moved farther into the house, trying to banish the dark thoughts from his head, and let his gaze wander around the interior.

The owner had clearly wanted to show off his wealth. The floor was beautifully tiled. Above the designer sofa hung a striking blown-glass chandelier, its unusual design reminding Jan of a weeping willow. The walls showcased two paintings that looked to his eyes like a jumble of color splashes, but he could guess they were valuable. Everything had a clinical cleanliness. Not one speck of dust anywhere. There were no streaks on the glass cabinets, and the carpet leading up the stairs looked immaculate, as if it had just been laid.

Chandu was clearly impressed by the pomp. "Looks like the judge pulled in a few. What do we do now?"

"We look for clues."

"I don't mean to say the obvious, Jan, but didn't your coworkers already go through the place?"

"Sure, but maybe they missed something."

"You're always telling me how thorough you guys are."

"The crime-scene techs might have been sloppier than normal. Plus, with me as the suspect, they probably viewed the case as easy to close. That might have tempted the guys into wanting to finish up quickly."

Chandu uttered a grumpy snort.

"I know there's little chance, but I had to come here. Even if we don't find a thing."

"Where was the judge murdered?"

"By the TV," Jan said, pointing to a flat-screen built into the wall. As they neared it, the antiseptic smell of cleaning agents grew stronger.

"Everything looks normal enough," Chandu said.

"The crime scene was cleaned. We won't find anything here. We'll have to look somewhere else."

"Today is my first day investigating a murder," Chandu said. "So I'd be grateful for any tips."

"We're looking for things that the judge might have hidden away. Every person has at least one dark secret. For some, it's just the porno sites they like to visit on the Internet—we'll never know in this case because they already confiscated the judge's computer. But lots of people have tangible stuff too—say, kinky sex toys, illicit photos, drugs."

"So where do we start?"

"Doesn't matter," Jan said. "Just focus on finding spots where something might be hidden. In a crawl space that's hard to notice, or behind books on a shelf." Jan shrugged. "Knock yourself out, but put on gloves. Your fingerprints are in our system."

"All right," Chandu said, heading to the stairs. "I'll start on the upper floor."

Jan nodded and then positioned himself in the middle of the living room, pivoting around. He tried to take in every detail. Then he closed his eyes.

"Where's your secret, George?" he whispered. He'd searched through plenty of homes and found more sick stuff than he cared to remember. Some people would just leave a snuff video lying out on a table next to a crack pipe. But a man like Judge Holoch was far too clever for that. His secrets would have to be sniffed out. Jan doubted the judge was so secretive that he'd have to bust open the walls, but the man would have known to hide things in a place where the cleaning lady wouldn't stumble on them.

Jan hadn't said it to Chandu, but he felt convinced that being in the judge's home would bring back a memory or two. The thing he wanted most was to recall some details, even if they incriminated him. Not knowing was the worst.

Just then, Jan heard Chandu calling for him.

•   •

Once they'd found the murder weapon in the Judge Holoch case, Zoe had dropped everything to drive over right away and pick it up. Two tickets for excessive speeding later, she was in the lab with gloves on and all the analyzers running.

She opened the plastic evidence bag, took out the hammer, and placed it, with due reverence, atop two little metal stands. Then she went around the table to verify its correct position. The apparent murder weapon was arm length and had industrial grip tape on the handle. Dried blood extended down to the tape. She focused on observing every centimeter of the surface. That completed, she pulled out of her lab coat a small tube topped with a cotton swab. She removed the cap and took a sample of the dried blood.

She handed the sample to her colleague Walter, who had arrived just after her. "DNA sample," Zoe said without turning, which Walter acknowledged with a crabby grunt. Walter hated being treated like an assistant, but Zoe didn't care one bit. When she was examining evidence, she didn't let anything interfere. A kind of symbiosis developed between her and the object if she concentrated hard enough. That was what she was after now. And there was no way she was going to let some Birkenstock-wearing bore wreck the delicate bond she was trying to forge.

As she examined the weapon, a clear timeline of the murder started to coalesce in her head. The tape revealed that the killer had brought along the hammer. The person had known in advance that he wanted to keep his grip. He'd also sensed that the victim might try to fight back when he realized the attacker had a hammer, not a gun. *That* would explain the minor burn on the neck of the corpse, which must have come from a stun gun. The murderer had probably been waiting in the house to attack the judge by surprise. Once he'd incapacitated the man with the stun gun, he'd smashed the knee and other body parts in succession. Not exactly a fair fight.

Zoe kept moving around the small table. She took a wide brush and began dusting off the handle. The first fingerprints became visible. Some were smudged and could barely be used, but two prints clearly stood out. She grabbed a piece of film and transferred the first print onto the see-through plastic.

She went to the adjoining table, took a magnifying glass from her pocket, and examined the prints. The loops and arcs were familiar to her somehow. They were identical to the ones found at the crime scene—and they belonged to Jan.

Zoe secured the second print and found Walter, who was busy analyzing the DNA.

"Run these through the print database," she said. "I'll take a few more blood samples."

The blood likely came from the victim, but you never knew. Maybe the murderer was injured in a struggle. Whatever she found, she'd have to call Jan right away. The guy was not going to like the results.

• •

After hearing Chandu call his name, Jan rushed up the stairs and into the bedroom. The decor echoed the upscale main story, with elegant floors, polished wood cabinets, and tiny halogen spotlights recessed in the ceiling. Only a set of branching deer antlers over the bed, which didn't seem to fit at all, disrupted the cold, stylized look of the place.

Chandu got up from the floor and held out a slim, leather-bound photo album.

"Where'd you get that?" Jan asked, taking the book into his own hands.

"There's a hidden compartment near the head of the bed. I just had to remove the board that covered it."

Jan whistled. "What clued you in?"

"Where you think I stash my piece?" Chandu said. "In the fridge?"

Jan carefully cradled the book. A photo album. Its brown leather was worn. He opened it and studied the first shot. A young woman, practically a girl, stared fearfully into the camera. Her right cheek was swollen. Under her left eye was a gaping slash. Blood was running out of her nose, and her upper lip was split open.

"My God," Chandu said. "She's fifteen at the most."

Jan turned pages. Another girl had been messed up the same way. Her blonde hair, wet with sweat, hung over her forehead. Her eyes expressed the same fear he'd seen in the first girl.

Chandu wiped his hands on his pants, as if touching the book had sullied him too. "Good thing that pig's dead, or I'd be paying him a little visit."

Disgusted, Jan shut the album. "We got what we wanted. Let's clear out of here and continue this back home."

He held the album under his arm and went downstairs. He'd seen a lot of sick crap in his day, but finds like this always left him shuddering a little. At least they now had a clue. This judge, he had a dark past.

Chapter 5

Once they were back in the car, Jan's new cell rang. He held the little phone to his ear. "Yup."

"Hi, Mister Yup," Zoe said. "Can I talk to Jan?"

"Cut the crap." He heard her snickering. "What's the latest?"

"They found the murder weapon."

"Where?"

"At your place."

"My house? They went all through my apartment and didn't find anything. All clear."

"Not in your apartment. In the basement instead. In your neighbor's storage room, to be precise."

"What?" Jan said, startled. "But the storage rooms are locked up."

"True. That's why investigators didn't find the weapon right away. When your neighbor went down to grab some potatoes this morning, her key fell right out of her hand. Seems she saw a blood-smeared hammer."

"Did you analyze it already?"

"Yes. Unfortunately, I don't have great news. The hammer has blood from Judge Holoch as well as your fingerprints. Wounds on the corpse match size and shape. This hammer is definitely the murder weapon."

"Fucking hell," Jan said.

"You're in a tight spot, yes, and it's getting tighter. Of all the cases I've worked over the years, yours is the most clear-cut. They catch you, they're going to lock you up and throw away the key."

"Someone wants to pin it on me."

Zoe sighed. "That may be, Janni, but we haven't found any evidence to suggest you're innocent. I'd love to help you, but the more I try, the tighter the noose around my neck if it gets out that I've been talking to you."

"I'm a homicide detective," Jan said, his voice rising out of frustration. "If I'd killed the judge, I would not have left my own car parked outside the crime scene and then tossed the murder weapon in my neighbor's basement storage. You have to give me that much."

"It's an investigator's dream, I'll give you that. What killer pulls every stupid move in the book? But you can't build a defense around that."

Jan rubbed at his eyes, weary. "Okay, Zoe. Thanks for the info. We found a book of photos at the judge's house, deviant stuff, shots of battered young women. Chandu and I will go through them all. Maybe we can ID a girl, then I'll report back in."

"Till then, Mister Yup," Zoe said and hung up.

Jan picked up the album. The photos were their only evidence. If this clue was a dead end, he was done for. He would just have to turn himself in, hoping. Maybe he'd get a milder sentence that way.

•   •

Each photo told a horrific story. The women were brutally beaten, but worse than their wounds were their eyes. Broken. Empty. Without hope.

Jan found it hard to look closely at the pictures, although his friend Chandu seemed capable of examining each photo precisely.

"It doesn't bother you?" Jan said.

"I've seen this too often. Lots of prostitutes get beat up by their johns or their pimps."

"You think these are prostitutes?"

"I know at least three of them are. There are a couple others I've seen around too. Besides, what other woman would undergo this kind of beating and end up being photographed—and never report a word to the cops?"

"Maybe some of the girls were secretly involved with the judge and didn't want it getting out," Jan said.

"Young things like that don't go having affairs with an old fossil like Holoch. Maybe one girl with kinky preferences, but definitely not twenty of them. These girls were paid for."

"Where can we find them?"

Chandu flipped back a few pages. "The first one was Manu. Nice girl from the country." He sighed. "She came to Berlin for an education. Met the wrong guy, he got her addicted, she ended up on the street at twenty-one. Three years later, she was drifting dead down the Elbe."

He flipped pages. "Jasmina." He pointed to a photo of a woman with eyes swollen shut from blows. "She's from the Czech Republic. Was turning tricks for this nasty scumbag while living in a cellar hole in Marzahn. Eventually she disappeared, never seen again."

"You think all the women in these photos are dead?"

"Manu and Jasmina are, I know that for sure. But this one here," Chandu said, turning the page, "I saw two weeks ago. Sarah, works an illegal streetwalk over in the poorest part of the Wedding District. We're lucky, we'll find her there."

Jan grabbed his jacket. "Come on."

A lead, finally.

• •

Patrick held his pistol out in front of him as he went up the grimy stairway. The wooden steps were worn and splintered, the walls smeared with graffiti. Overhead, the decrepit ceiling plaster was peeling off, and the whole place reeked of vomit and urine. On the second floor, a couple was having a shouting contest. If that wasn't nerve-wracking enough, the barking of a ferocious dog was interspersed with an infant's screams.

This was one of those Berlin buildings no one would ever enter by choice, but Patrick had a good reason. He'd traced the car Jan had climbed into during his escape; the trace led to this address. Considering how expensive that Mercedes had looked, Patrick could hardly believe the owner lived on such a run-down street.

He waved over two officers in bulletproof vests. One of them carried a metal battering ram. Without speaking, they positioned themselves next to a door. Patrick checked the safety on his pistol and nodded to the officers. The lock broke with a dull bang, springing open the door. The three men stormed inside.

"Berlin Police!" Patrick shouted. He stepped on an open blue trash bag and turned his face away in disgust. The little studio apartment was piled up with garbage. Cockroaches roamed over food scraps and empty beer bottles. It stunk of mold and feces. Rats scurried around between the shelves. In the middle of this shambles, a man lay on a tattered couch. He stared at the newcomers through bleary eyes. Patrick aimed his weapon, but the man just waved at him, smiling.

"He's no threat," one of the officers said. "Guy's all doped up."

Patrick lowered his pistol and navigated his way to the couch. Luckily he'd just gotten a tetanus shot.

"My name is Patrick Stein," he said, showing his badge. "Berlin Detectives. You're Peer Runge?"

"Yo, boss," the guy said. "Sit on down, help y'self." He pointed to a large pile of blue pills and a spoon that looked like it had been cooking heroin.

Patrick wrinkled his brow. He'd seen a lot of things, but no one had ever offered him drugs before. But he wasn't about to arrest this guy for possession. All he wanted were answers.

"Do you know a Jan Tommen?"

"Never heard of him, boss, but if he's a friend of yours, then bring him on over and we'll party."

Patrick sighed and stuck his pistol in his holster.

"Take this drugged-out idiot down to the station," he ordered the officers. "I'll question him once he's come down."

Patrick worked his way through the trash to get back outside. In frustration he kicked away a beer bottle, which clanked and shattered against the wall. The guy was just a goddamn drug dealer who hadn't even noticed that his car had been stolen. And given the bender the guy was on at the moment, Patrick couldn't hold out hope that his memory would be stellar.

"The first round goes to you, Jan," Patrick muttered. "But I'm already getting warm."

•   •

As Chandu slowed the car, Jan looked out the window at the desolate neighborhood. He hated run-down areas like this. The buildings' gray walls were smeared with graffiti, and not the artful kind. The glass windows of one of the now-closed storefronts had been replaced with plywood, and then pasted over with cheesy ads for an upcoming André Rieu concert at the O2 World arena. The bare trees looked hardly alive, and an uprooted "No Parking" sign lay out on the street. Near the curb, young women lounged around in way-too-short skirts. Their thick makeup masked the grief on their faces as their eyes followed the traffic. Jan watched a car roll to a stop alongside one of the young women. The driver opened the door, and she climbed in without a word.

Jan had been investigating scenes like this for a long time, but he still felt a little pang whenever he saw such young girls out on the sidewalk. No one deserved such a life.

Chandu drove at a snail's pace, eyeing each girl closely. "There," he said finally. "The blonde."

After a moment, Jan spotted a fair-haired woman leaning against an old plane tree. She wore a white skirt, a bright tube top, and knee-high boots with spike heels. Her tired stare was directed at the roadway.

Chandu stopped the car next to her. The girl tossed her cigarette, came out to the street, and forced a smile.

"Hi," Jan said, returning the smile.

"Youse a pig?" she asked in thick Berlin dialect.

"Uh . . ." Jan hesitated.

The woman rolled her eyes.

Chandu leaned to Jan's side. "Get in, Sarah." He held out a hundred-euro bill for her. "We just want to chat."

The woman looked around warily, as if no should see her talking to them. Then she tugged down her skirt, grabbed the bill, and climbed into the back.

"My pimp catches me talkin' to pigs, I'm dead."

"We won't keep you long," Chandu reassured her as he drove off. "You can be back hooking in five minutes."

"Whatever."

Jan said, "Miss, we just have a few questions about how long you've been working here."

The woman snickered. "Youse really are a pig."

"How can she tell?" Jan asked Chandu.

"There's a sign on your forehead," he said. "You can't help it." Chandu adjusted the rearview mirror so he could look the girl in the eye. "I'll answer the man's question, if you don't mind." He turned to Jan. "She's been around for going on five years."

"How old are you?" Jan asked her.

"Twenty-four."

"Sarah," Chandu warned.

"Nineteen," she corrected, her voice dropping an octave.

Jan shook his head. The girls were getting younger and younger. What a life they must have had to be tossed out onto the street at fourteen. He hated to imagine the kind of horrible parents they'd dealt with or the twisted scumbags they'd gotten to know.

He would've liked to have given Sarah another chance, found her somewhere to live, sent her back to school, and made a new life possible. But from his time as a patrol cop, he knew that that was just a romantic dream. The streets pulled these girls back in.

"You know Judge George Holoch?" Chandu went on.

Sarah's cold, apathetic expression turned fearful. "How come?" Her eyes darted around as if she was looking for a way to escape.

"Take it easy, Sarah," Chandu said. "You know that they bashed in the judge's skull?"

"He deserved it, fuckin' swine."

"The thing is, we want to find out who it was."

"It wasn't me, but if I woulda gotten the chance? I woulda slit him open." Sarah pressed her lips together tight. She had trouble keeping back her tears.

"We know what he did to you," Jan said softly. "And, yes, he did deserve to die. But we need to learn more about him and his . . . preferences."

"Hopefully youse got a strong stomach."

"When did you meet him for the first time?"

"I only met the sick fuck once. I was new to it, he was probably the fourth or fifth customer I'd ever had. I was impressed by his crib, but my pimp was barely out the door before he started hitting me. Just a slap at first, then harder and harder. With his fist, in the face, in the gut, till I was on the floor crying. Then he kept at it with a cane, till I passed out. Hours later, I woke up in some park in Neukölln. Clothes all ripped to shit, four broken ribs, and three less teeth. With all the swelling I had on my face, I couldn't work the street for six weeks."

"You were fourteen back then?"

Sarah nodded. "I wanted to go to the pigs, but my pimp, he threatened to beat me if I opened my mouth."

"You never encountered Holoch after that?"

"I was too old for him, actually."

"At fourteen?"

"I told you, he was one sick asshole."

"You know other women he beat up?"

"Two."

"How old were they?"

"Both no older than fourteen. Probably younger."

"My God," Jan whispered.

"Welcome to my twisted world," Sarah said, wiping a tear from her eye.

• •

Back at Chandu's place, Jan grabbed a beer from the fridge and drank down the bottle in one long swig. Whenever he thought of girls worked over like that, he felt ill. Every one of those images in the judge's picture album was a life destroyed.

In the bedroom, Chandu was comparing the descriptions and names they got from Sarah with the photos in the book.

"Nobody she identified is in here. It's a dead end."

"We'll have to keep looking," Jan insisted.

"That won't be easy," Chandu told him. "I'll have to go around, see what I can hear, find out if they're still in Berlin and where I can find them. For that I'll have to call in a few favors."

"Maybe the judge didn't keep photos of each and every victim," said Jan. "I'll come with you."

Chandu shook his head. "Way too dicey. Some folks wouldn't be too happy about me having a cop along. I have to do it alone."

Jan wanted to object, but Chandu held up a hand.

"I can watch out for myself. If there's trouble? I'll call you."

Jan gave in. "Okay. I'll stay home if it means getting a new lead."

"I wouldn't be too optimistic."

"How come?"

"Finding these girls won't help you," Chandu said. "I could find plenty of women who would've liked to see the judge dead, but there will be no link to prove you innocent. You don't know a single girl in those photos, and the descriptions Sarah gave us don't ring a bell with you, either."

Jan sighed. "Maybe something in all this will jog my memory."

"I just don't want you to get up your hopes. Whoever murdered Holoch knew about you having trouble with him, and seems to have easily gotten hold of your fingerprints. The hookers might supply us with more twisted details about Holoch's kinks. But they aren't going to get us closer to finding the murderer, or explaining why the crime was pinned on you."

"You're right, but it's all we have."

Chandu placed a hand on Jan's shoulder. "I'll find more of the women. You should get some rest. You've gone through a lot."

"I'm meeting Father Anberger later today. He was going to get me a few things from my apartment that I'm hoping will be useful."

"Don't forget, they're out searching for you," Chandu warned. "Avoid staying outside too long." He grabbed the car key and left the apartment.

Jan got another beer from the fridge and dialed Father Anberger's number.

.   .

For Chandu it was like old times. He strolled by the bars and bordellos, said hey to a few of the girls waiting for takers along the street, waved at the bouncers, and chatted a little with club owners. Most were happy to see him—he was still a known face in the scene. But the reality was that he hated this area. The hookers' empty faces, the rooms smelling like quickie sex, the criminal minds at work trying to find new victims to rip off or blackmail. From his very first day it had been tough for him to work here—but in the beginning, he'd had nowhere else to turn. So he had conformed and played along, following the underworld's rules to survive. He would've rather become a car mechanic or a race-car driver, but life had other plans for him.

It didn't take long for him to realize that searching for the girls would prove tricky. No one could get wise that his strolling around was really investigating, or he was going to end up with real big problems, real fast. Even after canvassing the whole street, he still hadn't seen any of the girls he was after.

"Chandu." A Russian accent made him spin around.

"Andrei," Chandu said. He hugged the powerfully built Russian as if they were old friends, but there was no one Chandu wanted to see less. The man was as big as he was. His tattoos included a star over his left eyebrow and Cyrillic script on his hands. The flashy rings on his meaty fingers had been sharpened to points to cause more damage when he hit someone.

Andrei was one of the meanest bastards in Berlin. In Russia, he had been sentenced to death for murder. Somehow he'd fled to Germany. Now he worked as a fixer for a ring that smuggled girls. His nickname, the Russian Bear, was far too nice for him. They should've called him the Russian Ripper. No one enjoyed violence more.

"What you doing here?" Andrei asked him. "You collecting dough again?"

"Things are quiet at the moment. No jobs going. I was just bored, so I'm strolling through the neighborhood."

"Stroll through the neighborhood." Andrei laughed and slapped him on the shoulder. "You look more like stinking pig who looks for something."

Chandu broke into laughter, but his eyes were taking in his surroundings, gauging his odds of survival. Beyond Andrei, inside the closest bar, sat two of the Russian's minions, types who were real quick on the trigger. Less than twenty feet away, another of his thugs was arguing with a Russian whore. Andrei himself always carried a knife, knowing a blade was more effective than any pistol at short distances. While keeping his right hand on Chandu's shoulder, Andrei moved his left suspiciously close to his hip. Chandu tried to recall if he'd seen a knife handle in the man's belt.

"What, you trying to insult me, brother?" Chandu replied, playing up the outrage. He worked himself loose from Andrei's grip, taking a step back—being that close to Andrei was never a good idea. "I've collected money for you, and you suspect me of being a pig?"

"You walk up street and study girls. Now you walk other side. Only pigs do this."

"I got to keep up on the latest," Chandu argued. "What kind of new girls are coming in, who's not working anymore, what kind of new players are showing up. You know how important it is to know the score."

"What do you have in your pocket?" Andrei said, unmoved.

Chandu knew that face. He had seen the Russian flip out enough times to know when he was about to lose it. The men at the bar rose from their seats. Their hands drifted under their jackets.

Chandu had only one chance. If Andrei saw the book of photos, it was over.

"You guys hear that?" He moved past the Russian, into the bar. "My old friend here, he hurts my feelings. He's calling me some kind of snoop."

The two thugs clearly did not like Chandu's maneuver.

He turned to the cocktail waitress. "Give me a glass of Andrei's best vodka. That's the least I get for the abuse."

Andrei was still standing at the entrance, still not moving. If the Russian went off on him now, he was as good as dead. With those two thugs at his back, he would never get out of there. He wouldn't escape outside, either. The street was too wide for good cover. Andrei's guys would blow him away before he'd gotten ten yards.

The put-on indignation was his only chance. Chandu kept up his insulted face, hoping Andrei was falling for it.

No one moved. The cocktail waitress was stiff with fear. Cheesy bar music clanged out of the speakers. Chandu shifted a little next to a beer bottle. He'd bring that down on the first thug's skull. He could deal with the second one too, but the Bear was a whole different caliber.

The tension faded from Andrei's face.

"Forgive me, my black friend," he said, smiling, coming all the way into the bar. The two thugs relaxed, taking their hands out of their jackets.

73

"Give him bottle of Kauffman," Andrei told the bartender. "This is only true vodka. Only best Russian wheat, with hint of honey."

Chandu grabbed a glass and toasted to Andrei. *"Za vas,"* he said, and tipped back the vodka in one swig.

"Za vas," the men replied, and drank.

Chandu hated vodka, but he'd have to permit himself a few. Maybe then his knees would stop shaking.

●　●

Jan's hair was disheveled and his unshaven face looked scruffy as he walked to his meeting with Father Anberger. He kept his head down and focused on his feet, wishing he were somewhere else. A million miles away from here. Away from murder charges, child abusers, and broken dreams.

In the Tiergarten, the priest was waiting with a large sports bag. As always, when he smiled at Jan, he radiated unshakeable optimism.

"You doing well, Herr Tommen?" he asked with concern. Jan's dark mood was not lost on the older man.

Jan waved it away. "So far, okay," he said wearily. "This has all been a little much for me."

Father Anberger didn't seem satisfied with Jan's answer, but he let it go with an understanding nod. He handed Jan the bag.

"It's all in there," he said. "Even that little plastic ice-cream cone thing. I hope it helps."

Jan felt a rush of gratitude and placed his hand on Father Anberger's shoulder. Only now did he realize how much he liked the old man. It was comforting to know some people would still stand by him in his dark hours.

"Thank you, from the bottom of my heart." Jan smiled. "When this is all behind me, I'll invite you over and we won't just talk briefly in the stairway like we do. I'll have a lot to tell you about."

Father Anberger touched Jan's hand in a friendly gesture. "There will come a time when you will make sense of all this. Then your life will be worth living again. And no matter how forsaken you feel, the Lord is with you."

Without another word, the priest turned and walked off, heading for the subway. Jan watched him go until the man disappeared among the throng of passersby. Jan shouldered the bag and made his own way back.

•   •

Chandu's tour through the red-light district had brought him little new besides waves of nausea from too much vodka. And he couldn't go back to Jan empty-handed. So he got in the car and drove to a neighborhood not far from the City Palace, parking in front of a villa.

As he approached the door, it struck Chandu that he hadn't been to the place for years. It was still a stunning home. He'd always admired its quiet elegance. Well-designed lighting illuminated the front courtyard, which was anchored by manicured shrubs. The exterior shutters were open, but curtains barred anyone from looking inside. He climbed the broad set of marble steps that led to the imposing wooden door.

The house fit in well among the old prewar buildings surrounding it, and yet, at a second glance, it differed from the others. Two cameras were mounted at the entrance. There was no bell or name plaque, just a bronze knocker mounted on the door.

Chandu knocked twice. He knew this door didn't open for just anyone. All he could hope was that the proprietor had not forgotten him. The woman who owned this place was his final hope for finding out more about the girls.

As the door gently clicked, he sighed in relief. A man in a dark suit opened up.

"She's expecting you upstairs." He motioned for Chandu to step inside.

The home's interior was as elegant as its facade. The floor was white marble. Dark-red columns nestled up against gold-trimmed walls. The stucco ceiling was embellished with a mural of a naked woman lounging lasciviously with a silk sheet. A corridor to the right was concealed by a curtain and guarded by a gorgeous blonde in a silk negligee. She had a model's looks and a slender, curving body that promised unimaginable delights, but Chandu didn't pause. He continued up the wide staircase, not stopping until he reached a white wooden door on the second floor.

He knocked.

"Come in," said a woman's warm voice.

A moment later, he was inside a small library with bookshelves to the ceiling and a cozy fire. In the middle of the room stood a heavy oak desk, its polished wood mirroring the flames. The woman who sat behind it still possessed the beauty that had enthralled him when they'd first met. Her black hair was combed back severely into an elegant violet head wrap. Her face had a perfect symmetry, barely any makeup, and an immaculate clarity. Her intelligent gaze and confident manner made her beauty even more extraordinary. As Chandu entered, she set aside her golden fountain pen and closed a leather folder.

"Chandu," she said graciously. "It's nice to see you again."

"Lady Samira." He gave a little bow. "The pleasure is all mine."

The woman gestured to a leather chair. Chandu settled into it, grateful to be sitting.

"What can I do for you? I assume you'd like an appointment with one of the girls. I'm guessing that your sexual inclinations haven't changed."

The big man smiled. "Thanks for the offer, but whips and chains still scare me."

Lady Samira returned the smile.

"A friend is in trouble. I want to lend him a hand, and I need your help."

"An unusual request, after all these years."

"Apologies. If it wasn't important, I would never bother you."

Lady Samira leaned back, weighing her options.

"He has a name, your friend?"

"Jan."

"The policeman who saved your life?"

Chandu nodded.

"You do know I don't exactly have a friendly relationship with the police."

"It would kill me to ever get you into trouble. Jan doesn't know I'm here, and he won't ever know. The only reason I'm sitting here is because I see no other way."

Lady Samira steepled her hands below her chin, studying Chandu from over her finely manicured fingers.

"I'll listen to what you have to say. Then I'll decide if and how I can help you."

"Thank you," Chandu said, relieved. He pulled the photo album from his pocket. "It's about the murder of Judge George Holoch."

"No loss there," Lady Samira said. "He was a nasty sadist, with poor manners."

"He was a client of yours?"

"He wanted to book one of my girls, but I could tell at once he would only cause trouble. His ego couldn't handle me rejecting him. He threatened me and told me that I'd regret the decision, but after I showed him the door, I never heard from him again. What did this policeman have to do with it?"

"He's suspected of murdering the judge."

"That does make me like him."

"But Jan is innocent. I'm helping him find the actual murderer."

Chandu set the album on the desk and pushed it over to Lady Samira.

"What is it?" She opened it.

"This shows Judge Holoch deserved to die. It's his trophy collection. Nothing but girls all beat up. I know three of them, and I wanted to see if any of the faces looks familiar."

Lady Samira paged through the photos, impassive.

"I have little to do with these types of prostitutes," she said. "Why come to me?"

"I was hoping that Judge Holoch had been one of your clients. Since you rejected him, though, you can't tell me much. Do you know where he might have gone?"

"George Holoch was a pathetic creature," Lady Samira said without raising her voice. "Some women do offer services to sadists like him, but none would willingly endure his level of cruelty. Few procurers would seek him out, either. They don't view it too kindly when someone breaks their girl's nose or brings her back with a black eye. It's bad for business."

"Where did he get the girls, then? He can't have kidnapped them."

Lady Samira closed the photo album. "Don't look for the girls, but rather the person who took them to the judge."

"So I should blame all the local pimps?"

"Judge Holoch wouldn't have had enough money to reimburse each procurer for such a large number of maltreated girls. That nice house he had alone was more than he could afford."

"Who should I look for?"

"I don't have a name for you. However, you must know that not all the girls in these photos are whores."

"You mean . . ."

"Most of those girls were procured privately. Children of fathers who don't care if their daughters are roughed up. The main thing for them is, they earn a few euros for their next fix or that bottle of schnapps. Search for the fathers. Then you might find an avenging angel."

•   •

Michael Josseck woke up. Sweat drenched his white shirt. His face was flushed red and he panted heavily, making his thick body shudder. The whole room spun around him. Harsh ceiling light pierced his eyes. He had no idea what had happened. He had come home, left his coat on the chair, and poured himself a cognac. With glass in hand, he'd turned on the TV and flipped through the channels. At some point he must have nodded off.

Now he lay in front of the sofa on the floor, his feet tied up, his hands bound behind his back. The TV was still on, though now the volume was unbearably loud. The bass boomed; the news anchor's voice hurt his ears.

"What the hell?" He tried to break his restraints. The plastic ties wouldn't give.

A military boot planted itself atop his chest. It belonged to a masked figure with mirrored sunglasses. The figure was wearing a black jumpsuit. There was a hydration pack on its back. Michael had seen those things on joggers along the Spree.

"Take your fucking boots off me," he barked, "and cut off these straps or you're going to get it right in the face."

The figure shook its head a little. It appeared to be smiling under the mask.

"Let me go, you motherfucker, or—"

The attacker dropped and pressed Michael's face between its thighs, making it impossible to move his head. He tried to twist his way out of the hold but found he couldn't move. He strained with all his power and felt the plastic ties cut into his flesh. He couldn't get free.

"Motherfucker," he groaned, squeezing out the words. Something was shoved into his mouth. He tried to close his jaw tightly but some kind of metal barrier forced his mouth open.

"I thought you were into oral action," the figure said. "Be good, hold still."

Michael's eyes opened wide. He knew this voice.

A sweetish liquid was sprayed into his mouth. Like the stuff he'd had to ingest for that gastroscopy.

"Wouldn't want you to have to gag," the figure chirped.

Michael's thoughts raced. It couldn't be. Not after so many years. He fought against the straps on his hands until blood dripped onto the floor. No matter how much he tried, the relentless squeezing of those thighs made it impossible to turn his head.

A plastic tube was inserted down his throat. Michael convulsed as the tube was forced into his esophagus.

"Good, swallow," his attacker said and uncapped the hydration pack. A gritty pulp ran through the pipe and into his stomach.

"Wouldn't want any to miss."

Michael fought one last time, but the thighs kept him pressed to the floor as the mix kept flowing down his throat.

Chapter 6

It was only 7:00 a.m. and Jan had already been awake for two hours. His insomnia was really starting to worry him. He wasn't going to get any more sleep, so he opened the bag from Father Anberger.

He pulled out what appeared to be a plastic toy that looked like a vanilla ice-cream cone. Then he uncapped the end of the cone to reveal a USB flash drive. It contained files from most of the cases Jan had worked on. It had been handy for his investigations because it was a way to reference old details at home, without needing to drive into the office and look them up. Taking out records was strictly forbidden, of course, but the fact was the flash drive had helped him solve several cases. Sometimes he had his best ideas for breaking a case on the weekend or at night.

It was a stroke of luck that the data hadn't been discovered by his coworkers when they'd searched his apartment. He had his friend Max to thank. Max had given him the fake ice-cream cone a couple years ago.

Jan connected the flash drive to Chandu's computer. As the laptop started up, he pulled clothes from the bag and placed them in the cabinet his friend had freed up for him. Now he could finally change.

He was enjoying the scent of fresh new clothes on his body when his phone rang.

"Hello?"

"It's Zoe here. We have another dead."

"Who?"

"I don't know yet. I'm on the way to the crime scene now. But homicide squad has been knocked for a loop. Seems Holoch and dead guy knew each other."

Jan cursed under his breath. This new murder could have been his chance to rule himself out as a suspect. If he were in custody right now, he'd have the perfect alibi. Instead, here was another crime they'd probably want to pin on him.

"I don't have much time," Zoe continued. "I'm going to take a few photos, but we should meet in person. E-mail is too risky for me."

Jan paused. He wasn't sure if he could trust Zoe, but she was his only link to the homicide squad. Without her, he had zilch.

"My hideout is tough to find," Jan told her. "Send me a text if you want to do it tonight. If so, I'll be waiting in front of the Absolut Bar on Oranienburger."

"Okay," Zoe said and hung up.

Jan set down his phone, his dark mood gone. He had the urge to drive over to the Homicide offices to find out more about the victim. And discover whether his own fingerprints had once again turned up at the scene.

Whoever had murdered Judge Holoch had probably pre-planned this new murder the same way as before, to make him look guilty. Jan pounded on the coffee table. His inability to act was driving him nuts. There was a lunatic running around and he couldn't do a thing about it. He turned on the TV and flipped channels, hoping to distract himself as he waited to hear from Zoe. Then he heard Chandu's heavy steps coming up the stairs.

• •

Once Chandu shut the door behind him, he let out an audible sigh of relief. It had been a crazy night.

"You're home late," Jan said.

"Early, you mean," Chandu replied.

"You were gone a long time, either way. Did you find out anything?"

"I'm not sure yet." Chandu went into the kitchen. "I went poking around the red-light district and hit up every contact I got, but I didn't find any more girls."

He pushed buttons on the coffee machine to get the brew going.

"I did learn more about Judge Holoch," he said. "It seems the upstanding fellow didn't have as much dough as you might think from that sweet crib of his. Apparently to procure girls that he could abuse like that meant having to shell out a hell of a lot."

"Maybe he simply picked up girls off the street."

"That wouldn't have worked for long," Chandu said. "For one thing, word would have gotten out and hookers would've refused to get into his car. Plus, pimps don't like it when a john beats on their girls, because they can't make money off damaged goods. They'd find the guy and take revenge real quick."

"What else is there?"

"Private procurement."

"Private?" Jan said in surprise.

"Fathers, handing over their daughters for whatever."

"Who would do such a thing?"

"Addicts, drunks, and other losers who don't give a shit. They're happy to take the payout and let some degenerate do whatever they want with their kid. They tell Child Services the kid took a fall, and they believe it."

"What a shitty world."

"I'm sorry, Jan, but I just don't know how we go about this one. I was hoping for more."

"It's not over. Look, somebody was dealing those girls. Judge Holoch didn't just run ads for that in the *Tagespresse*. We find that dealer, we know who the girls were."

"So how do we find him?"

"I got no idea, not yet, but Zoe's coming this evening. There's another dead man. She's bringing crime-scene photos. Maybe they'll get us that much closer."

• •

Klaus Bergman flipped through documents for the Josseck murder case. Maybe it sounded cynical, but he was glad the latest victim had not been another prominent judge. The department couldn't take a second George Holoch case. The last few days he'd done nothing but fend off prying reporters, reassure politicians, and report their progress to the police chief.

Patrick Stein knocked on the doorframe. The lead detective looked tired. His eyes were bloodshot and his suit rumpled.

"You need to get some sleep."

"When we have Jan."

"It seems there's another lunatic loose in Berlin." Bergman held up a photo of the dead Michael Josseck.

"It was Jan."

"What makes you think that?" Bergman shot back in surprise. Jan did have a possible motive for murdering the judge, but nothing connected him to Josseck.

"It's only speculation, but I'll deliver you the proof soon."

"If you don't have it, I suggest you start thinking more broadly."

"I am certain that Jan is behind this. That's why I propose to make it public."

"A public manhunt?" Bergman blurted, startled now. "That is the last thing I will do."

"It would make our work—"

"I don't think you recognize the situation we're in," Bergman cut in. "My job is to pacify the media and what feels like five hundred political committees. I can't even go take a piss because one of my detectives is the main suspect in a murder case. With that kind of manhunt? It would turn Jan into a serial killer, and the case would make headlines all over the country. And we might as well build a moat around the station."

"But what if I can confirm my theory?" Patrick said.

"My God, Stein, come off it. With all due respect to your commitment. Jan is not the next generation of Red Army Faction killer." Bergman slapped the photo of Josseck on the desk. "All right? Now get this idea of a public manhunt out of your head."

He grabbed for the new phone. He'd had this one brought in after he'd destroyed his old phone in a fit of rage a few days before. "Right now, I get to go kiss the police chief's ass. Concern yourself with Josseck. You have something firm, come on by, otherwise keep your wild theories to yourself."

He waved Patrick out.

"Public manhunt," Bergman grumbled. "Like a rabid dog."

•   •

The table was covered with pictures and crime-scene reports. Zoe was enjoying sipping her coffee, gazing around the apartment while Jan looked at the photos. The shots showed the dead man from every possible angle. Michael Josseck had been the victim of a clearly sadistic murder. His thick body was bound up with plastic ties. His thin hair was sticky with sweat. A gray, gritty substance oozed out of his wide-open mouth.

"Is that concrete?" Chandu asked her.

"He was a building contractor," she said. "Took a couple hours to get the stuff out of him." Zoe pulled out her pack of cigarettes, stuck one in her mouth, and lit it with her waterproof lighter.

"I hate people smoking in my apartment," Chandu growled.

Zoe blew smoke into the air, ignoring him. "We even found concrete in his stomach," she went on. "The esophagus was filled with it too."

"Was it the cause of death, or did someone pour the stuff into him afterward?"

"Michael Josseck asphyxiated. The murderer poured concrete into his mouth when he was still alive."

"What a sick bastard," Chandu said.

"I've seen worse," Zoe said, unmoved.

"You find concrete on his clothes, in his hair, or on his face?" Jan said.

"Why do you ask?"

"I want to know exactly how the murderer did it," Jan told her. "No one just lets himself have concrete dumped down his throat. Michael Josseck looked like a big strong guy. He would've defended himself no matter what. If no specks of concrete were discovered on his clothes and face, then presumably he was lying steady."

"The toxicology analysis is ongoing," Zoe said. "If he had any drugs or poisons in him, we'll find them."

She raised her coffee mug and tilted it toward Chandu, showing him it was empty. The big man waved away cigarette smoke in a huff and got up.

"He have any indentations inside his mouth or missing any teeth?"

Zoe narrowed her eyes. "We actually did find indents in his jaw, but we weren't sure what caused them."

"Indentations could be from a jaw spreader. The perpetrator could hold his mouth open that way, then pour in the concrete."

"My God. Why kill a man with concrete?" Chandu asked from the kitchen. "Why not just slit his throat or put a bullet in him?"

"Gruesome murders are usually personal," Jan explained. "The murderer spent a long time planning the act and wanted to savor Josseck dying. An atypical murder weapon often says something about the perpetrator or points to there being an unusual motive for the deed. But concrete for a building contractor? It's hardly specific. The murderer could be any angry former customer who got cheated by Josseck." He turned to Zoe. "Are there suspects?"

"No idea. I only have the exam results, these autopsy photos, and a few crime-scene pics I shot."

As Chandu set down Zoe's mug for her, Jan picked up the crime-scene photos and spread them out over the whole table, trying to piece together the facts. Michael Josseck had been killed in his living room. It was a large space with white furniture and a silvery light fixture. His head lay on a bright-white flokati rug. Only a still-life painting and a flat-screen TV stood out in the colorless landscape.

"Notice anything?" Jan said. Chandu and Zoe moved closer, scrutinizing the photos.

"He had some real bad taste in furniture," Zoe said.

Chandu shook his head.

"It's all neat and tidy," Jan told them. "Michael Josseck was bound and choked in agony. But if you retouched the picture to remove the corpse, the apartment would look in perfect order. There are no bloodstains, and the furnishings are all intact. Even if the murderer was really strong, he wouldn't have had an easy time with the likes of Josseck. How tall was he—six foot two?"

"Six three."

"And his weight? At least three hundred pounds."

87

Zoe flipped through the autopsy report. "Three fifty-nine."

"The murderer didn't go at Josseck head-on. No, there were drugs or narcotics at work here." Jan leaned back on the couch. "Plus, I bet nothing was stolen."

"How come?"

"Josseck was supposed to suffer and die. The money wasn't important. The crime scene suggests extensive planning, not spontaneity."

"So?"

"That's good news," Jan said. "In a robbery, there's rarely a relationship between victim and perpetrator. Here, the murderer watched Josseck a long time before striking. The two probably knew each other, or at least had some contact before the murder. So maybe a neighbor noticed something."

Jan felt the thrill of the hunt surging through his veins.

"Can you access what the investigators have found so far?" he asked Zoe.

"No idea. Never tried to, but supposedly they've approved a new authorization for this. So it could be tougher than with previous cases. What would you need?"

"All of it. The blood analysis won't help, since Josseck had to be stunned somehow. What I really need is the crime-scene analysis as well as any evidence that can link the perpetrator and the victim."

"I'll see what I can do. I'll call you tomorrow on my break." Zoe stood, tossed her cigarette in her coffee mug, waved good-bye, and left the apartment without another word.

Chandu opened the window, letting in fresh air. "You should teach your friend some manners."

"Yeah? This was one of her better days," Jan told him. "You should see her in a bad mood."

"Can hardly wait," Chandu growled. "I have to go take care of some business now. Make yourself at home." He took his jacket and left too.

Jan rubbed his hands together. It was time to get things going.

• •

After Zoe and Chandu were gone, Jan sat at the computer and searched the Internet for George Holoch. He came across a seminar the judge had offered on issues surrounding defective construction. The web page included a bio. In his photo, Holoch had dark, thinning hair and an unsympathetic, artificial smile. His suit and his tie lent him a certain integrity. Jan read the seminar description:

George Holoch studied in Munich and joined the Berlin District Court after completing his Second State Legal Exams. He's known for numerous published works on construction law. His seminar is an introduction to the relationship between the law and construction engineering. It's designed to illustrate practical examples based on specific trades.

Jan saved the document on the flash drive and then returned to the search engine and entered the name "Michael Josseck." The first hit was the home page of Josseck Construction. Under the company name were pictures of construction sites.

For years we've stood for quality construction, the marketing copy proclaimed. *We specialize in building repairs and drywall jobs. We also provide additional construction work as part of a partnership with other contractors, so you can get all services under one roof.*

Below that were the physical address, a phone number, and an e-mail address. Jan jotted down the location and typed both men's names into the search engine together. He got 1,600 hits. Apparently some blogger had the same name as Josseck, and he quickly realized that none of the results pointed to any common ground between the two murder victims.

It wasn't hard to imagine a connection between a judge special-izing in construction law and a building contractor, of course, but for now, it was only speculation. He would just have to wait for Zoe.

Frustrated, Jan shut down the computer. He lay on the couch and compared the two crime scenes in his head. Soon he fell asleep.

•   •

Klaus Bergman had feared this day. He was barely out of his car when the reporters stormed him like a horde of squealing teens. Microphones thrust into his face, questions pelted him.

"Is it true that a police detective is a suspect in the Holoch mur-der case?" a small, stocky woman asked him.

Bergman smiled, not discussing it, and kept pushing his way through the throng.

"Is he also suspected of having killed building contractor Michael Josseck?"

"What's the officer's name?" another reporter shouted.

"Do you feel personally responsible for the murders?"

Bergman balled his fists. These were not journalists, these were animals. They were just waiting for the tiniest lapse, and then they'd pounce on him like a pack of hyenas. He wouldn't do them the favor.

A cameraman shoved toward him. A microphone brushed his head, but Bergman didn't let it get to him. He plowed on, aiming for the door. Twenty yards.

"Shouldn't you have selected officers more carefully?" the woman asked. "Essentially you carry a share of the blame for a murder."

Bergman sighed. He could just see the headline: "Berlin Detectives Train a Murderer!"

How liberating it would be to drop one of these vultures to the ground with a straight jab. He pictured himself doing it.

Ten yards to go.

"Don't you think the public has a right to know more about the murderer?"

The photographers fired away as if their lives depended on it. The flashing got to his eyes. The clicking cameras were drowning out the reporters' increasingly hostile tones.

Five yards.

Almost there, he told himself. In front of the department, the throng closed around him, the reporters trying to keep him from getting away easily. Bergman could hardly breathe. He lowered his head and rammed himself through the wall of people with microphones. He used one arm to shove a couple of extra-pushy guys with cameras.

"You see any fallout yet from the scandal?" the woman shouted after him. And then, finally, he made it. Four uniformed men stood before the building, keeping the overeager reporters outside. Bergman pushed inside the lobby. In a rage now, he kicked at the nearest table.

"Fucking vermin!" he shouted. A few more curses later, he was feeling somewhat better.

Most of his colleagues had been able to keep well outside the range of fire now coming at him. Only his assistant was sticking by him, he thought, as he saw her waiting to speak with him. She'd been in her job far too long to feel threatened by any of it.

"What?" he barked.

"A story's about to air on RBB—apparently, an insider wants to talk about Jan."

Bergman shut his eyes. Whenever he thought it couldn't get any worse, fate just laughed in his face.

"When's it airing?"

"One minute."

Bergman went into his office, slammed the door shut, and turned on the TV. He switched to Berlin's regional channel.

In a studio, a young woman sat in a chair, note cards in one hand. The moderator's grave expression didn't match her bouncy hair and stylish suit.

"Good morning," she began. "Everyone in Berlin has heard about the murder of Judge George Holoch. Already, rumors are making the rounds that the main suspect was working for Berlin Detective Division. Now there's been a second murder, and we've heard suggestions that the same person is behind the crime. The detective division has not yet commented on the accusation, but we were able to interview an insider who has some alarming events to report."

The camera pulled out. Just beyond the moderator was a partition of white paper. A person's silhouette was shadowed onto it.

Bergman shook his head. Cheap sensational journalism. It worked without fail. The man behind the paper wall was likely more of a scandalmonger than any insider. Probably just a coworker from the TV station's editorial team.

"To protect our whistleblower, we'll call him Herr Müller," the moderator continued. "We've also disguised his voice." She turned to the shadow.

"Herr Müller. You've worked at the detective division for several years. Is it even conceivable that the murderer could be a police detective?"

"Detectives are only people too," a mechanical-sounding voice replied. "When you're working in an environment involving violence, you can become capable of violence yourself."

"But isn't this a horrifying notion, that even the police cannot be trusted?"

"It is. It's unsettling. The alleged murderer worked on the homicide squad. There can't be a better training ground for killing than that. After years learning investigative techniques, it would be possible to map out a strategy that would leave behind no clues."

"Are you saying that this cop could commit the perfect murder?"

"Well, this murder was not perfect. But it's always going to be tougher to catch an experienced officer than a simple criminal."

"Didn't the police already fail by hiring this person to work for the department? Are selection criteria too lax?"

"I wouldn't condemn the police as a whole. The fault lies with the Berlin Detective Division, who laid the worst of all possible eggs right in its own nest."

The moderator turned to face the camera.

"We'll take a short break. When we come back, our whistle-blower will reveal more misconduct inside the Berlin Detective Division. I promise, you will be shocked."

Bergman turned off the TV and fought an urge to smash the remote against the wall. His phone rang. He didn't have to look to know the chief of police was on the line.

"What a lovely morning," he muttered and lifted the receiver.

•   •

Jan's ringing phone jolted him from sleep and he quickly pressed it to his ear, despite not being fully awake. "Hell-o," he mumbled, drowsy.

It was Zoe. "You still sleeping? It's ten a.m."

Jan yawned, sitting up. He had slept twelve hours but still felt wiped out. "Find out anything?" he said, rubbing his weary face.

"No."

"Why not? There still no reports up on the server?"

"There could be."

Jan sighed. "Man, Zoe, I'm not myself yet. Okay, what's going on?"

"I'm not getting in with my username."

Jan was afraid of this. "They removed your access."

"So, what now? Without those homicide files, we're nowhere."

Jan stood and stretched. His brain was starting to work again. "Here's the deal. I know someone who can help us. Can you come by again this evening?"

"I'll be there at seven." The line went dead.

Jan put his cell aside and went into the kitchen. Without his coffee right after getting up, he was only half a man. He thanked God that Chandu believed in the power of caffeine. The African blend he favored was so potent it probably violated certain weapons laws. He started brewing the coffee and savored the aroma that filled the room. He would do research the whole day long. And that evening, he would bring a brand-new player into this game.

Chapter 7

Jan, Zoe, and Chandu climbed the stairs of the old prewar building. The stone steps were worn down, the ornate metal railings looked to be a hundred years old, and the old brown wallpaper on the walls really needed replacing. It smelled of onions and garlic. The happy shrieks of children filtered right through the door to the second floor.

"Good God, how much farther?" Zoe growled. Climbing stairs was clearly not her thing.

"I can't help it if the elevator's out," Jan told her.

"Smoke less, you'll walk easier," Chandu remarked.

"If I need advice, I'll ask my hairdresser," Zoe replied.

Chandu looked around the stairwell. "I like it here. It's got a certain . . . permanence."

"You mean it's old."

"Old doesn't have to be bad."

"Old is crap," Zoe said. "My apartment has an elevator, it's soundproof, and it came with air conditioning. I wouldn't even dump my garbage here. What the hell are we doing?"

"I told you," Jan said. "We're meeting a friend who knows his way around computers. He might have an idea how we can get to those files in Homicide."

"I just hope, for you and your front teeth, that this hike is worth it."

Jan stood at a door, catching his breath. "We're here." He rapped on the door. "Max? It's me. Jan."

Two tiny cameras in the corners of the doorframe pivoted on him. A robot-like voice sounded: "Identify yourself."

"Who is this guy?" Zoe said. "Yoda?"

"You mean C-3PO," Chandu corrected her.

"What, you think I fucking watch *Star Trek*?"

The big man sighed.

"Cut the crap, Max," Jan said into a camera. "Let us in."

"Who are the others?" the mechanical voice asked.

"They're with me and it's fine."

"Show me your IDs, please."

Chandu nudged Jan aside and stood before the camera. Despite the tall door, he was almost eye level with the lens.

"Listen up, Robot Man. We're not here for some kid's birthday party. Open up this door or I'll kick it in, grab you by the ears, and stomp all over you so long that not even your mama's gonna know you."

For a moment, silence prevailed in the hallway. Then a short click sounded and the door opened up.

"There you go," Chandu said.

Inside the apartment, Jan held a hand over his mouth. It reeked like food going bad, onions, and something indefinably sweet.

Zoe scrunched up her face. "Your friend doing experiments on rotting meat?"

"Some fresh air would help," Chandu remarked.

They went down a narrow hall, the only light coming from the room ahead of them. It grew unusually warm. Jan heard the soft hum of numerous fans.

They entered a room that had windows covered with aluminum foil. Across an entire wall were tables set up with monitors connected to computers of various shapes and sizes. Hundreds of yards of cable snaked along the floor. A large flat-screen TV was mounted to the ceiling with chain. On it, a cartoon show flickered in English, with two strange-looking mice in the lead roles. Piled in front of the tables were blank CDs along with magazines and small mountains of printouts. This was striking enough. Yet dominating one end of the room was a man-high mountain of pizza boxes surrounded by a sea of empty nonreturnable cola bottles.

"Classy," Chandu muttered.

"Glad I got the heavy-duty hand sanitizer," Zoe added. She turned to Jan and gestured into the room smiling. "After you."

"Hi, Max!" Jan shouted.

A young man peeked out from between two narrow cabinets. He had a full cola bottle in one hand, brandishing it like a truncheon. His long, black hair hung down his forehead in strands. His pale, hairless face probably hadn't seen any sun for weeks. He wore thick, dark sunglasses, the frames held together with white tape. Fluttering from his gaunt upper body was a tatty black T-shirt printed with the words "There's No Place Like 127.0.01." His too-wide jeans were worn out, and faded sport socks could be seen under his Birkenstocks.

"Put the bottle down, and take it easy," Jan said. "And open a window."

"The windows are screwed shut," Max said in a hushed voice. "The CIA is everywhere."

Jan turned to Chandu and Zoe. He forced out a pained smile. "May I introduce—Maximilien, or simply Max?"

"You can call me Maximum," he said, straightening up.

"Maximum?" Zoe asked, raising her eyebrows. "Like, Maximum Loser?"

"Maximum Power, more like," Max corrected her. "The name is famous in all the hacker community."

"Rather be stuck in the lab," Zoe grumbled and lit up a cigarette.

"Smoking is not allowed here." Max seethed, wagging his cola bottle.

"Shut your trap, Maximum Moron, or I'll come shut it for you."

"Be nice to him," Chandu said, grinning. "You're probably the first woman who's entered his apartment willingly."

"And I'll be the last too."

Jan changed the subject: "We need your help."

"With what?" Max said, still looking to defend his life with that cola bottle.

"Well, you are one of the world's best hackers, and we have a problem that only the best can solve."

The flattering words had the desired effect. Max squared his shoulders and lowered the bottle.

"Don't you have police people for that?" he said.

"Sure, but not as good as you."

Max scratched at his chin. "I be paid for it?"

"At the moment, I'm having a little trouble with my account."

"Is it illegal?"

Jan nodded. "You're going to hack the police server."

"Ha!" Max shouted. He let the bottle drop and sprung into his office chair. He pushed off and rolled over to a computer screen. "That's not a problem. Berlin police admins, they think their firewalls and anti-Trojan software are getting it done, but I'll jimmy their servers faster than they can say 'Atari ST.'"

"Did you get anything that freak just said?" Chandu asked.

Zoe shrugged.

"Have yourself a seat," Max told them. "But not that brown chair. The spring's shot and I don't know what'll happen if you sit on it."

"We'll remain standing," Jan replied, eyeing a plastic chair with pizza sauce smeared all over the backrest.

Max's fingers flew over the keys. Then he pushed off to another computer and typed something in with preposterous speed.

"What should I hack for you? You want the latest police reports? Or a wanted list?"

"I need access to the Homicide server."

Max drew in a deep, noisy breath. "The Homicide server, that's a tough nut. Almost a puzzle of its own. Not much you can do there."

"I thought you were the best hacker in the world," Zoe sneered.

"This isn't *WarGames*," Max snapped at her. "It takes a lot more than pressing a few keys to get us that kind of info." He turned to Jan. "Give me five minutes. I got something to try out."

He pointed at his cardboard pile. "You want, you guys could have a piece of pizza. Anchovies and onions. It's this morning's."

"Thanks." Jan declined with a wave. "We're not hungry."

Max sank into his work. His eyes lit up and he hammered at the keyboard as if his hacking alone could prevent an evil mastermind from destroying Planet Earth. Now and then he rolled around the room on his chair and typed on various keyboards.

"Oh, man," Zoe said, lighting another cigarette.

While Max was busy with the computers, Jan found it hard not to fall asleep. It felt like the stale air and Max's nonstop typing were putting him in a trance.

"He going to get there some time before tomorrow?" Zoe asked after her second cigarette.

As if in reply, young Max whirled around in his chair. "I'm not getting in," he said. "But while Smoker Lady there was spouting her stupid comments, I did come up with an idea."

He reached for a tiny circuit board. "I crafted this little wonder a few weeks ago. I'll have to do a few mods to it, but if you just hook it up to a Homicide computer, I'll only have to hack the password. Won't take an hour."

"And how do you expect that to happen?" Zoe said. "Go right in, crack open the computer, and solder the thing on?"

"I'll tweak the board so any amateur can hook it up, of course," Max said. "It'll connect through a USB port. You do know what that is, right?"

"I'm about to smack you upside your noodle, Zit-Face."

Jan raised his hands, planting himself before pissed-off Zoe. "Easy, easy. How long do you need to convert it or whatever?"

"Twenty minutes," Max said.

"We'll wait that long."

Max rolled over to a workbench, grabbed a little screwdriver, and got down to work.

Jan turned to Zoe. "Can you find a spot to hook up that thing?"

"No problem," Zoe said, taking another cigarette from her case. "I hooked up my iPod to my computer in forensics and no one's ever noticed. The machine is back in a corner, under an old table. And my coworkers are pretty much dead themselves. They couldn't tell a pocket calculator from a DVD player. Even if they found Genius Boy's little invention, they wouldn't know what to make of it."

Jan smiled. Tomorrow evening, at the latest, he would have all the files he needed. But first, he was really going to need some fresh air.

•   •

Patrick chewed nervously at his fingernails. His hair hung over his forehead. His dark-blue suit was wrinkled, and his tie hung loose at his neck. The collar of his white shirt was greasy. Under his desk lay a sleeping bag and an old jacket that served as a pillow.

He stood before three monitors connected to various computers. As he clicked through surveillance videos on the screen in the middle, the one to the right showed the autopsy photos of Michael Josseck in all their revolting detail. The man lay on a metal autopsy table with his upper body opened up. His organs had been removed and the concrete from his stomach and esophagus cleared out.

Patrick glanced at the computer on his left. He called it his "alarm detector" because it was the place he'd gathered together all the details that related to Jan. If someone drew money from Jan's account, called from Jan's landline, or used Jan's credit card, it would show up on the screen.

Next to the computers sat a telephone with a number that was known to all police stations in Berlin. Every tip as to Jan's whereabouts would come straight to it.

Patrick took a sip of his strong coffee. But not even that could make him ignore his lack of sleep. His three hours' rest under the desk had given him no comfort. He'd started whenever the computer had made a noise. Once he'd even dreamed the phone was ringing. In a panic he'd picked up, but he only heard the dial tone.

Patrick continued looking at the surveillance videos at the main train station. The first feed showed the atrium with its brightly lit glass facades and walkways hovering above the escalators. Around this time, the stream of commuters was waning, although the station had not yet completely settled down. Patrick let his eyes wander, watching anyone who seemed to want their face concealed. Plenty of young people roamed around, the hoods of their jackets pulled over their heads. None resembled Jan.

Patrick switched views to the platforms. On track three, an older couple stood at a vending machine getting drinks. A preteen leaned against an ad board, gesturing wildly while holding his cell to his ear. Next to him, an elderly lady in fur showed clear annoyance with the phone call. Then an ICE train rolled in and spit out a handful of passengers, only to take in a few new ones again.

Patrick shoved the mouse across the desk in frustration and knocked back all his coffee in one gulp.

He opened the word processor and started a new document. Whenever he didn't know how to proceed on a case, he wrote down whatever thoughts came to him under the header "Brainstorming."

Surveilling prominent destinations like the main train station would get them nowhere. Jan wasn't stupid enough to show himself there.

Capture at camera-surveilled targets unlikely, Patrick typed.

It was the third day since Jan had fled. Even with cash he wouldn't be able to survive for long, unless he was living on the streets. Therefore, that unknown man or woman in the black Mercedes was not only helping him escape, but also providing him with a hideout.

Escaping Berlin? he wrote. That would be Jan's safest bet. In the country, out in Brandenburg, he could go underground quite easily. But the man had few friends out there.

Unlikely, he added.

He could try all he wanted to put himself in Jan's shoes, but the only way of apprehending him for sure would be by finding his abettor. Whoever had been driving that Mercedes.

Driver? Patrick typed. The getaway car had still not been found. Its owner was a dead end, as was the location of the cell phone Jan had used to write his final text.

Patrick pounded on the desk. Three days of manhunt and they still had nothing to show for it. His head felt like a balloon filled with syrup. He was getting nowhere this way. He kicked off his shoes, shrugged out of his jacket, and crawled under his desk. Inside his sleeping bag he could smell his own sweat, but he had to forget about personal hygiene for now. Only when Jan was in handcuffs could he spend time on himself again.

"I'll find you," he murmured, half-asleep. "You're not going to spoil my plans."

•   •

Light from fluorescent tubes reflected off the dull chrome autopsy tables. The tile floor was freshly scrubbed, the grout still wet. It smelled of chlorine. The room was filled with cabinets where scalpels, saws, and pliers waited for their next assignment, as well as computers and all kinds of other tools used in forensic analysis.

Normally, Zoe was the last one to make it to work. She hated having to get up early. Today, though, she had to be there before anyone. She turned on the computer and waited till the log-in screen appeared. Then she got down on one knee and connected the cable for the little gray case into the USB port. She hid the slim box behind the plug strip. As long as no IT tech was checking out the computer setup, no one would notice a thing.

The nerd had said that she only had to log in to get him into the system. After that, she could log herself out again. He told her something about it making a permanent connection too, but at that point she had already stopped listening. She had just wanted to escape his horrible place and that mixture of stale air, lack of personal hygiene, and pizza smell.

"Good morning," said a voice behind her.

Zoe started but kept typing like normal. "Morning, Walter," she replied without turning around. Walter was that classic divorced man in his midforties who imagined himself hotter than he really was. He liked to wear cardigans and sweater vests over his washed-out T-shirts. He combed his hair to the side, to cover up his receding hairline. Oral hygiene had always been an alien concept to him, and his crude jokes were older than the Old Testament. He was always trying to chat her up. Apart from that disheveled preppy look he had going, he had all the charm of a diesel locomotive.

"What are you doing here already?" He was trying to start a conversation.

Zoe closed her eyes and exhaled, remaining calm. She hated conversations like this. She just wanted to do her work and not chat about trivial crap.

"I couldn't sleep," she said. She logged herself out again.

"We're getting new work in any second now," Walter said. "Some case from the Wedding District."

"Huh," Zoe replied. The info wasn't worth any more than that.

"Snazzy shoes," Walter said, winking at her.

She moved away from the computer. Coffee time.

"Snazzy sandals," she responded with a glance at his feet. "Rivet them yourself?"

Walter's hateful look was reward enough for her. Maybe it would be a good morning after all.

She just had to get her caffeine level up. Then she'd lose the need to stab Walter's eye with a scalpel. But since the machine in the next room wasn't working, she had to head up to the third floor.

On the way up, she ignored the "No Smoking" sign and lit up a cigarette. Maximum Nerd now had all he needed to make himself real happy. Her job here was done.

• •

The sunny day did not match Jan's mood. He had to find peace somehow, and it occurred to him that he hadn't been to church for a long time. Yes, he felt a little seedy only seeking out God's help in times of need. But he didn't know where else to go. Besides, he felt indebted to Father Anberger.

As he opened the door to St. Sophia Church, he was received by a room bathed in light. Rows of dark pews extended to the altar, divided down the middle by a long red carpet. The green of the walls harmonized with the stucco ornamentation on the ceiling.

On another day, Jan might have taken his time checking out such beauty. Today, though, he just ducked into the last row, bowing his head. He caught the scent of incense mingling with the smell of cleaning agents. He lowered to his knees and folded his hands.

"I haven't prayed to you for a long time," he whispered. "Maybe because things were going too well and I didn't need your help, or because I still do believe that evil will lose out in the end. But the last few days have made me doubt.

"I did not tamper with the gas line, but I do feel guilty for Betty's death, like I killed her with my own hands. She always seemed so happy and content. Maybe I was only telling myself that—and stayed blind to her problems on purpose, out of wishful thinking. How could I have ever known that she'd want to kill herself?"

Jan cleared his throat.

"I'm not asking for you to forgive me. I'll have to spend my whole life living with this guilt. But I am asking for leniency for Betty. She was depending on me, and I let her down. A less selfish friend maybe could have saved her.

"I know that suicide is a cardinal sin, but Betty was a good girl who earned her place in paradise. If you are the Lord that Father Anberger always tells me about, then you've forgiven her already and she is with you now."

He wiped at the tears on his face.

"Let her know that I miss her, and that I'm sorry I never told her how much I love her."

Jan crossed himself and sat back up on the pew. He shut his eyes, grateful for the silence. The weight on his conscience, it seemed a little bit lighter.

•   •

When the connecting signal turned green, Max leapt from his chair.

"Direct hit!" he yelled, balling his fists. He mimicked a sequence of punches and kicks that looked exactly like a computer geek imitating a ninja. Then he sat back down on the wobbly office chair and let his fingers fly across the keyboard.

"You *are* good for something, Hottie," he muttered. He hadn't believed that Zoe would pull it off. He'd made the box idiotproof, sure, but with chicks like that, you never knew. She looked like a model, but she clearly had no clue about computers.

Two input fields appeared, labeled "User" and "Password."

"That all you got?" he roared at the monitor. "I am Maximum. King of Hackers! I'll take on ten of you amateurs."

He pressed keys and a program with the name "Maximum Password-Killer" appeared. He clicked the "Let Me In" button and jumped back a step. His chair had clattered to the floor, but Max kept his eyes steady on the long, wide loading bar as it changed from red to green. He paused, motionless. Only his foot tapping nervously on the laminate floor disturbed the total calm.

After a minute, his computer speaker emitted the devilish laugh he'd built in to signify the program's success. He watched the bar. Before his eyes, the whole thing turned green. Max turned and slid down the hall on his knees, hands above his head like a prize boxer who'd just killed his opponent.

"Yet another win for the hacker—over the system of oppression!" he shouted.

"Shut your face, asshole," came a voice from the other side of the wall. "Trying to crash."

Ignoring his neighbor, Max went back to the computer and clicked around the Homicide server. And he found just what he needed.

． ．

Jan strolled closer to the location of Michael Josseck's construction company. While many detectives focused on the perpetrator, Jan wanted to know all about the victim. Every detail, no matter how trivial. If he could find out the motive for murder, the number of possible perpetrators would shrink significantly. The contractor had been dead two days now. And unfortunately, Jan's colleagues had already wrapped up the questioning of Josseck's employees, so it would have looked suspicious if Jan had tried to interrogate them. Luckily Max would secure the interview files so he could look them over later.

Today, he wanted to survey the bigger picture around the contractor. Maybe there were neighbors or workmen who knew him, but who hadn't been questioned. Something like that often got overlooked in the course of the investigation.

The noise of the industrial neighborhood around him drowned out the rush-hour traffic. Thick smoke billowed from the chimney of a factory building. Beyond it he saw an auto-repair shop, a paint facility, a motorcycle store, and a pipe distributor. Some buildings didn't even have a sign out front on the fence, so Jan didn't know if they were empty or not. At the end of the road stood Josseck's construction business, a one-story building with three garages of corrugated metal. Jan suppressed the urge to head inside and ask questions directly. Instead, he turned around and walked back using the path along the other side of the road, past a tire dealer, a fleet of mobile homes, and a small Italian restaurant.

He stood before the restaurant. The Italian joint was the only spot in the industrial zone that offered anything to eat. Since Michael Josseck apparently spent more time at his office than out on job sites, he might have eaten lunch here. His physique did indicate a major passion for food.

Filippo's Place had a small, plain-looking exterior. Inside, the interior was similar, with brown carpet, cheap wood furniture, and low-hanging lamps that took Jan straight back to the 1970s. Only the wall of souvenirs from Italy broke up the dated decor.

An elderly man was wiping a table. He had graying dark hair and wore a dapper vest over his white shirt. When he saw Jan coming in, he set down his rag.

"The kitchen doesn't open for fifteen minutes," he said, smiling, "but if you like, you could wait till then." He gestured to a little bar overloaded with wine and grappa.

"Thanks, but I'm not here to eat," Jan said and showed his badge.

The man stiffened up.

"My name is Jan . . . Schmitt. I'm with Berlin Detectives, and I have a few questions about a case. Are you the owner of this restaurant?"

"Filippo Rotolo," the man said, shaking Jan's hand. "I've owned this restaurant for eleven years. How can I help you?"

"Did you know a Herr Michael Josseck? He owned a construction business here."

"Naturally I knew him. Is it true he was murdered?"

Jan nodded.

"How terrible. It's hard to imagine that he's dead now. I'll miss his visits."

"So he was a guest?"

"Regularly."

"How often?"

"At least three times a week."

"So what was he like, then?"

"How do you mean?"

"Well, was he friendly? Did he give good tips or complain about the food?"

"Herr Josseck was never a problem."

"Herr Rotolo," Jan sighed. "I know one is not supposed to speak ill of the dead, but in a murder investigation we do require the truth, even when it's none too pleasant."

Filippo's face lost the friendly expression. "I hated him from the first moment on," he said. "He wore suits that sat all wrong, showing off his belly. He reeked of sweat, and whenever I took his order I had to stand on the other side of the table because his breath was insufferable."

Jan smiled. He loved this Filippo's honesty.

"The other thing is, he had no culture for eating. Always demanding ice cubes for his red wine, rarely giving a tip."

"Why did you let him in your restaurant?"

Filippo shrugged. "A customer is a customer. As long as he doesn't disturb other guests, his money is good. Me, I'll run this restaurant for a few years more. Then I'll buy a little home in Tuscany and leave all this behind. No more working in a drab industrial neighborhood with depressing views. No more guests smelling like torn-down buildings and trash, and no more people like Michael Josseck to cook for." He sniffed in disgust. "People who can't tell the difference between plastic wrap and pasta."

"Do you think he had enemies?"

"Certainly. People like him are the kind who will walk over a cold corpse or sell their own grandmothers."

"Nasty enough enemies that someone would want to kill him?"

"You know, Herr Schmitt, an industrial zone is basically a village. Everyone knows everyone. At some point, you learn everything. Who's mixing bad concrete, not repairing cars right, getting around paying taxes. This is a nice thing about my job. To the guests, I'm invisible. No one changes the subject just because I come to the table."

"So what did people say about Herr Josseck?"

"He was a cheat—used shoddy materials and invoiced the high-end stuff. No one wanted a thing to do with him, but somehow he kept getting new jobs. His business got bigger, and in court he always escaped the noose."

"Didn't that seem strange to you?"

"Naturally. But I don't ask. The less I have to do with such things, the better. You see where that leads."

"Is there someone in particular who might have had it in for Herr Josseck?"

Filippo thought about it a moment. "No one comes to mind. There were always disagreements, again and again, but if word had made it around that Herr Josseck wasn't trustworthy, he would have stopped getting clients. Yet he always got more business."

Jan tapped his pen on his notebook, thinking this over. "Thank you for being so open about this, Herr Rotolo," he said, shaking the man's hand again.

"If you're looking for someone who could have murdered Herr Josseck, you won't have to dig too far. I do know a nasty human being when I see one, and Michael Josseck was one of the worst kind."

Chapter 8

Chandu schlepped bags full of groceries up the stairs. He'd actually only wanted to buy a few small things, but on the way to the supermarket Jan had called him and told him he had invited Father Anberger over for lunch on the spur of the moment. The priest wanted to bring the mail by and, as thanks for his unshakable trust, Jan had promised him Chandu's outstanding *isombe*.

Like I have nothing better to do, Chandu thought, testy about it. The thing was, his apartment was supposed to have been a hideout. First, that weird chain-smoker came over. Then they visited that high-tech freak with no personal hygiene, so that was one more person in the know about their connection. Now Jan's neighbor was about to show up. Only thing missing was a high-school reunion hosted at his place. As he opened the door to his apartment, fully loaded down, Chandu wondered if maybe he shouldn't go buy a cap that said "Doorman" on it.

"You were gone shopping a long time," Jan said.

"That's because cassava isn't exactly widespread in Germany," Chandu snapped. "Fortunately for us I have this friend from back home who always has some on hand."

"Want me to help you cook?"

Chandu wrinkled his forehead at him. "How well you know your way around Rwandan cuisine?"

"Not very."

"Then it's better I cook and you go gather up those clothes of yours that are spread all over the living room."

"Okay," Jan said.

"And your shoes," Chandu went on. "Then hang your bathrobe back up and clear the beer bottles off the table."

Jan saluted.

Chandu sighed, put on a pot of water, and unwrapped the cassava. He took two knives from the block and got to work.

The time flew by. Chandu was barely finished when Jan came through the door with the priest.

Father Anberger was exactly how Chandu had imagined a man with such a name might look. Pale, haggard, with a sunken face and an unreadable expression. His gray hair was combed over his balding head. With longer hair and a dark beard, he could pass as the suffering Jesus. Chandu didn't much like priests or any other agents of the church. Too earnest, too dogged, and not very tolerant of those of other religions.

"This is my friend Chandu," Jan said. Father Anberger nodded pleasantly enough but couldn't conceal his mistrust. Chandu smiled as he imagined the man's thoughts: that big, dark-skinned men with tattoos on their faces probably didn't come to Mass very often.

Chandu raised a hand. "Just about done. Have a seat."

The priest didn't take his eyes off Chandu, as if expecting he might come after him with a machete at any moment.

"Going to be a real pleasant afternoon," Chandu muttered under his breath. Still, he would try to be patient. Jan needed every friend he could get, and if Chandu's cooking skills helped the man get his clothes and mail, it was all good with him. He would just keep on cooking and keep his mouth shut.

• •

When they'd finished eating, Father Anberger leaned back and sighed with delight.

"I've never eaten anything that exotic. That was outstanding."

Chandu accepted the compliment with a nod. He might just get to like this starched, stiff priest.

"What kind of dish was that again?"

"*Isombe* with *ubugali*," Chandu explained. "*Isombe* is a fish dish seasoned with leaves from the cassava root. The gray porridge was the *ubugali*. The cassava root gets shredded and cooked into it. You have to be real careful cooking it, since cassava is poisonous in its raw state and only becomes edible after heating."

The priest nodded approvingly.

"You're still looking quite depressed, Herr Tommen," he said, turning to Jan. "You know, you should consider yourself lucky to have such a friend."

Jan got carried away and actually smiled. "Without Chandu here, I would've put a bullet in my brain a long time ago."

"Suicide is no path any man should take," Father Anberger said solemnly.

"I know," Jan said, his tone apologetic. "But I'm feeling a lot of doubt. I used to see myself as one of the good guys. Now there's a lunatic running around out there who doesn't just think it's fun to kill, but enjoys taking revenge on me in a most malicious way."

"Perhaps it's simply a former criminal, seeking gratification after a prison stay?"

"I keep saying that to myself too," said Jan. "But what if I put someone in prison wrongfully, or harmed someone in a manner they could not forgive? That would make me to blame for the judge's death and for Michael Josseck's."

"You didn't kill the men, Herr Tommen."

"If it were only that simple," Jan said, despondent. He turned the fork in his hand, deep in thought. "I respect you, Father Anberger, but I doubt you've ever loaded so much guilt on yourself that you just about fall apart because of it."

The priest looked away. "You think that I'm infallible, just because I'm a man of God," he muttered. "But don't fool yourself. I have done things that robbed me of sleep, and I asked myself whether I was possessed by some kind of demon. I'm just a human too."

"So what's a person do?" Jan asked. "When you know you're to blame and you know you can't ever make up for it?"

"A person should never stop believing in atonement. At some point, the Lord shows the path. It may be painful and unbearable, but at the end there waits salvation. I firmly believe in this."

"And a person should take this path? No matter what happens?"

Father Anberger nodded. "Without hesitation."

• •

Zoe had refused to ever enter Max's apartment again, so they met at Chandu's. The big man fumed at having to host another gathering inside his personal space as he handled the coffeemaker. Zoe smoked her second cigarette while Max hooked up a mini projector to his laptop.

Jan could not hide a grin. Here sat the world's strangest detective team. He had a bouncer and debt collector with numerous connections to the underworld, a nicotine-addicted medical examiner who looked incredible in stiletto heels and was bored to death with her job, and a childlike hacker who took great delight in cracking the Homicide server, even though the stunt could get him decades in the pen.

Chandu came out of the kitchen with four cups of coffee and took a spot next to Zoe. He saw her lit cigarette and frowned. Zoe returned the look, unperturbed, and blew smoke past his ear.

Max spoke up. "Allow me to introduce—George Holoch." All eyes turned to the wall, where the hacker was projecting a picture of the judge. Jan recognized the photo as one he'd already seen online.

Max turned to Jan. "Your fellow officers were busy. They went through his verdicts looking for any irregularities. They focused on who benefited and who was aggrieved."

"That's logical," Jan said. "The murder has a personal component. With the judge, the murderer was probably someone he'd convicted who felt they hadn't been treated fairly."

"In fact, Judge Holoch was quite controversial. His sentences varied wildly between very mild and exceedingly tough. He never crossed the line into obvious corruption, but even a legal layman like me has to shake his head at some of his decisions."

"Why?" Jan said.

Max pressed on the mini remote in his hand, replacing the judge's picture with a photo of a house.

"This is a single-family home in Karlshorst. At first glance everything looks good, but the builder did shoddy work on the foundation. Even before the family was all moved in, the walls had become damp and mold was starting to form. It wasn't livable after a few weeks. The family went to court and got Judge Holoch. He did rule for the plaintiffs, but he only sentenced the builder to a laughable fine of ten thousand euros."

Chandu let out a whistle. "Ten thousand euros for a total restoration? You're better off leaving it there, buying a tent."

Max nodded. "The family was heavily in debt, had to move out."

"But is that enough to motivate a murder?"

"I know people who've killed for less," Chandu remarked.

"Maybe in your circles," Zoe said. "But that homeowner was a family man, not a pimp or a drug dealer. This murderer is a sadistic bastard. It doesn't make sense."

"The case is a good example of the judge's dubious verdicts."

"In other words, there are more than enough suspects who could have wanted revenge on George Holoch," Jan said.

"Actually, yes, but now comes the most interesting part." Max pressed on his remote again. A picture of Michael Josseck appeared. "The guy who botched the single-family home in Karlshorst was one Michael Josseck, our recently murdered builder. So with that in mind, I checked all of Holoch's verdicts—and found fourteen intersecting with Michael Josseck."

"Let me guess," Jan interrupted. "All these verdicts were just as favorable as the one for that family from Karlshorst."

Max pointed at him. "Bingo."

"Hmm," Jan said. "That leaves only two conclusions. Either Holoch and Josseck were in cahoots to make money, or the builder was blackmailing the judge."

"Your fellow detectives were thinking that too," Max said. "They checked the judge's bank-account transactions over the last five years, but they didn't find any transfers between the two men."

"Then Josseck was blackmailing the judge," Chandu remarked. "One favorable verdict might be a coincidence, but fourteen?"

"Where's the investigation going with it?"

"All your colleagues' records and e-mails indicate they're trying to find out more about the connection between the two."

"That's it?" Zoe asked. "They're looking for connections and hoping to stumble on the murderer?"

"It's a lot of work," Jan said. "They have to review all fourteen judgments and talk to each person involved. That will take a while. So. Am I still the main suspect in the Holoch case?"

Max nodded. "That's why it's progressing so slowly. In the homicide squad's view, you're either Holoch's murderer or at least aware of the motive for the murder. Once they have you? Case is solved. So they'll keep searching for you."

Idiots, Jan thought. There was a moment when he'd considered turning himself in. Now it was becoming clear that that would have been a stupid move. He didn't have anything to do with the crimes. Yet until he was ruled out as a suspect, he'd be taken right into custody the minute they found him. He'd have no chance to clear his name once he was in prison.

Max clicked on his remote. The document of a court decision appeared on the wall.

"What is it?" Jan asked.

"The only case where the verdict against Josseck's company was somewhat harsh."

"You just said that all legal decisions against him had been mild," Zoe commented.

"True. This one too. That's because the sentence wasn't actually directed at him, but rather at his construction supervisor, Horst Esel." The picture of a man popped up. He was midfifties, with a coarse face and hair shaved short. He had a three-day stubble and a cigarette in the corner of his mouth.

"Horst Esel worked for Josseck for twenty years. As supervisor, he was in charge of countless projects. Among those were some that had defective work. His greed eventually led to his doom."

Esel's picture was replaced with a factory building in dismal condition. The windows were broken out. Metal supports were scorched.

"Not too pretty," Chandu said.

"Esel built this new glass factory using low-grade materials. He only incorporated a fifth of the required metal supports and sold the rest of the steel for cash. Plus, the conduits were installed poorly, which eventually led to a short circuit and a fire. Fortunately, production in the factory hadn't begun yet, so no one was injured. The damage amounted to two million euros."

"Then what?" Jan asked.

"Judge Holoch sentenced Esel to one year without parole. He more or less declared Josseck free of guilt, forcing him to pay eight thousand euros in damages."

"If that's not a reason to be pissed at someone . . ." Chandu said.

"Now comes the best part," Max added, grinning. "A week before Judge Holoch was murdered, Horst Esel was released from prison. No one's seen him since."

Chandu sipped at his coffee. "In that case, it's clear what we do now."

"We have to find this Horst Esel," Jan said. "He's our man." He turned to Max. "They have a manhunt for him?"

"Not an intense one, but all patrols have been informed."

"We start with his last known address?" Chandu asked.

"That won't help us," Jan replied. "My colleagues will already have been there and followed up on any workable leads. They questioned the neighbors for sure."

"You know another way to get at him?"

"We have to go about it differently. We search out friends who did the crooked jobs with him. I won't find out much if I show up at some job site waving my cop badge. Half the workers will take off because they're illegal, and the rest will be reluctant to give answers. In my situation, it's not like I can go applying a lot of pressure. Did Esel have any known associates?"

"Yes. A man named Manuel Floer. He was given a suspended sentence. He sounds like Esel's gofer."

"Can you find out his address?"

"I'll try."

118

"The other thing is," Jan said, "I'll need an overview of Josseck's company's current job sites. Maybe Esel's hiding away at one."

"Will do, but it's not going to work here with the laptop, not with this lame-ass connection. I'll go home real quick and call you."

Max waved at them and left the apartment.

"Some personal hygiene would make meeting with him more pleasant," Zoe remarked.

"He doesn't reek any more than your cigarettes," Chandu said.

"Tobacco smells comforting. No reek. And a man whose kitchen stinks like an otter died in there should be careful what he's talking about."

"That's the scent of tamarind, coriander, and cassava. Why am I not surprised that someone who probably considers fish sticks a culinary delight would have no clue?"

Zoe lowered her cigarette. "Listen here, Mr. T. You might have arms like elephant legs, but that wide nose of yours will break just the same when I go bashing it in."

Jan groaned. Zoe was back in top form. He dropped down on the couch between the two contenders. "Listen, you two, I got enough problems." He turned to Zoe. "You, why don't you head over to Forensics and ask around? Maybe there's something new that's not in a report yet. And you," he said to Chandu, "can go get a car. Max will call soon with a few job-site addresses. We'll drive to some tomorrow morning."

A tense silence persisted a moment. Jan just hoped the two of them weren't about to gang up on him. It was a disturbing thought, to be sitting between a six-foot-six mountain of muscle and a bad-tempered coroner who liked to give her scalpels pet names.

A minute later, Zoe stood up. "Keep me updated, you wussies." And she left the apartment.

"Such a charming assistant you've picked up for yourself there," Chandu said.

"Don't be fooled. She's always in a nasty mood, but she's an ace technician."

"Huh," Chandu grunted, not too convinced. "If you say so."

Jan, meanwhile, let out a deep sigh of relief. He finally had a new lead.

• •

Patrick contemplated the photo in his hand. Jan had an arm around a tall, muscular black man and was toasting the photo taker with a beer bottle. A colleague from Vice had identified Jan's friend as one Chandu Bitangaro, a known bouncer and debt collector. He was assumed responsible for several auto thefts, but no one could ever prove it was he. His record was clean.

Patrick had someone retrieve the man's address, and he drove over right away to take a look. The apartment house was a washed-out gray darkened by years of exhaust fumes. The plaster was flaking off and the windows were dingy. It was a clearly a crumbling neighborhood with plenty of the usual problems.

The doorbell panel names didn't get Patrick very far. Names were either wiped out or not there at all. He was about to just try all the bells when a teen boy came running out, his cap pulled down low on his face. He turned away from Patrick, rushing in for the back courtyard.

Patrick held the door open and went in. The stairway smelled musty and was in worse shape than the exterior. According to his records, Chandu lived on the fourth floor. Patrick went up the stairs and came to a stop before a scuffed wooden door. He adjusted his tie and knocked.

A moment later, a dark-skinned woman opened up. Her long hair was knotted in pigtails running down her shoulders. She had an athletic figure and garishly painted red fingernails. She was wearing a white bathrobe and was clearly irritated by the nuisance.

"What?" she barked at Patrick.

He held up his badge. "My name is Patrick Stein, from Berlin Detective Division. Could I please speak to Herr Chandu Bitangaro?"

"Ain't here."

"Where would I find him?"

"I'm not his fucking babysitter. No clue."

"Are you married to him?"

The woman chuckled. "Listen here. I ain't seen Chandu for a long time now. Leave me your number. He comes around, I'll call ya."

She went to shut the door in his face, but Patrick held it open with a hand.

She went off on him: "I got no time, man. If you got no search warrant, then go fuck off."

Patrick grabbed at her arm and twisted it behind her back until she screeched in pain. He kicked the door open all the way, shoved her inside, and pushed her to the floor.

"Okay, now let's talk," he told her. "And by the time I leave, I expect to know where he is. Anything less? Would not be good." Then he closed the door.

•   •

Chandu got to the disco's vast parking lot around 9:30 p.m. He lurked in the shadows, waiting for an opportunity. Luckily the place was underneath a bridge and the lighting was sparse. With no video surveillance and several hard-to-see spots, he felt confident he'd be able to work unnoticed.

Chandu waited a half hour without seeing any car pull in that was worth stealing. Irritated, he checked his watch. When a silver-gray Toyota Auris compact came around the corner a minute later, Chandu sighed with relief. Finally, a ride he wouldn't have trouble with.

From his pants pocket he took a black box that was barely bigger than a cell phone, and he pulled back deeper into the shadows.

The car zipped into a parking space. The headlights went off, and a young guy in a suit stepped out. He was wearing dark sunglasses and had a flashy watch on his wrist. His hair was combed severely to the side, and a gold chain glittered on his white shirt. As he went to slam the car door, Chandu activated his jammer to interrupt the key's signal to the car. Walking away, the driver pressed his remote to lock the car. He didn't notice when the usual flash failed to happen. He was singing some song or other and doing a few dance steps as he headed for the disco. Chandu waited until he was out of sight, emerged from his hiding spot, and opened the driver's door. Inside he found the right lever and popped the hood. A minute later, he had hooked up his laptop to the engine's distributor box. Then he started a program called "Toyota Auris" and waited. After a moment, the engine fired up.

Satisfied, Chandu packed away the laptop and shut the hood. He pulled a screwdriver from his pocket and swapped the Toyota's plates with those of the car next to it. Even if they did start searching for the Auris, the fake plate would keep him safe for a few days. He just needed to make sure he didn't get stopped at some police checkpoint.

His job done, he tossed laptop and screwdriver on the passenger seat and drove off the premises, grinning.

• •

While Chandu was out getting a car, Jan was watching a boring reality show. He hated these crappy talent competitions, but it was the best thing on at the moment. His cell phone rang. The screen showed a picture of his kooky computer buddy.

"What's new, Max?"

"I found something," the hacker said. "Michael Josseck's construction company is building a row-house development in Friedrichsfelde."

"How did you find that out so easily?"

"I called their office earlier—said I was an investor and asked if I could have a look at a building project before I put in a bid."

"And they gave you the job site's address?"

"Yup."

"They mention that the company's owner was just murdered?"

"No. You'd think nothing had happened. I wonder if the people there refuse to believe that their boss is dead."

"Weird," Jan said. "But, okay, give me the address."

Max described how to get there. He hung up.

Jan was jotting down a note when Chandu came in the door.

"Was that Max?"

Jan nodded.

"We know where we're going?"

"To Friedrichsfelde. Some dinky row-house development. We'll head out tomorrow morning."

•   •

"I don't know why you're so worked up," Chandu said, handing Jan a cap. "We're just going out for a quick drink."

"Maybe you forgot, there's a manhunt on for me? Going for a little stroll? Maybe. But staying a long time in one place, it's stupid. Anyone could drop in on us."

"You don't need to worry. It's my local bar. I know everyone personally, and newcomers rarely come in."

Jan pulled on the hat and looked at himself in the mirror. "This is supposed to keep anyone from recognizing me?"

"With this it will." He gave Jan a pair of eyeglasses. Their angular frame was basic, almost cheaply so. The lenses were tinted.

"Reading glasses?" Jan said. "Really?"

"The lenses aren't prescription," Chandu explained. "I got them for a costume ball."

"You go to costume balls?"

"Long story. Put 'em on."

Jan looked in the mirror, the glasses resting on his nose. "I look worse than Max."

"Precisely." Chandu grinned. "It's not like we're out on the prowl—we're just getting a drink, so you can relax a little. Anyone there will only remember some unshaven freak with a stupid hat and even stupider glasses."

"Sounds killer."

"Come on, don't be like that. Used to be a phone call was all it took and we were on our way out."

"I wasn't the main suspect in a murder case back then."

"Tonight, we're going to block out that little detail," Chandu said, smiling. "Two beers and we come home."

Jan sighed. "All right, fine."

Chandu grabbed his jacket. He was glad to be providing his friend with a little diversion. Zoe and Max didn't know Jan well enough to see the weight on his shoulders. Jan was barely sleeping, and if it weren't for the light sleeping pill he was swallowing down with his beer, he wouldn't be getting any shut-eye at all. Chandu knew it was tough for him to be off the detective squad, not to mention being a murder suspect. Then there was Betty's suicide. It had almost shattered him, partly because he seemed to feel responsible for her death.

"Not more than two beers," Jan said. "We have to get to the job site early tomorrow."

Chandu gave a thumbs-up and pushed Jan out the apartment.

"I'm still not sure I like this idea," Jan said as they headed down the stairway.

"Man, I do miss the wild times in good old Kreuzberg."

"Once I'm not a suspect any more, we'll make up for it."

On the way to the bar, Chandu tried to drive away Jan's dark thoughts with a few of their stories. He talked about those massive outdoor viewing parties during the World Cup, swimming naked at night in the Spree, even that brawl they'd gotten into with some bikers after one of their leather-clad girlfriends had hit on Jan.

Chandu's local bar was a small joint with darkened windows and two tall bar tables at the entrance. The small nameplate-style sign was illegible. It was not the kind of place a guy would just stumble into, but Chandu loved it. Soul music boomed from two speakers. A smell of deep-fry grease hung in the air, and the dim lighting resembled a hazy twilight.

"Where to?" Jan asked.

"Standing tables in back," Chandu said. "That way we'll be away from the entrance, and it's so poorly lit that no one will recognize anyone, even if detectives do come." He pressed a bill into Jan's hand. "Grab us two beers. I'm going to say hi to a couple dudes. I'll be waiting over there for you."

Jan left Chandu waving at friends and starting to shake a lot of hands. By the time Jan made his way back with two beers, Chandu was deep in conversation with a few guys about Berlin's bar scene. He was about to introduce Jan when his eyes roamed toward the entrance—and his smile went cold. Chandu grabbed Jan by the collar, opened the nearby restroom door, and heaved his friend inside.

"Stay in there," he hollered after him. Chandu slammed the door shut before the sound of beer bottles crashing started disturbing the regulars.

A man in a suit had come in. He pushed on through the regulars, looking disgusted, and came directly for Chandu. With his bright tie and standard oxfords, he looked like an alien being in the bar.

"My name is Patrick Stein." He showed his badge. "I have a few questions for you."

Chapter 9

"Why didn't you look me up at home?" Chandu asked Patrick, taking a useful look around. "A bar isn't exactly the right place."

"Your housemate told me that you're rarely home and you could be found here."

Sakina, Chandu thought. He'd have to threaten to increase her cheap rent when he got a chance—not that he'd ever have the heart to go through with it. Still, thank God she didn't know about the apartment on Oranienburger. He glanced at Patrick. There was no sense in putting him off. The more helpful he was, the sooner the man would be gone.

Chandu put on his friendly face. "How can I help?"

"I'm investigating two murder cases in which a friend of yours is a main suspect."

Chandu said nothing, maintaining his noncommittal expression. He wasn't going to make it easy for Patrick either.

"Jan Tommen."

"Jan?" Chandu made a surprised face. "Doesn't he work as a detective?"

"Used to. He changed sides."

"Really? Who got murdered?"

"Not important." Patrick waved it aside, growing impatient. "Have you seen Herr Tommen recently?"

"Not for two weeks now."

"I don't have to remind you what happens when you lie to a police officer."

"It's the truth, Herr Kommissar." Chandu raised his hands in defense. "We know each other, go drinking now and then, but we were never close friends. Why are you after me?"

"I found a photo of you and Herr Tommen together. You looked like real good friends."

"I'm a bouncer. Jan helped me out once, when I was having trouble with a couple drunk dudes. Wasn't a big deal. He was just doing his duty."

"Uh-huh," Patrick muttered, unconvinced. Chandu forced himself not to turn to his right, look toward the toilet. Hopefully Jan was heeding his warning. If he as much as peeked out, they were screwed.

"What kind of car do you drive?"

"I don't have a car. Mother nature is dear to my heart, which is why I use public transportation." Chandu fought a grin. He was proud of how easily the lies passed from his lips.

"You don't drive a tuned-up black Mercedes?"

"You must have me confused with someone else. Check my registration. I don't have a car."

And why would he? Patrick thought to himself. *Borrowing is cheaper.*

The door to the restrooms opened. Chandu's heart stopped a second, but instead of Jan, a young blonde came teetering out on high heels.

"Sicko perv!" she shouted, slamming the door. Only now did Chandu realize that he'd shoved Jan into the women's restroom.

With an angry snort, the blonde pushed on through between them, left the bar, and slammed the front door too.

Patrick kept looking between Chandu and the toilets. His sense of duty as a police officer was apparently fighting with a dread of entering the women's restroom.

"Hey, why don't you leave me your number?" Chandu said, pulling the man's attention back his way. "I'll get in touch if I hear anything about Jan."

"Er, all right," Patrick stammered. He reached in his pocket and handed over a business card. "Jan Tommen committed two murders. He is dangerous. Stay out of his way and call me at once if you see him."

"Will do, Herr Kommissar." Chandu gave a casual salute. "You can depend on me."

Patrick nodded and made his way back out. After a couple steps, he turned around.

"And one other thing." He pointed a finger, threatening. "Don't call me Herr Kommissar." And he slammed the front door shut as well.

•   •

Jan's sudden appearance in the women's restroom hadn't been well received. Chandu's shove had sent him crashing into the door of a toilet stall, where a pretty blonde was just fixing her top. While falling, he had tried to save his beer, but the two bottles had foamed all over his shirt. Thus drenched, he'd winked at the young woman cheerfully enough. As his reward, the blonde started beating him with her handbag so hard he'd fled into another stall. That was where Chandu found him.

As Chandu relayed what had happened, Jan was again reminded just how dangerous it was to be out in public. A hat and glasses would not have fooled his fellow cops.

Out of fear that Patrick could still be creeping around outside by the door, Chandu had grabbed a case of beer and moved the party into the women's restroom. His friends kept joining the festivities until all the regulars were hanging out with them. It wasn't till 3:00 a.m., when the bar closed up, that Chandu and Jan sneaked out the rear entrance.

Jan was going to have a hell of a headache the next morning, but he didn't care. For a few hours, everything had been like it used to be. Before the murders. When Betty was still living.

.   .

Jan lay in bed, breathing in the subtle aroma of basil. Sunlight brightened the main room that was bedroom, living room, and kitchen in one. Betty stood at the stove, cooking her special breakfast. Ham omelet with fresh herbs. She had a tiny garden growing along her window ledge. She loved the smell of plants. Flowers, miniature trees, and shrubs were spread out all over, and she was devoted to caring for them. At Jan's, even the fake tulips died, but Betty always knew when a plant needed water or a few days in a sunnier spot.

She smiled over at him. Jan's heart threatened to burst with joy. She was so gorgeous, with her long hair and her sparkling eyes. Jan could still taste her lips and feel her warmth on his fingers, as if their bodies were still united in their lovemaking. He wanted to take her in his arms again and savor the taste of her skin.

Jan wanted to stand, but something was pressing him to the bed. An unseen force held him there without mercy.

Betty didn't notice any of it. She scattered rosemary in the pan, its aroma mingling with the basil. She turned a knob on the stove and the burner flame grew larger. The fire only licked around the pan's edge at first, but it grew with every breath of air it got until the exhaust hood was turning black. Betty's good mood remained. She kept on cooking as if the flames were just an illusion. Her arms caught fire. The fresh scent of the herbs was driven out by the stink of burning flesh.

Jan screamed, but the pressure on his chest only grew stronger. He could hardly get any air. He tried to wrench himself free and get up. But the more he tried, the harder he was pressed down into the bed. The flames shot higher and set the kitchen on fire. Betty's arms were scorched black. Her hair blazed. Her faced seemed to melt. Then the stove exploded in a ball of fire.

Jan jerked awake from his dream, screaming. He'd kicked the covers off the couch, but his T-shirt was soaked with sweat. His hands trembled. Only slowly did he become aware of his surroundings. The streetlamps outside illuminated the dim outlines of Chandu's living room. Then his memories overtook him—the murder cases, his escape, Betty's death. His stomach rebelled, and he vomited onto the coffee table.

• •

Jan hadn't been able to fall back to sleep after the dream. His head ached and he felt dizzy, the images on a recurring loop in his head. Even after the hour it took him to clean up the table, he still could hardly walk straight. Only when Chandu brought him a cup of coffee did he start to feel recovered.

On the way to the car they spoke little, and the trip passed in a shared silence. Judging by how many aspirin Chandu had taken with his morning brew, he wasn't feeling great either. After an hour, they found the development. It stood in the middle of cleared land surrounded by trees on all sides. A rutted, trash-strewn road led to the site, where most of the houses were under construction. Some already had windows, but all were missing the exterior plaster. There were no vehicles apart from a crane and a backhoe. No lights were burning, no chimney smoke rising into the sky. No one had moved in yet.

"Who'd pay for a shack like this?" Chandu asked.

"There are worse places."

"Guantánamo?"

Jan laughed but regretted it instantly. His head punished any sudden movements.

Chandu pointed to the last house. "There's a few people over there." He drove the Toyota up to the sidewalk, and they got out. The sandy earth was mushy, dotted with little puddles of muddy water filled with building debris. Jan looked for a path that wouldn't ruin his shoes.

Chandu put on dark sunglasses. With his hair cut short and his broad back, he looked like the perfect bodyguard for a Bond villain. He motioned for Jan to go first.

Four workmen leaned against a delivery van, smoking and looking bored. Judging from the number of butts on the ground, they'd been at it awhile already.

"Morning, guys," Jan said. None of the men reacted to him.

"You working for Michael Josseck?"

"Might be," one of them grunted. He had a scrawny build and uncombed long, blond hair. His lower arm sported an indistinguishable tattoo. Possibly a lion's head.

"Not to worry. We're not building inspectors. We just have a little . . . job."

That perked them up. "What's it about?"

"Nothing big," Jan said. "Restoring some old prewar in Charlottenburg. Twenty an hour."

"Why come to us?" the scrawny one asked. He wasn't looking convinced.

"Buddy of mine worked with Manuel Floer and was happy with it."

"Manuel ain't here."

"Where do I find him?"

"Why's it have to be Manuel? Guy ain't even a super."

"I only work with recommended guys. He brings you along to work? It's all good by me."

Scrawny eyed Jan, sizing him up.

"Fair enough." He threw his butt on the ground. "You all ears? Here's what you do . . ." He rattled off the way to an industrial building site.

"In Marzahn?" Jan asked.

Scrawny nodded. Jan sighed. From here, it was going to take forever to get there.

"You don't got a phone number for us?"

"I don't. You gotta go there personally." Scrawny pulled a pack from his pocket and lit up another cigarette. "Manuel's there till quitting time."

A man didn't have to be a psychologist to see the guy was lying somehow, but Jan wouldn't be getting any more than that out of him. At least it was an address.

"See you around." Jan raised a hand and went back to the car. Had he turned around, he would have noticed the worker make a call on his phone and watch them warily as they drove away.

. . .

On the drive to Marzahn, they had to pull over to the side of the road twice. The night before was still exacting its toll. After yet another coffee from a snack stand, Jan's headache began shrinking to a bearable degree.

When they arrived, Chandu parked the car in front of an industrial building that was clearly under construction. A huge tarp covered the framework of the main building, and the other structures around the site looked abandoned.

"No one's here," Chandu said. "There's not even a concrete mixer or a crane. Maybe we head back to Friedrichsfelde, break some bones."

"Let's go on in first," Jan proposed. "I want to take a little tour."

The industrial building appeared empty. Dust covered the floor, and it smelled moldy. The tarp barely let any light through.

"You looking for someone?" a voice echoed through the space.

Four husky men came up to them. They wore work clothes and big safety boots.

"Are you Manuel Floer?"

"Tell me who you are," the strongest-looking one demanded. He had on white overalls splattered with fading paint. His nose was crooked, and he was missing several teeth. His unshaven face and shifty expression made Jan dislike him instantly. Types like this got their fun bullying others. Normally Jan would take this as a challenge, but he needed information.

"A friend tells me you'd like to take on a little side job."

"You a fucking pig, what?" He pushed at Jan.

"No," Jan said calmly. "A builder looking to work around the taxman."

"I know that face you got," the man continued. He shoved Jan backward. "You're a filthy pig."

Jan fought his urge to slam this guy down with a head butt.

"So who's this supposed friend anyway?"

"Peter," Jan said without pause. He'd thought about putting Horst Esel into play, but decided to wait.

"Who in the hell is Peter?"

The guy never got an answer, because a hard blow from Chandu knocked him off his feet. His fist made a loud crack as it connected with the man's face.

"Enough chatting," Chandu said, ripping off his jacket.

"What the hell you—" Jan began to say when one of the men jumped him. His head hit the concrete, hard. For a moment he saw stars, was disoriented. A punch to the stomach brought him back. His attacker was on top of him, working him over with punches. Jan grabbed hold of the man's head, jerked him toward himself and hammered an elbow into his back. That earned him a loud groan.

Jan thrust the man's head to the right and twisted free of his grasp. Then he grabbed the punching arm, swung his leg over it, and stretched himself backward. An arm lock. Jan applied pressure on the man's shoulder. Two seconds later, the thug was pleading for mercy.

Jan released his grip and stood up. The man rolled to the side, holding his shoulder. Chandu stood next to Jan, massaging his knuckles. Their three opponents lay on the floor.

"You already done too?" the big man said, grinning.

"Why did you do that?"

"Do what?"

"Start a brawl."

"These boys weren't nice," Chandu said with a shrug. "Plus, they were going to attack us anyway. I just beat them to it."

Jan sighed. Diplomacy was never Chandu's strength.

"I never know what you want," the big man protested. "Now they'll be nice and cooperative."

• •

Manuel Floer held a dirty rag to his nose, his head back slightly. The bleeding was slow to stop. Jan would rather have gotten by without a brawl, but Chandu was probably right.

"Why were you looking for trouble?" Jan asked.

"Because I don't fucking like pigs."

"Maybe I'm not one."

Manual snorted a laugh. "You stink like a whole room of them."

Jan fought an urge to sniff at his clothes. He waved away the thought. "Screw it. Just answer my questions, and we're gone."

The man nodded, scowling.

"Where is Horst Esel?"

"No fucking clue."

"You should be more cooperative," Chandu threatened, "otherwise there's seconds."

Manuel was clearly intimidated by Chandu. "I really don't know," he said feebly. "I saw Horst a few days ago. He visited me at a job site and started telling me all about his time in the big house. I asked him if he was gonna work construction again, but he just laughed. He was 'sitting pretty,' that's what he said. Then he grinned all stupid."

"What did he mean by that?"

"How should I know, man? Horst always skimmed off the top by moving this or that building material, but he didn't get rich off it. Don't ask me where he got the dough."

"You have an idea where he is?"

"Not a one, man. I'm telling you. Apparently he and his wife moved out of his old place."

"Why did he come to the job site?"

Manuel shrugged. "For old time's sake, maybe. Didn't give me a number or any kind of clue where I could find him."

Jan had done enough questioning to see Manuel knew nothing. Another dead end. He pulled a pen from his jacket and took Manuel's hand.

"Here's my number." He wrote the number on the man's palm. "Something comes to you or you see Horst, call me."

"Be better for you if you did," Chandu added.

Manuel nodded. And they left the building.

•   •

"What do we do now?" Chandu asked on the drive home.

"We have to get back to Josseck. Going after Esel's lackey Manuel wasn't a bad idea, but we might be looking in the wrong direction."

"It is interesting that the murders coincide with Esel getting free."

"But he had no real reason to kill Judge Holoch and Josseck. And he had no connection to me."

"Connection to you?"

"I didn't kill Judge Holoch, so we know the murderer got a hold of my fingerprints, my blood, and my car somehow. It had to be someone close to me or someone who caught me in a moment of weakness."

"You blacked out for thirty-six hours. Could be that Esel was lying in wait and slipped you something."

"But how and why would he have targeted me? We had nothing to do with each other."

"You could have run him in before on some raid, or knocked up his sister, or screwed up some deal he had going."

"I've put a ton of losers in the pen. If each one wanted revenge, half of Berlin would be pinning me with murder."

"In the pen, he did have plenty of time to think it out."

"A simple construction guy is supposed to figure out a scheme like that?"

"There's more than enough sickos in prison. He only had to have the right cellmate, with connections to the outside."

Jan pondered that thought, hemming about it. There could be something to what Chandu was saying. "How fast can you get me another police ID?"

"The basic kind that won't pass a test? Three hours. If I put down two hundred it'll go faster."

"Can your counterfeiter make forged passport photos too?"

"You'd be surprised just how fast he can do it. He'll turn you into a cross between a squirrel and a Martian if you want."

"I don't need it that hard core. Just make my hair a little longer and give me a trimmed beard. And come up with a new name for me."

"What's your plan?"

"I'm going inside the pen."

"I thought prison is a place you don't want to be."

"I'll explain later," Jan said. "Let's meet back at the apartment in three hours. Let me out at Oranienburger. They got just the shop I need there."

•   •

Jan felt like a kid in a toy store. Latex masks hung all over the walls. A laughing pig stared at George Bush. An old man with a beard rested next to Venetian masks with gold ornaments that clashed with the zombies lurking above a doorway. A colorful clown grinned demonically at Batman, while the superhero's indifferent gaze was set on a bimbo wearing a feather boa.

Jan wanted to roam the store and try on every mask, but time was short. He tried on a few select wigs until he found the right one. He threw in some makeup and checked out. He hadn't worn a disguise for a long time.

● ●

Chandu, yawning, climbed the stairs to his apartment. He still felt the drinking, right down to his bones. At the counterfeiter's place, he'd nearly fallen asleep in his chair, even though it had only taken an hour to create a cop badge for one Martin Müller. In the doctored photo, Jan had a beard that made him look ten years older and totally changed his face.

Chandu was turning the key in the lock when the door flew open, a gun aimed in his face. He cursed his slow reaction, but with that .45 barrel at his nose he didn't exactly have time for reacting anyway.

He raised his hands. "Okay, man," he said to the intruder. "Just don't be getting nervous now. Who are you, what do you want?"

"Fldya," the intruder said, waving the pistol around.

"Wha . . . ?" Chandu stammered. He was obviously dealing with some kind of weirdo. He weighed his options. He'd have to move all in one motion, yanking the man's arm to the side to take him.

The intruder stepped closer. A broad grin showed on his bearded face, and he pocketed the gun.

"Fooled ya," Jan chirped.

"You fucker." Chandu sighed in relief. "I just about shit my pants."

"How you like my new disguise?"

Jan had long brown hair. The beard looked real. Put an old shirt on him and he was some lazy clerk who called it quits every day at three.

"Learn that in detectives?"

Jan shook his head. "In German class."

"German class?" Chandu said, puzzled.

"In eighth grade our teacher made us put on a play. My role was old vagabond with beard. I had to paste on a thing like this for every show. Together with the wig, no one knew who I was."

"Why not just keep it on all the time, then?"

"A glue-on beard is a nasty deal. It itches like hell for hours and you break out in a rash. Get my new ID?"

"Yes, Martin." Chandu pressed the plastic in his hand.

"Martin?"

"Martin Müller. Whenever you're sporting that sweater on your face, that's your new name."

"Not exactly creative."

Chandu shrugged. "I'm guessing you plan on questioning Horst Esel's cellmate?"

"Precisely. If the guards just look at my badge, it'll be easier. The ID is only backup."

"Don't the guys know you in there?"

"I haven't visited the pen for two years now."

"What are you hoping to get?"

"A possible motive. A year in the pen doesn't turn a crooked construction supervisor into some sick serial killer. On the other hand, it's bizarre that Esel went into hiding right after being set free. Plus, I want to find out more about this thing Manuel mentioned, that Esel seemed to be acting flush."

Jan checked himself out in the mirror, satisfied. The disguise fit perfectly. "If nothing else, maybe I'll find out more about any connection between Judge Holoch and Josseck. There has to be more than a few court decisions. I called Zoe and Max. We'll get together tonight. I'll tell you how my questioning went."

He faced Chandu, grinning. "Till later then."

"Take care, Martin."

Once the door clicked shut, Chandu shuffled into his bedroom. He pulled off his shoes and dropped into bed. Until Jan was back, he was going to have himself a little nap.

· ·

Jan let his gaze roam the empty visiting room. Visiting time was over now, but his badge had granted him access anyway. He anxiously patted his beard, hoping the glue wouldn't lose its stickiness.

The door opened. Horst Esel's cellmate was an obese man, with thinning hair and an unshaven face. He sat down looking grumpy.

"I already told the tax people everything," he began. "What do the police want from me?"

Jan glanced at his notes. "Gregor Linz, I take it?"

"Yes. I'm hoping you have good news about my motion for reduced sentence."

"I'm not here because of you."

"Why, then?"

"Because of Horst Esel."

"Horsti? What's up with the guy? Was he moving goods again?"

"I can't tell you, because I don't know where he is," Jan explained. "Maybe you can give me a tip."

"I'm sorry, boss." Gregor held his hands up in defense. "Got no idea."

"Herr Linz," Jan said gently. "If you help me, I will speak up for you about that reduced sentence. Otherwise you'll have to sit out the full sentence, because I'll tell the review committee that you weren't cooperative."

Gregor pinched his eyes shut, and then opened them wide and glared at Jan. His indignation at this veiled threat was clear.

"Fine," Gregor said, the tension draining from his face. "Well, so? What do you want to know?"

"The whereabouts of Horst Esel."

"I can't help you there. Horst did tell me about his house, though. Built it with a guy he worked with. In prison he even worked out plans for a swimming pool. If you can't find him there, something must have happened after he got out."

"Okay," Jan said. "Now, tell me about your stay together in here."

"He got a cozy deal. Someone had seen to it that he was put in with me."

"What's so special about that?"

"Me, I'm sitting here because of tax evasion. I don't hurt a fly."

"And that's it?"

Gregor shook his head. "He was always getting all kinds of stuff. Magazines, food, that kind of thing. Don't ask me from who."

"That didn't bother the other prisoners?"

"That was the thing. One of the baddest guys in the joint was watching out for him."

"Who?"

"I only know him by his nickname, Troweler. Real name Otto or something. Skinhead. Over six foot six with hands like sledge-hammers. Broke two guys' necks. A goddamn plague, but he always kept an eye on Horst."

"So, why?"

"Word was, there was lots of dough flowing his way. Hundred a day."

"Who paid him?"

"Some kind of builder type guy."

"Michael Josseck?"

"That's it." Gregor clapped his hands. "Horst was always telling me how he'd gone to prison for the guy."

"Just because? Brotherly love?"

"No. Horst got dough for that too. Plus this Josseck had promised he'd get him work right away once he was out."

"Did he say anything about what kind of work?"

"Something on a building site. I'm sure Horsti doesn't know anything else. He seemed along for the ride."

"Nothing else? Maybe ripping off building materials? Or some other big scam?"

"I never knew of anything like that. His time in the joint was earning him a tidy little sum. That was the main thing."

"All right, thanks a lot, Herr Linz." Jan put away his notebook and stood. He wasn't going to get any more than this out of the man.

"Hey, boss," he shouted after Jan. "You will put in a good word for me. Without Horsti's food donations I'm croakin' on this grub here."

"First thing tomorrow," Jan lied.

He left the room. He waved to the guards. He hadn't gotten much closer to Horst Esel. Tonight, he hoped the combined forces of his whole ragtag team could make sense out of all the puzzle pieces.

Chapter 10

The gatherings were almost falling into a routine. Zoe and Jan made themselves comfortable on the couch while Chandu fiddled with the coffeemaker. Max stayed absorbed in the tech, fine-tuning the images coming from his little projector. With the smell of cigarettes in the room, the whole scene reminded Jan of a night of poker with friends. The only things missing were cards and beer.

"How did it go with Esel's cellmate?" Chandu asked from the kitchen.

"I didn't get much further. Josseck was making sure, from the outside, that Esel had a pleasant prison stay. There's no reason Esel would want to kill the builder. More like the opposite."

"So, another dead end," Zoe remarked.

"It's conceivable Esel took off for vacation. We should focus on Josseck. Meantime, maybe Max finds something on the Homicide server."

Max sensed he'd been called upon. "Your fellow officers have been hard at work," he said. He was wearing the same threadbare jeans he'd had on when they first met. His unkempt hair was sticking up all over, and his attempt to let his stubble grow was looking pathetic. His T-shirt boasted a *Sesame Street* character aiming a pistol. Underneath it read, "Make My Day."

The first image Max showed was of a big, burly man. The guy's sparse hair was combed back with gel. A wide grin split his flabby face, which captured a mix of arrogance and lechery. His shirt was open. Almost lost among his thick chest hair was a gold chain.

"That loser washes less than you do," Zoe commented.

"Thanks for that expert criticism." Max pointed to the picture. "Allow me to introduce—Michael Josseck. Former building contractor, now harp player in heaven. Was sent from this life to the next with concrete in his stomach."

"You going to tell us something new while you're at it, Maximum Nerd?"

Max pressed the remote and the image of a tube appeared. The gray plastic was smeared with concrete. He gestured at the wall with both hands. "Ladies and gentlemen—the murder weapon. A plastic tube, found with Jan's fingerprints on it."

"Ha!" Jan sprang up from the couch. "That's good news."

"Doing all right there, Janni?" Zoe asked, mystified.

"Yep." He sat back down wearing a satisfied grin.

"I think maybe you didn't quite get all that," Chandu said to him. "Your fingerprints were found on the murder weapon. Which means you're the main suspect in not just one murder case, but now two."

"Not a big deal." Jan waved away the thought. "The main thing is, now I know that I'm not Judge Holoch's murderer."

Zoe and Chandu exchanged telling glances. Max, unsure, scratched at his head.

"My God. Do I have to explain everything?" Jan moaned. "I had a mental blackout lasting about thirty-six hours on the weekend that Holoch was murdered. From Friday night till Sunday morning, I was blacked out. I have no idea what I was doing. I would swear on my life that I'd never kill the judge in a sober state, but clearly I'd been drugged. They found ecstasy in my body, something I would never take, so it's possible other drugs were put in me too. All this means I couldn't be fully sure that I was *not* at the judge's house on the night he was killed. But now that my fingerprints were found at this builder Josseck's place, it's clear that someone's trying to put the blame on me. I haven't had any blackouts the last few days. Most importantly, I was of sound mind and body on Tuesday night when Josseck was killed."

"So where is this person getting your fingerprints?" Zoe asked him.

"No idea. The perpetrator was planning both murders for a long time. When he got my blood and fingerprints for the first murder, he must've pressed my hand onto that tube there too."

"Huh," Chandu said. "Your hunch might sound logical, but I'm guessing it's not going to be enough in court."

Jan waved it aside. "Not important right now. At least I wasn't completely berserk last weekend."

"That's nice for you," Zoe remarked. "But this doesn't get us any further."

"But it does help, because now we know that the murderer was planning to pin both crimes on me all along."

"You must have really stepped on someone's toes," Chandu said.

"Not necessarily. Revenge is the obvious motive, but maybe the murderer was simply able to get at my fingerprints and blood easily. Add my connection to Judge Holoch and I'm the perfect fall guy."

"This does narrow down the possible suspects," Zoe said.

Jan turned to Max. "Write this down." He raised a finger. "First off, the perpetrator comes from my environment. That can mean my circle of friends as well as my fellow cops, but also persons nearby like neighbors, the baker around the corner, people at my local bar."

"Second, he must have insider knowledge," Zoe interjected. "Your relation to Judge Holoch wasn't the talk of the town. Just your circle of friends and your lawyer knew about it."

"And your fellow cops," Chandu added.

"There's more than a few wusses on the Homicide squad," Zoe said. "Plenty in Forensics too. I have a hard time imagining any one of them as a serial killer."

"You know the hammer murderer?" Max asked them.

"We haven't been introduced yet," Zoe replied.

Max's fingers flew over the keys. Soon an image appeared of a black-haired man with a full beard. He wore a dark suit and tie. His piercing glare was directed sideways.

Max pointed to the picture on the wall. "Allow me to intro-duce—Norbert Poehlke. The hammer murderer. Good old Norbert was a police sergeant in Stuttgart, got deep into debt and saw no other option than to start committing murder-robberies and holding up banks. He killed three people total. Once they were hot on his trail, he murdered his wife and his eldest son. After doing that deed, he fled with his youngest kid to Italy. After they'd finally cornered him, he went and killed the kid too before blowing his own head off."

Max clicked the image away. "What I'm saying is, we should disregard no one. Even Jan's coworkers in Homicide. Who knows what depths this person will sink to?"

. . .

"I'm telling you, the guy has gone nuts," Andreas whispered, exchanging secret glances with the colleagues who'd joined him in the investigations room. Every photo of Jan's apartment had been painstakingly pinned to the wall. Most of the photos were sharp, but some looked like shots taken with a disposable camera. Yellow

Post-it notes were attached to some photos taken elsewhere, bearing titles such as Potsdamer Platz, Oberbaumbrücke, or Tiergarten. Others had red Post-its with probable locations. The rest of the photos were unmarked.

Patrick stood before a shot showing Jan and a friend in front of a cabin in the forest. The identity of Jan's friend and the location of the cabin remained unknown.

"Where are you, Jan?" Patrick muttered. The detective's dark hair hadn't been combed in some time. His eyes were rimmed red, and he was chewing his fingernails. He hadn't shaved in days, and his gray suit bore a big coffee stain.

"He didn't go home last night," Andreas whispered to the female detective next to him.

"I've never seen him like this," she responded. "He's even wearing his sidearm, like the murderer's going to ambush us in here."

"It's his first case as head of a homicide squad. Up till now, Jan was always standing in the way. Now he doesn't just get the chance to solve a highly public case, he gets to remove his biggest competition."

"But why is he so . . . fanatical about it?" The detective raised her eyebrows. "The evidence in the Holoch case was damning enough. Now we've got fingerprints on the murder weapon used on Michael Josseck. At some point, Jan's going to turn himself in or get caught in the dragnet. Then Patrick can celebrate."

"I don't know." Andreas shook his head. "I just don't feel right about this. Something's off."

• •

"Let's turn to Michael Josseck," Jan proposed. "What's the investigation turned up so far?"

"Like with Judge Holoch, everything centers on you. They found your fingerprints, which makes you the main suspect. Now they're looking for a motive, trying to figure out why you'd kill the builder."

"Hasn't it occurred to any of them that I don't have a motive?"

"It looks like any leads that didn't point to you were put aside."

"Oh, man," Jan said. "Patrick is even stupider than I thought."

Max clicked the remote. "I concentrated on the leads that they tossed." A list of e-mails appeared. "These are threatening hate e-mails Josseck received in the last few months," he explained. "They range from threats to kick his ass, to murder."

"We know who sent them?"

"Partly. Your fellow cops didn't try too hard. I went rummaging around and figured out a few of them."

A new list appeared. Jan scanned the names.

"I don't know a single one. Who are they?"

"All had done business with Josseck, either as partner or as the builder's client. I searched for any connections to you but found nothing."

Jan sighed. "So that's a dead end. We got anything else?"

"Only Josseck's notebook."

"What about it?"

"I don't know, not exactly. I could only find a comment in the investigation files saying that Josseck had written down incoherent stuff, in some little book."

"Incoherent?" Chandu asked.

"Probably some type of code. No one had bothered to decipher the entries."

"What's this code look like?" Jan asked.

"That's the problem. There's only a photo of the notebook, of the cover."

149

Jan folded his hands together. He had to find out more about Josseck's crooked business dealings, about his connection to the judge. If he nailed that piece, the murderer would emerge from the slew of potential perps.

"We need that notebook," Jan declared. "Or at least we have to know what's in it."

"I hate to tell you this," Chandu said, butting in, "but you can't exactly go back to your old workplace."

"I'm not getting the book. Zoe is."

The blonde medical examiner coughed. "Excuse me? Are you on something?"

"You're the only one who can go prowling around CID without it looking suspicious."

"I work in Tempelhofer Damm," Zoe said. "I get over to your offices maybe twice a year."

"Then take some evidence over to CID," Chandu suggested.

"I'm a medical examiner, Mr. T, not a courier."

"Maybe the courier will be busy, so you'll have to bring something by in person."

"It's not a bad idea," Jan said.

Zoe rolled her eyes. "Transferring evidence has a procedure. People have to sign for it, keep a list, stuff like that."

"It's a risk we'll have to take."

"So what do you propose? That I go marching into Homicide, wave nicely to everyone, then make myself copies of the murder victim's little book?"

"We'll have to proceed with subtlety," Jan said. "You'll have to go there at a time when they're all out. Tomorrow is Saturday, so I propose the evening. By seven, few people will still be hanging around, since there's no new evidence that really needs going over."

"What do I do then? Just walk up to a copier and lay the book on it?"

"You can take good photos with that cell of yours," Chandu said. "Our computer freak here can edit them how we want them."

"You did want to get out of Forensics," Jan added. "Now you have your chance."

Zoe blew cigarette smoke toward the ceiling. "Bad fucking idea."

•   •

Zoe took an evidence bag from Forensics and filled it with fibers from an old sweater. She put on a white lab coat with her name printed on it, and she slipped into white clogs. She looked like the perfect stereotype of a scientist. She hadn't felt this stupid since she was eight and wore a pointy princess hat and veil for Mardi Gras.

Still, she felt okay about the plan as Jan had laid it out. She strolled past the guards at the entrance, giving a little wave, and made for the investigations room. A light was on, and Patrick was looking at a photo. He looked exhausted, but the energy drinks on the table told Zoe he wasn't intending to go home.

She cursed to herself, fighting an urge to just toss the evidence bag on the floor. She had to photograph that notebook. With Patrick in the room, it was impossible.

She caught her breath, disappeared into the next room, and called Jan. He picked up after the second ring.

"What's up?"

"I got a little problem. It could be solved, if you tell me what kind of car Patrick drives."

"Why you want to know—"

"Quit babbling. Model and color."

"Audi A3, metallic blue. Rear right, there's a Coldplay sticker."

"Thanks," she said and hung up.

151

"Coldplay," she grunted. "Then it won't be too bad about that clunker."

She left the station and made her way into the neighboring park. For this, she was going to need a little help.

•   •

Patrick laid photos out on the table. He sat down and was taking a sip of the nasty-tasting energy drink when a car alarm went off. He went to the window and pushed the curtains aside. The lights of a dark-colored car were blinking wildly. With horror, he saw why. A skater was using the Audi's hood as a ramp. Only now did he realize it was his car.

"Damn bastards," Patrick hollered. He ran out of the room and sprinted down the corridor for the exit, his fatigue totally gone. At the entrance, a young woman in a white lab coat held the door open for him. She held an evidence bag in her hand and had on weird shoes.

He sputtered a quick "thanks" without stopping. Then he was out on the street. The skater was about to make another jump. He'd show the little shit. This would be his last run.

•   •

"Say again? You got a few kids to trash that detective's car?" Chandu said.

"It wasn't that hard," said Zoe. "I told them the pig had nabbed my brother skating, just because he'd bumped into a pedestrian on the Ku'damm. They started freaking out about it. I had to hear about the surveillance state, skaters being oppressed, and the fascist police structure; by then they were all piss and vinegar. Once I added in a few more euros for a case of Red Bull, the deal was done.

Barely ten minutes later Patrick came flying out like Superman and ran after them in hot pursuit."

"Then what?" Jan asked.

"CID offices were as good as dead. In Homicide, the book was lying there in a box along with other evidence."

"Did you take photos of all the pages?"

"Yes," she said with pride, holding up her cell. "In color and in focus." She tossed the phone to Max and stood. "Now, I gotta get to work. I'll be here tomorrow at nine. Pretty early for a Sunday, but I can hang."

Before she left, she turned to Chandu. "Buy some croissants, will you? Without breakfast, I get cranky."

With that, the door shut. Silence reigned for a moment.

"Well, guess I'll get after it," Max said to break the silence. He connected the phone to his laptop.

Chapter 11

Jan stirred his coffee, half asleep. He'd spent the night looking over the illegible writing in Michael Josseck's notebooks with Max and entering it all into the computer. The hacker had eventually cracked the code. It had been a simple character shift.

A loud knock on the door made Jan jump. Chandu came out of the kitchen and opened the door.

"Morning," Zoe said. She tossed her jacket on a chair, opened a window, and sat in an armchair.

"Black with a spoonful of sugar," she shouted after Chandu. "Hopefully you remembered my croissants."

Chandu's response was a crabby growl.

"Well, Maximum Computer Freak," Zoe said. "Find out anything?"

"The photos were good ones," Max replied wearily. "You do seem to have certain talents."

"I'm about to smack you upside your—"

"Please, no fighting," Jan broke in. "I'm too tired."

Before Zoe could talk back, Chandu handed her a cup of steaming hot coffee. "Here, Sunshine."

Zoe took the cup without responding and took a sip. The coffee clearly calmed her.

"So," Max began, turning on the projector. A photo of Josseck's notes appeared. "That notebook was packed. After we deciphered the code, it turned out to be a bribe log, including cash amounts and dates of payment. That's the bomb right there, but it doesn't help us find the killer. Anyone he was bribing wouldn't want him out of the game. Who would murder a cow he could milk?"

"Maybe Josseck wanted to take the bribes public," Zoe said.

"Unlikely," Jan said. "Evidently, a large part of his jobs came via bribes. If he'd made that public, he would have gone broke immediately. Not to mention he'd be under criminal investigation."

"More interesting were the addresses and phone numbers," Max continued. "I haven't had time to check the background on each one, but they don't seem to fully match the list of people he paid off. So who do they belong to? Maybe our murderer's among them."

Max clicked his remote and a list with names and phone numbers appeared. "Do these names mean anything to you guys?"

Jan added, "I looked through the list but—"

"Goddamn it," Chandu interrupted. Their eyes found the big man.

"You know someone?"

He nodded. "Nathan Lefort. Better known as French Nat."

"What's his deal?"

"A goddamn son of a bitch. Lefort comes from Algeria originally, I think, or maybe Tunisia. He was a pimp in Marseille for a long time before coming to Berlin. Assembled himself a little gang of buddies, running a prostitution ring with illegals who could only be booked over the Internet. Exclusive, for people with special requests."

"Special how?" Zoe asked.

"Any and every sexual deviancy, most of which you can't even imagine."

"I can imagine."

"You'd be surprised."

"Then we should talk to him," Max said.

"It's not that easy," Jan interjected. "If Nat is some underworld big shot, he's never going out the door without a bodyguard. It's not as if he's going to provide us the info like it's his civic duty."

"I got an idea," Chandu said, looking at the clock. "I just have to make a call, but what do you guys think about a little café breakfast? We might just meet a few interesting people."

·   ·

Jan sat in a wicker chair, sipping an espresso. It was a lovely morning. The sun warmed his face and the wind caressed his cheeks. Only the smoke from Zoe's cigarette disrupted the harmony. He watched as the medical examiner coated a croissant with Nutella, poured cherry jam on it, and then ate it with her scrambled eggs.

"You know what cholesterol is?" Jan asked her.

"You know what my heels could do to your shins?" she replied with her mouth full.

Jan gazed around. The café was full of customers. Children played out on the green. A riled-up dog's bark mingled with the beats coming from an Opel with its stereo way too loud.

Jan had hidden his hair under a cap. He was wearing narrow sunglasses and several days' worth of stubble. Despite this camouflage, he did not feel secure. He used to enjoy summer mornings like this. Starting off Sunday in a café, enjoying the warm temperatures and the food. Now his eyes darted around, out of fear that a police vehicle could pass through Leipziger Platz.

Jan heard Chandu's voice in his ear: "Turn your head to the left." His friend sat in a car not far from them, staking out the street. Max had attached a tiny camera to Jan's sunglasses, feeding a picture to a monitor Chandu had mounted on the dash.

"The guy with jaw-length, blow-dried-back hair."

Jan turned inconspicuously. The man might have been attractive if his nose were smaller and his teeth weren't yellowed.

"The one with the open shirt and glitzy Rolex?" Zoe whispered into the microphone under her collar.

"Yes."

"Oh, dude. Like in some bad movie."

Nathan Lefort sat down at a table. Following him was a Mediterranean-looking man, about Chandu's size.

"I was right. This joint is the son-of-a-bitch's breakfast spot."

"What now?" Zoe said. "We're not finding out anything watching him drink coffee."

"Bisacodyl," Chandu said.

Zoe raised her eyebrows. "What's a laxative have to do with it?"

"I know two of the servers. For a kindly gratuity, they'll help us cause problems with our friend's digestion. Plus, they've been wanting to get back at the not-so-charming Frenchman for a while now."

"Where did you get the bisacodyl?"

"Here and there," Chandu hedged.

Zoe kept at it. "Then what? We analyze his stool?"

"Please have a little more faith in my plan," Chandu said. "I'll sneak in the back and wait in the restroom while Jan stalls the bodyguard. You stay in your seat, so our man Max can record it all from your lapel camera. Some other guys might be coming wanting to meet up with Nathan."

A blonde woman approached Nathan's table and took his order. After she'd turned back around, French Nat stuck out his tongue at her lewdly and laughed out loud about it.

157

"Nice guy," Zoe remarked.

"Don't stare at him so much," Jan warned. "Types like that are paranoid."

Jan nervously tapped his fingers on the table. He hated sitting here doing nothing while the others did all the work. The server finally brought two coffees to Nathan's table.

"Is she one of the ones you know?" Zoe asked.

"Yes," Chandu replied. "That's Sandra. Sweet thing, really gets up and goes. You can't imagine what she—"

"Don't want to know," Zoe cut him off. "Main thing is, she got the bisacodyl in there. If she did, you should head on in. That stuff works fast."

Jan checked the time. The plan was not perfect. Countless things that might go wrong had occurred to him, but this was their only chance to get close to Nathan. Jan would have liked to interrogate the Frenchman personally, but two people waiting for him in the men's restroom would have been too conspicuous. Besides, Nathan had been in the French Foreign Legion, so Chandu was the better choice. Jan only had to keep the bodyguard at bay.

•   •

Chandu was waiting in a stall in the men's room. His legs anxiously shifted back and forth. He composed himself like before a fight, blocking all else out. This Nathan was no weakling. Anyone who'd fought with the Foreign Legion for ten years knew all the tricks. In a fistfight he'd slaughter the Frenchman, but Nat was sure to have a knife or even a piece on him.

Everything had to go just right. The café was busy and bright, not some dark, secluded underpass. If just one customer came into the restroom along with Nathan, the whole thing was finished.

Chandu had only one shot. He had to overpower the Frenchman before he knew what was coming.

"He's getting up," he heard Jan say in his earpiece. "The way he's holding his stomach, our pharmaceutical magic is working."

The door to the men's restroom opened. A man was cursing in French.

Chandu bounded out of the stall, lunging at the startled Nathan. He grabbed the Frenchman by the collar and kicked open the stall door. Chandu rammed Nathan's head into the toilet bowl and flushed. Nathan twisted and jerked to fight Chandu's hold, but Chandu drove his knee into Nathan's shoulders and held him down. Once the water emptied, he pulled Nathan up and slammed Nathan's forehead against the stall wall. Then he plunged the Frenchman's head back into the toilet again. The Frenchman floundered in Chandu's tight grip. The African was merciless. He counted to ten, then yanked Nathan from the bowl and looked him in the eyes.

"Listen up, son of a bitch. You're going to answer a few questions. I don't like an answer? I drown you in this toilet."

Nathan's eyes were wide with fear. He coughed up water. Blood ran from his forehead. And he nodded.

• •

Nathan's bodyguard seemed to suspect nothing. The thug drank his coffee leisurely, setting his feet up on the chair opposite. He pulled a pack from his shirt and lit a cigarette.

The things Jan was hearing through his earpiece made him cringe.

"Your homeboy is not too squeamish," Zoe remarked, grinning. "When he's done with that asshole, he'll have to go have that talk with my neighbor."

After the bodyguard had allowed himself a couple puffs, he glanced toward the restroom, looking anxious. Evidently his boss's toilet break was lasting too long.

"Damn it," Jan said. "I'm going over to him." He stood.

"Just wait," Zoe said, trying to hold him back.

Jan shook his head. He didn't want to take any risks. Chandu needed every second. Jan maneuvered around the chairs and tables till he was at the bodyguard's table. The man was about to rise, but Jan sat down and showed his police badge.

"Berlin Detectives," he said. "Please remain seated."

The man was taken off guard. He looked around as if reconning possible escape routes, but he sat back down in his chair.

"I haven't done anything wrong," the man said.

"Possibly," Jan said, "but we've received a terror warning, so we're watching all public squares and gathering places."

The bodyguard reared up. "I look like a fuckin' A-rab?" He'd clearly recovered from his initial shock. "What, you think I got a bomb strapped on under my shirt?"

The toilet flushing roared in Jan's ear. He could barely focus on their conversation.

"Measures include weapons checks. Are you carrying a weapon on you?"

"Not a one," the man said, holding up his hands. "I swear."

"So what's making that bulge in your jacket, at the left hip?"

The bodyguard turned his head toward the street again. He seemed to be entertaining more thoughts of fleeing.

"It's jus' a little club I got," he whispered. "No one's assassinating anyone with a thing like that."

"A little club." Jan raised his eyebrows, disapproving. "You planning on killing your own breakfast? Why else would you carry that on you, and at a place like this?"

Jan could practically see the man's thoughts racing. Meantime, Nathan had become talkative. Jan had to play for more time.

"There's a few bad guys in Berlin," the bodyguard explained. "It's jus' self-protection."

"Can I see this club?"

The man grumbled something and set a slim plastic stick on the table. Jan knew the style of weapon. It could be whipped out in one quick movement. At its tip was a heavy, round ball, good for breaking bones. Jan took a good, long look at the blackjack.

"Cudgels and steel rods are prohibited. Purchase and ownership are forbidden. You do know that, right?"

The bodyguard nervously wrung his hands. "Listen, Herr Police Detective. I'm sorry, but there's people I got trouble with."

Jan suppressed a grin. When thugs started getting civil, you had them in the palm of your hand.

"I got it all," he heard Chandu saying in his ear. "We can go."

The plan had worked. Now Jan only had to get something good out of his situation. He gave the bodyguard a stern stare.

"All right, fine," he began, sounding generous. "We are searching for assassins, not heavies. Since I dread all the paperwork involved, I'm going to let this pass. I'll confiscate that blackjack, but don't ever get caught with this again."

The big bodyguard nodded and thanked him profusely. "Promise, Herr Police Detective. Won't happen again."

Jan stood, went back over to his table, and waved at Zoe.

"We're out of here," he whispered. He set a twenty-euro bill on the table and left the café. Out of the corner of his eye, he observed the bodyguard heading for the restrooms. Whatever the guy found in there, it was sure to end his career in the underworld.

• •

Chandu sat on the couch and sighed.

"If I would've known how much fun you have solving cases, I would've joined the detectives."

Jan ignored the remark. "What were you able to find out? On the recording we only heard the toilet flushing and a bunch of French cussing I didn't understand."

"Oh, our friend got quite creative," Zoe explained. "In one part he's calling Chandu an African locust muncher whose dick is the size of a—"

"That's about as much as I need to hear," Jan interrupted. "Just tell us what info he spat out after downing that toilet water."

"One thing I have to make clear first," Chandu told them. "I don't usually go in for violence, but Nathan is a bag of shit even for the Berlin underworld. So it was my duty to treat him like that."

"You're the kind of good Samaritan I don't want to meet in a dark alley," Zoe said, which earned her another deprecating look from Chandu.

"I have to admit it was a tall order, but after that toilet bath he started singing like a lark," he said.

"Michael Josseck was one of his clients. The guy did four thousand euros a month in business with him. As far as his sexual requests, he was into gay sex, rough S&M, and even pedophilia. Apparently Josseck tried everything Nathan had to offer."

"He know the judge?" Jan asked.

"No."

"Could it be that one of the girls was abused by the both of them and decided to take her revenge?" Zoe asked. "She could have come to the judge some other way."

Chandu shrugged. "That would be one possibility. Over the years, Nathan has pimped hundreds of girls whose names he never bothered to get to know. He can't help us any further, toilet bath or no. Prostitutes won't get us anywhere."

"Damn it," Jan said. "Keep thinking. The two murders must be connected. There's more to it."

"I might have something to offer," Max broke in. They all turned to the hacker.

"I checked out Nathan Lefort. As you guys might imagine, he's been to court countless times already. Assault, money laundering, inciting prostitution. Nothing special for him, but one time he was under suspicion of murder. It was for a woman named Stein. She was his drug courier."

The name struck Jan like a bolt through the head.

"You mean Marie Stein?" He jumped from the couch.

"Yes," Max said. "You know the case?"

"Marie Stein was the sister of Patrick Stein, my fellow cop."

Chapter 12

"Patrick Stein joined the Detective Division because of his sister's murder," Jan began. "Supposedly, an illustrious career as a lawyer was in his future. He was the family's golden boy, but his sister had gone off the rails. She was taking hard drugs and ran away at sixteen. Next two years, she kept getting arrested for drug-related crimes, casual prostitution. She must have met Nathan somewhere in there. He got her working as a drug courier. She allegedly smuggled heroin from Russia to Germany. Her parents had already given up on her by then. Only Patrick stood by her. She was found in a gutter eventually. Someone had beaten her to death and cut open her stomach to retrieve the dope."

Jan turned a beer bottle in his hands, deep in thought.

"The case was never solved. Her pimp, who we now know as Nathan, was the main suspect, but the evidence was sparse and he was let go. On the day the verdict came down, Patrick broke off his studies and applied for the police. He worked hard from the very first day and passed with flying colors. He got into Homicide. The first few years went well, but then his rise got the brakes put on it."

"Why?" Chandu asked.

"He lacked the instinct," Jan told them. "Patrick knows all the rules, regulations. He is a good cop, but when standard operating procedures fail him, he gets nowhere."

"And you were better at it, and you spoiled his career?" Zoe asked.

"I'm not better, just more driven by instinct. Which meant I made progress on cases when he was never able to. I didn't destroy his career. He's the one still working as a detective."

"So why does he hate you, then?"

"Two reasons for that. First, I made jokes at his expense. That's an initiation ritual. Nothing dramatic, but he took it the wrong way coming from me. The final break came when I interfered with one of his cases. His investigation had gone down the wrong road, but thanks to my help, the case was solved. But it made Patrick look stupid. He'd wasted two weeks without getting any results, and I got it done in one day. I can get where he's coming from, but we're in Homicide. All that counts is catching who did it. It doesn't matter who gets the credit for solving the case. That's the way I look at it."

"Patrick sees it otherwise," Chandu said.

"I dismissed it all so easily. I never would've thought it would lead to something as big as this."

"You're saying he's behind all of this?" Zoe said. "That's a pretty harsh allegation." She blew cigarette smoke at the ceiling. "I hardly know Patrick, but he doesn't seem like a psychopathic murderer to me."

"There's a madman inside all of us," Chandu stated. "You only need that trigger. His sister's brutal murder might have done it."

"I don't want to go suspecting anyone too easily," Jan said. "But with Patrick, we have found the connection to me. Plus, he's the perfect murderer."

"Because he's with detectives?" Chandu said.

"Who can pull off a murder better than someone who's pre-occupied with it all day long? He'd know crime-scene methods, forensics, how to track clues. He'd know how to observe a target, figure out their weaknesses, and determine just the right moment to commit murder. Patrick possesses all the skills for going on a killing spree."

"And since he runs the homicide squad, that caps it all off," Chandu said. "He just diverts the investigation away from himself and straight to you."

"I feel so much safer now," Max remarked.

"I still don't see why he decided on you," Zoe said.

"I was an easy target," Jan said. "He knows my apartment, my car. He knows all my colleagues and friends—he easily could have found out that Judge Holoch and I had a history."

"How did he get at your blood and fingerprints?" Max asked.

"It must have happened sometime after Betty and I went out Friday. He could have spiked something I drank with knockout drops, at my place even."

"They wouldn't have seen that on a blood test? They found the ecstasy, after all," Max said.

"No," Zoe said. "Gamma-hydroxybutyric acid, for instance, one of the most common knockout drugs, is only detected in the blood for twelve hours maximum. They would have had to check Jan's hair."

"Let's assume that Patrick is the murderer and wants to take revenge on you," Chandu said. "What's the connection between him and the two victims?"

"It's pretty apparent that Marie wasn't just a drug courier; she was also a prostitute," Jan contended.

"That I get," Chandu said. "But how did Patrick know that Marie was abused by Judge Holoch and Michael Josseck?"

"She would have told him," Zoe said.

"Really?" Chandu said. "Would you tell your own brother that you were doing tricks with all kinds of perverts to fund your drug addiction?"

"He was all she had," Zoe argued. "Her parents didn't want anything more to do with her, and if she was a true addict, she didn't have any real friends."

"There are unanswered questions," Jan said. "But since Nathan Lefort is a dead end, Patrick is the best we got."

Max turned on the projector. A picture appeared of Jan's fellow cop wearing a suit. "Ladies and gentlemen. Allow me to introduce—our new main suspect, Patrick Stein."

"So what do we do now?" Zoe asked. "We can't go ambush Patrick in a café and stick his head in a toilet bowl."

"Although that does work on cops," Chandu said, grinning.

"We have to be careful," Jan warned them. "Right now the homicide squad is only focusing on me. If someone guesses that Chandu's hiding me or that Zoe's helping me, we're all going to be in big trouble."

"We wouldn't be personally introducing ourselves to him," Chandu reassured Jan. "Patrick only needs the slightest suspicion to launch an all-points dragnet. The fact that he's seen Zoe once isn't that bad. But another encounter would get him suspicious."

"That supposed to mean I can't take part in the plan?"

"I'm eternally grateful that you've been helping me, Zoe, but I won't allow you to ruin your career and end up on unemployment."

Zoe laughed, choking on smoke.

"That really is sweet of you, Jan, but I don't need you to protect me."

"If you get thrown out of Forensics, you'll have trouble finding—"

"What kind of shoes are these?" she cut in, raising her right foot.

Jan blinked, confused. "Black boots?" he tried.

"I love guys like you. Know the soccer scores going back ten years, yet think 'sneakers' is a shoe brand."

Jan couldn't see anything special about her boots. The leather looked well made. The boot had a slightly raised sole and a metal ring on the upper.

"Those are Gucci," Chandu said. "From the winter collection."

Zoe nodded approvingly. "I didn't know they had Gucci in Africa."

"Oh, there's loads. See all the things you don't know?"

"So, Jan," she said. "The million-dollar question: How can a medical examiner with the police department afford sixteen-hundred-euro shoes?"

"Sixteen hundred euros for a lousy pair of leather boots?" Max blurted.

Zoe punished the hacker with a disparaging glance. It shut him up instantly.

"Uh, medical examiners make that much?" Jan ventured.

Zoe rolled her eyes. "Have you ever seen me wearing the same pair twice?"

"Well, for what it's worth, I don't—"

"Forget it. Obviously you can't follow my train of thought. I'll put it in a way that your simple male brain can grasp." Zoe glared, searching Jan's eyes. "I do the job for fun. I have enough dough that I never actually have to work."

Max began to say, "So where did you—"

"None of your fucking business, Computer Brains," she shot back. "Best you start thinking about how we nab Psycho Patrick."

She leaned back on the couch. "Am I actually going to get any more of that jungle sludge you call coffee, or do I have to run to Starbucks?"

Chandu stood and took her empty cup. "It would be my pleasure, Zoe," he said with excess hospitality, adding a bow.

As the big man went into the kitchen, Jan turned to the image on the wall. "So. How do we close in on Patrick?"

"You can forget about a stakeout," Chandu shouted from the kitchen. "He'll notice."

"What good would that do, anyway?" Zoe asked. "Even if he returns to the scene of the crime, he can always justify it as head detective."

"Maybe he's not finished yet and already has a third victim in mind," Chandu said.

"You mean Nathan?" Jan wondered.

"Would be a clear candidate." Chandu set down a cup in front of Zoe. "He might even know who really murdered his sister."

"It wasn't Nathan?" Zoe said.

"No, that's not his style. He might well have killed people, but he would never bother with a small-time drug courier. He has a staff for that."

"Then you guys are going to have break into his place," Max offered.

"Max," Jan said in a fatherly voice. "This is not *CSI*. Patrick surely doesn't have the kind of door you can just click open with a matchstick. And he's not leaving his balcony door unlocked, either."

"Then present yourselves as police detectives to the building manager and get the door opened. By the time he comes home, you'll have any evidence you need."

"A bad idea," Jan replied. "The building manager would be able to describe me, and Patrick would be tipped off. He doesn't know that we're on his trail. The element of surprise is the only advantage we have."

Jan stood up and paced. "How do I avenge my sister's death?"

Max began to say, "I didn't know your sister—"

"It's hypothetical, nerd," Zoe snapped at him.

"Ah," Max said. He went back to the computer in his lap.

"You'd have to know everything about your target," Chandu said.

"That's not a problem. I can find all important files on any police computer. In my free time? I study the victim and record his every movement."

"You have to write it down somewhere," Max said.

"What do you mean, write it down?"

"You want to kill two or more people and go about it painstakingly, you have to make notes somewhere. Nobody can keep all that in their head."

"So where do we find notes?" Chandu asked.

Max said, "Either Patrick is supercareless and keeps his notes at work . . ."

"Or they're at his place," Jan finished.

"Exactly," Max said. "Which means, there's no other option but to break in."

"I'm afraid Max is right." Jan turned to Chandu.

The big man sighed. "My record is nearly spotless. But since I've been chilling with you? Seems I'm just dying to get into the big house."

Jan gave a sheepish grin.

"Make all of yourselves comfortable," Chandu said. "I have to go visit a friend, get up to speed on the latest in security systems. Tonight we'll plan some more." He took a key, pulled on his jacket, and left the apartment.

"Any more coffee?" Zoe said.

• •

Chandu wasn't gone long when someone knocked on the door.

"You expecting anyone?" Zoe said, stubbing out her cigarette in the ashtray.

"Maybe Chandu forgot his key," Max suggested.

Jan bounded over the couch and pulled out a pistol from under a pillow. He rushed to the door and gestured Zoe over.

"I hope it's not Jehovah's Witnesses," she muttered, went over to the door, and pulled down the handle.

"Is Herr Tommen there?" Jan heard Father Anberger's voice ask. "I have mail for him."

Jan sighed in relief, set his gun on the entry table, and stood next to Zoe.

"Well, Father Anberger," he said, to make the priest feel welcome. "Come on in."

"I hope I'm not disturbing you, but your mailbox was full, so I came by after church service."

"That's kind of you." He waved Father Anberger inside. As much as Jan liked the priest, this visit wasn't exactly well timed. When Chandu came back, they were going to figure out how to break into Patrick's apartment. And before then, Jan had a lot of thinking to do.

"I'd like to introduce you to my friends Max and Zoe." The hacker gave the father a friendly wave. Zoe lit up another cigarette.

"Pleased to meet you."

"Have a seat." Jan gestured to an armchair.

Father Anberger sat down, handing Jan the mail.

"I know that, at the moment, you're having some . . . trouble coming back home," the priest said in a secretive whisper.

"You don't have to worry. Max and Zoe know all about it."

"Ah," Father Anberger said. "Are you doing well, Herr Tommen?"

"Despite my situation, I've been lucky enough. I have a place to sleep and friends helping me look for the real killer."

"Do you know who it was?"

"We only have guesses as of yet, but we're hoping to have something concrete soon."

"Things are getting worse all the time," the priest said. "I just read about another murder. Some building contractor was tortured to death."

"Ah, you mean Michael Josseck?" Max said.

"I think that's his name. You knew him?"

"We're working on that case too," Jan explained.

"Is it the same murderer?"

"Possibly." Jan was a little surprised the priest was interested in the murders.

"Why would a person do such a thing?"

"Certainly not because he's possessed by the devil," Zoe said, clearly annoyed by the conversation.

"Can I offer you anything to drink?" Jan said, hoping to sidestep the remark.

Father Anberger shook his head. "Thanks. I just wanted to bring you your mail." He rose from the armchair. "I will pray that you find the murderer." He nodded at Max and Zoe and left the apartment.

Jan closed the door and leaned on it, feeling relieved. He did not want to drag the priest into this.

"Somehow I get the feeling the old man wasn't just looking to bring over the mail," Zoe said.

"Father Anberger is a good-hearted soul," Jan said in his defense. "He cares about all of his flock. Even if the mail was a blatant excuse to drop by, his motives are selfless."

Zoe raised her eyebrows and dedicated herself to another cigarette. She wasn't looking too convinced. But Jan didn't have time for head games. All that counted was getting ready to break into Patrick's house.

• •

Chandu returned from his expedition that evening.

"First, we have to find out where Patrick lives," the big man said.

"In an apartment building, in Kreuzberg," Max said. "Not a bad neighborhood, but not exactly kick-ass."

"Good. I'll need a photo of the lock at the front entrance. Then I'll know how we're getting in, because the unit locks will have a similar setup."

"What options are we looking at?" Jan asked.

"We can first try to electropick it," Chandu explained. He held up a little device that looked like a handheld milk frother but a little bigger. "This thing generates vibrations from a mechanism rapidly moving up and down. Using this tensioner on the front here, the cylinder core can be manipulated to turn and the door opens right up."

"Sounds like child's play," Zoe said.

"It kind of is. But most cylinders have a safeguard against this. This only works if the lock on Patrick's door is old enough."

"And what if it isn't?" Max said.

"Then we go with the lock-bumping method. For that we use a key blank with special notches, a so-called bump key." Chandu held up a key with teeth that were beveled down.

"Basically, every lock has five pins that need to be pushed upward. If any one of them is higher or lower than the key, the lock will not budge. The notches on this key are designed so that when I give it a bump and jolt it hard, the pins inside jump up because of the thrust. Then I can turn the lock real quick."

"Is that it?" Zoe asked.

"Basically, yes. I need a photo of the front lock because I'll choose a blank based on its looks. It should work. Then, a minute later? We're in."

"Awesome. Can I come too?"

"Zoe," Jan reminded her. "We already talked about that."

"And I told you that I don't rely on my job."

"It's not just about money," Chandu told her. "They catch you on a break-in with Jan, they'll run you in."

"Don't you worry yourself about me, Mr. T," Zoe said, teasing.

"Don't go flattering yourself, Carcinogen Queen."

Zoe fluttered her eyelashes, all flirty.

"Besides," Jan weighed in, "I need you over at CID. You have to keep an eye on Patrick, give us a warning in case he decides to go home early."

Zoe, sulking, breathed out cigarette smoke. "So how will you guys sneak inside?"

"I may have a plan for that," Jan said.

• •

Max almost dropped the package from nerves. He hadn't been this worked up since he'd faced off with his final opponent in *Diablo*. Of course, that was a role-playing video game and this was real life. His hands wet with sweat, he walked over to the building and read the doorbell nameplates. He tried to remember the plan, but his mind was a blank. Then he heard Jan's voice behind him.

"Nice and easy, Max. You can do this."

Jan wore the reflective outfit of a city street cleaner. He stood at the curb with a leaf blower. Once Max got the door open, the sound would bluster in through the entryway and cover up any noise Chandu made breaking in to the apartment.

Max took a deep breath. He had to work his way down the names from top to bottom until someone let him in the door. On the way up, he'd write on the package the name of whoever had buzzed him in and then deliver it to them. The cardboard box was all bound up, with practically an entire roll of packing tape. This would give Max enough time to disappear before the recipient had unpacked the scraps of useless computer parts inside.

Max started with the first bell. *A. Regner*. He pressed the white button and waited. Nothing happened. He wiped his moist hands on his pants. Then he tried the next bell.

"Let's see if you're home, P. Walter," Max muttered. Two seconds later a woman's voice blared out from the speaker. Startled, Max almost dropped the package.

"Hello?"

"Uh, hello there. Max here. I mean the mail, of course. I have a package for you, Frau . . . Walter."

The door was activated to open. Max nearly whooped with joy. Now he had to fix the door so that Chandu got in and the racket from the leaf blower would echo down the corridor. Max pressed on the door and it clicked open.

"Ha," he blurted in triumph. He quickly wrote Frau Walter's name on the package and got ready to complete his job.

• •

Jan took out his cell and tapped on a Favorites icon. Zoe answered.

"We're inside," he said. "What's up with Patrick?"

"He's still in the building, though I don't see him," the medical examiner replied. "His car is still here and I'm keeping an eye on the entrance."

"Good. We're going in."

175

"I'll wait thirty minutes. Then I'll go to work. Tell me how it went later tonight." Zoe hung up.

Jan turned on the leaf blower. The machine howled and blustered, drowning out all sound. He was blowing gum wrappers around in front of him as Chandu approached the stairway.

The roar of leaf blower turning on was the signal they'd worked out. Without looking over at his friend, Chandu entered the building. He wore a borrowed blue work jacket with various tools sticking out of it, passing himself off as building maintenance. He climbed the stairs swiftly, but without running. If all went according to plan, Max would be delivering his package and Chandu would be inside the apartment before the hacker was back downstairs. Jan would toss the blower in the car and come up to the apartment.

When he got to Patrick's apartment, Chandu pulled out the bump key. He stuck it into the lock, a screwdriver ready in his other hand. Holding the key in place, he pounded against the door lightly, turning the key. The little metal thing wouldn't budge. He tried again, but again he couldn't get the key to turn.

Chandu cursed under his breath. He had the right blank. He'd practiced it yesterday and had no problems.

Something was stirring at the door next to Patrick's.

"Honey," he heard a man's voice say over the noisy blower. "I'm going shopping real quick." The door opened a crack. Chandu's thoughts raced. Should he break it off and split?

He pounded on the blank harder.

"Don't forget bread," a woman's voice answered.

He had one, maybe two more tries. He drew out the key a little. He jerked his wrist, but the metal wouldn't budge. The blank bent under his strong grip.

"Dude, relax," he reminded himself. If he broke off the key, it was all over. They wouldn't get into the apartment and Patrick would be tipped off.

"See ya soon," the man said, opening the door.

Chandu pounded at the key. The blank turned. He shoved the door open, rushed into the apartment, and pulled the door shut in one quick motion. He heard footsteps passing in the hall. Then everything was still. He breathed out, trying to calm his thumping heart. Break-ins really were not his deal.

He took his cell from his pants pocket. He dialed Jan's number, let it ring once, hung up.

The leaf blower went silent. So far so good.

• •

"Good morning to you, Frau Walter," Max said, smiling wide.

The elderly lady inspected him with suspicion. "Morning," she replied grumpily.

"Your package." He pressed the box into her open arms.

"Thanks." The woman, curious, turned the box in her hands. "Where do I sign?"

Max's smile faded. "What's that you want?"

"To sign," the woman explained. "Normally a person acknowledges receipt."

He'd never considered that part. "No, no," he gushed, "we got this new technology. All you do is receive the package and it's all good."

"Which carrier you working for again?"

"The post office."

"You mean DHL?"

"Exactly."

"Don't they wear those yellow uniforms?"

"Me, I'm . . . freelance. Only permanent employees get those outfits."

"Uh-huh," the woman said. She studied Max as if he wasn't quite right in the head. Then she shut the door.

Max wiped sweat from his forehead. He had to clear out before the old woman opened the package. He hurried down the stairs and almost collided with a man carrying a shopping basket. He apologized and kept moving. Outside, he rushed around the corner and leaned on an ad column. His knees were shaking. The real world out there could get pretty damn exciting. It was time he got back to his computer.

• •

The air in Patrick's apartment was stagnant. It smelled like fried meat. On a wall, jackets hung in a precise row. Next to them stood an empty umbrella stand and a little cabinet of worn slippers. The laminate flooring was shiny, as if making up for the apartment's odor. When Jan came into the living room, Chandu was sitting at a desk. He had connected his laptop to Patrick's computer and started to copy files. Max had gotten them set up so that the hard drive would download without Patrick noticing it was copied over.

Jan took a good look around the room. The walls were covered with bookshelves holding stacks of legal journals, scientific magazines, travel guides. An old leather couch and the computer desk were the extent of his dull furnishings. Only a picture of Patrick and his sister gave the living room a personal touch. Patrick looked to be about fourteen years old, his sister just a little younger. They were darkly tanned, sitting near a cliff. Behind them lay the blue sea of what looked like the Adriatic. Their smiles were those of two happy teenagers who had no clue just what sort of troubled fate might await them.

"What are we looking for?" Chandu said, interrupting his thoughts.

"We need the data on that computer." Jan slipped on a pair of gloves. "Also crucial are any handwritten notes or anything else that could connect him to the murders. You keep looking in here. I'll be in the next room."

Jan went into the bedroom. The room was bleak. A simple bed with a blanket and an armoire were the only furniture. The bed linens were faded, the pillow shabby. A large punching bag hung in a corner of the room. A pair of boxing gloves and a towel lay on the floor. Jan pulled his cell phone from his pocket so he could document it all. He had to record everything. Interpreting it would come later.

Jan opened the armoire to find a jumbled mess of underwear, socks, and T-shirts. Defying this chaos, two dark suits and four ironed shirts were neatly draped on hangers.

The mess of clothing bothered him. He had always considered Patrick a middle-class conformist, the type who sorted his socks. Evidently that was only an appearance he wanted to maintain. Jan took photos of it all and went back into the living room.

Chandu had laid a photo album out on the table and was taking shots of the pages. Most of the pictures were faded and old. Many of them featured Patrick's sister.

"He seems to really have liked her," Chandu said. The album was tattered like it got used a lot.

"We still have twenty minutes," Jan said, looking at the clock. "I'm going into the bathroom to see what I can find."

The bathroom was small and much too warm. A ratty bathrobe hung on the door. The moldy smell of the shower curtain was partly masked by Patrick's aftershave. To Jan it was too tangy and too cheap, yet somehow it fit the bleak apartment. He opened the cabinet under the sink. There were cotton swabs, hankies, a little first-aid kit, and a package of aspirin. While taking photos, he noticed a black plastic bag stashed behind the first-aid kit. He

179

carefully extracted the bag and opened it. Seeing the contents, he let out a low whistle. He grabbed his camera and took photos. Maybe this was the proof they needed.

Chapter 13

The image Max projected on Chandu's wall showed a black plastic bag full of pills and vials.

"Okay," Zoe began. "We got ecstasy, marijuana, blister pack of Valium, and two vials of knockout drops, probably benzodiazepine."

"Your colleague likes to party hard, looks like," Chandu said.

"Indeed he does," Zoe said. "With that much ecstasy, he won't be coming down for six months."

"I don't believe he's taking drugs," Jan said.

"Why not?" Chandu said.

"So why have all that stuff in his bathroom?" Zoe added.

"If Patrick was on ecstasy, I would've noticed somehow. To me it looks more like he busted some dealer."

"And kept the stuff for himself?" Chandu asked. "But why?"

"It was the best way to get the drugs. You can't get knockout drops and ecstasy at the pharmacy. Say he took it from the evidence room. It would have been noticed. Patrick probably knew a dealer. He relieved the guy of his goods."

"Not a bad theory," Zoe said, "but what does it prove?"

"It proves that Patrick could be our serial killer. If he was taking the ecstasy himself you could say it's an unfortunate coincidence, but if he's drug free, why's he stashing the stuff away at his place?"

"But we don't have any other evidence," Chandu said. "There was nothing else in that apartment that could connect him to the murders. No picture of the victims. No bloodstained clothing or anything else suspicious."

"Maybe, though . . ." Max ventured. All heads turned to him.

"I checked out his hard drive. There weren't any fishy docs or incriminating photos, but part of the hard drive is encrypted."

"Can you decrypt it?" Jan said.

"The problem is, you can't copy the encrypted partition. You'd have to install a password cracker. That would have taken a long time at first, and Patrick would've noticed, anyway."

"Damn it," Jan said. "So we're still not a step further."

"But we can assume, from this, that Patrick is involved."

"It's not enough," Jan said. "We need something concrete, otherwise I don't dare break cover."

Jan's cell interrupted them. For a moment, everyone just stared at the small, ringing device.

"I thought only we had your number," Zoe said to break the silence.

"Might be the phone company," Max said.

Jan took the call. "Hello?"

"Hello," answered a faint voice, a woman. "Are you the man who gave Manuel his number?"

"And who are you?"

"Sarah Esel."

"Sarah Esel?"

"He's here." Sarah Esel was crying. "I don't know how he found us, but he's torturing my husband, to death, here in the living room."

Jan set the cell phone on the table, switched to speaker.

"Who's trying to kill your husband?"

"No idea. He's wearing a mask. I can't make out his face."

"Where are you?"

"In Charlottenburg. We just ate. Then suddenly he was standing there in the living room and he attacked Horst with a stun gun."

As if confirming it, a loud scream interrupted their call. Sarah started wailing hysterically.

"Frau Esel. Tell me where you are. Your street address."

Jan turned to Max. "Call Homicide. Use your cell, get connected to Patrick Stein."

"Help me. I'm lying under the bed . . ." Sarah let out a loud scream. "Let me go," she pleaded. A loud slap followed. The attacker must have hit her in the face.

"No. Please no," Sarah pleaded. "I'll do anything . . ." Her pleading descended into shrieks of pain.

"Frau Esel," Jan yelled out, but the woman couldn't get to the phone. The call stayed connected, transmitting Sarah Esel's suffering till the very end.

Her death didn't come for seventeen minutes.

Then someone took the phone. Faint panting came over the line.

"You hear me, you twisted bastard?" Jan said.

Silence.

"I will find you. You can put all the blame you want on me, but I will get you."

The call ended. The murderer had hung up.

•   •

Max came out of the bathroom at Chandu's place, wiping his mouth. He'd just vomited for the third time, and it looked like it wouldn't be the last. His face was waxen, like a corpse's. Sweat stood on his forehead and his eyes were red. Zoe wasn't doing much better. She kept sipping at her cup even though it had been empty a while. Her hand trembled as she directed a cigarette to her mouth.

"Fucking hell," she mumbled. She pressed the half-smoked cigarette into the ashtray and hurried to light up a new one.

Chandu was sitting on his sofa, staring at the floor with vacant eyes, as if the woman's shrieking had provoked some long-forgotten memory in him.

The murder had shaken up Jan too, but then he had already seen some fucked-up things in his life. He envied his friends, that they could still feel so much horror. Their world was a nicer place. They had not yet stared into the abyss.

Jan loved his work, but it exacted a price. It was physical at first, and then emotional, as each new death ripped a little more from a detective's soul. His fellow cop Simon hadn't been able to stand it. After twenty-four years on the job, every murder had cut into the folds of his face. He was at his end. He'd already had one nervous breakdown. If a second one had come, Bergman wouldn't have been able to contain the problem. So he'd offered Simon an early retirement. At fifty-one.

Jan had never gone in for philosophy much, but he once read a famous quote from Nietzsche that made him feel close to that unhinged detective now: "He who fights monsters should watch out that he himself doesn't become a monster. And if you stare into an abyss long enough, the abyss will stare back into you." Many people knew the saying. But few grasped the reality behind it. Jan did. Simon too.

"Patrick Stein wasn't at CID." Max's voice jolted Jan from his dark thoughts. "I called the homicide squad during the murder. He'd been gone for an hour."

"Fuck," Zoe said and sipped at her empty cup.

"I'll call a few guys," Chandu said. "Real nasty types. Then we'll wait for the bastard. An hour later? Whatever is left of him will deliver us a detailed confession."

"That does not help us," Jan said.

"Forget about human rights, man. That woman's screaming is still ringing in my ears. We stick him on a spit and let him roast in the sun."

"We do not know if it was Patrick."

"Jan, come on," Zoe fumed, blowing her angry smoke into the room. "How much proof do you still need? Let's mess up this scumbag for good."

Jan held up his hands to calm the others down. "Patrick may be implicated, but what if he's hired some hit man to do his dirty work for him? What if there are more on the hit list? The killer could already be staking out the next victim."

"I'm not going to listen to this shit anymore," Chandu said, standing up. "Bastards like this deserve to be taken out." He grabbed his jacket from the chair. "I need fresh air, otherwise I'm taking me and my gun and heading over to CID." The door banged shut.

"He's right," Zoe said. "I can't imagine, not even in my darkest thoughts, just what he was doing to her. Give me one reason why we shouldn't send Chandu after Patrick. We just prove Patrick guilty, he goes to the pen. Either he'll be declared mentally incapable at trial or he'll go inside and walk after fifteen years, strolling the streets of Berlin as if nothing ever happened. You call that justice?" Her face was flushed with rage.

"Nothing is simple," Jan said, glaring at her. "It drives me crazy when I find a child's body and know that, even if I find the murderer, they'll be set free again at some point. But people like you and me, we have to separate ourselves from the lowlife scum. If we use the same methods, we're no better. Then everything's just a huge heap of scum."

185

"You don't think he deserves to die?"

"Of course he deserves to die!" Jan roared. He kicked the table. "But I'm still a cop and not some goddamn avenging angel. Sure, it's tough on me in moments like this, but I do believe in the system. I will prove Patrick guilty of murder. Then I'll hand him over to the authorities and watch him marched into the pen."

"I'm going back to work." Zoe stood. "Two corpses will definitely be coming in within a few hours, I can tell you that."

As she was leaving, she turned to face Jan. "I'll send you a few nice color pics. Then you can ask yourself whether we should take out the bastard or not."

And the door banged shut again.

•   •

Chandu parked his latest car in the visitors' parking lot and got out. He walked a narrow path between two oaks and reached the brightly lit entry area. A checkered pattern of paving stones showed him the way, past precisely trimmed hedges. A broad door with motion sensors opened up. Chandu waved at the woman at the entrance desk, who smiled back. He breathed in the odor of cleaning agents mixed with the scent of the fresh flowers that filled the terra-cotta vases. The deep red light of a beautiful sunset streamed through the windows.

Chandu crossed the big, open hall and stepped onto a balcony with a view of forest. Sometimes he missed his homeland, Rwanda. Especially during Berlin's cold winter months. Yet this vista of leafy trees relieved his longing for the more open canopy of the savanna. Whenever it all became too much for him, he got in his car and left the city behind him. He marched beyond the paths and into forest, searched out a big tree, and lowered himself down beneath it. Soon he found his burdens eased.

At the edge of the balcony sat a dark-skinned woman in a wheelchair. She appeared to be bathing in the light of the setting sun. Chandu stood behind her and kissed her on the forehead.

"Hello, Mama."

"Chandu." She smiled without averting her gaze from the sun.

"I knew that I'd find you here. Not a cloud in the sky, and look at this view stretching over the forest, all the way to the horizon."

"The sunset is lovely here," she murmured, as if in a dream. "When you kids were young, we'd always go out in the early evening and wait till it grew dark. You'd all watch with your eyes aglow as the great red ball sank beyond the sand dunes. You kids never wanted to leave there until the last ray of sun had vanished. Your brother always carried your sister; you walked along with me, holding my hand. You still remember that?"

Chandu gently stroked her hair. "It's been a long time."

"Sometimes I still dream about her. How she ran through the hut, with that wild hair of hers and her joyful laugh. She could not sit still for one second."

Chandu closed his eyes and tried to block out the images of his sister. The memory was just too painful.

He changed the subject. "How are you doing, Mama?"

"You haven't come to visit for a long time now."

"I've been very busy. I haven't even had a chance to work. I must help a friend who's gotten into some trouble."

"The main thing is, don't get yourself in trouble," his mother said, her tone full of warning. "You still working for this debt collector?"

"No," he reassured her. He didn't like lying to his mother. But this nursing home was not only the best in Berlin, it was the most expensive. He couldn't have paid for one week here doing a normal job, so he had to work where he could make big money. And the Berlin underworld had more than enough options to choose from.

"You do not need to worry yourself."

She reached up to squeeze his hand. "You are the only one I have left, Chandu. I just want you to be well."

"I know, Mama. I'm doing well."

"You still have some time?"

"The whole evening."

She beamed. How easy it was to make her happy.

"Then let's stay out here. Until the sun goes down. Like we used to. When we four were all still together."

Chandu placed his hands on her far-too-scrawny shoulders. He raised his gaze to the sun, feeling grateful that he was standing behind her. This way, she could not see his tears.

•   •

After Max left, Jan sat on the couch for a long time and stared at the wall. He held his photo of Betty in both hands. He had been distracted by the murder investigations and had blocked out her death. In solitary moments like this, though, his memories caught up with him. He'd called her cell a few times just to listen to her cheery outgoing voice mail message. Even in death, she hadn't lost her good mood. But today he couldn't bear to make the call. He dialed Father Anberger instead.

"Hallo? Father Anberger? It's Jan."

"Hello, Herr Tommen. Nice to hear from you. Should I get you something else from your apartment?"

"Not for now. Thanks a lot, though." Jan was searching for the right words. "I know it's getting late already, but do you have time to meet today? There's some things I can't get out of my head, and I have to talk to someone about it."

"Of course," the priest replied, as if he'd expected this very thing. "Should I come to your place?"

"No, that's too far. Let's meet in the church, the congregation you used to serve? I'll be there in an hour."

"All right."

"Thanks a lot," Jan said, choking up.

"It's not a bother. Till later."

Jan pocketed his phone. It was dark outside. With the hat and glasses on, he felt safe enough to take the subway without being spotted by a patrol cop. He stood wearily, waiting for the train.

•   •

Zoe got a message on her cell. A new murder case. Two bodies. A text from Walter came at the same time. Just two words. "Need help."

She dialed his number. He picked up on the second ring.

"I've never seen anything like this, Zoe," her coworker said, out of breath. "I thought this only happened in movies."

She'd heard how long the woman was tortured, so she could imagine how maimed the corpses were.

"Calm down, Walter. What's wrong?"

"I can't tell you on the phone. Come into Forensics and take a look at it."

Then he hung up.

Zoe pulled on her coat and left her apartment. She slammed the door in rage. If Jan didn't have the balls to take out Patrick, she would do it herself. It was easy to get a gun. Even if she wasn't a good shot, she wouldn't miss from six feet away.

•   •

Max nibbled at his pizza. He had hoped that he'd feel calmer being at home, but he still couldn't get the woman's screams out of his head. Even his music at maximum volume couldn't drown out the sounds of her drawn-out, painful death. Normally, when he was in a bad mood, he'd just kick some ass playing *Counter-Strike*. But now he couldn't so much as look at that violence. He might even have to give up first-person shooters altogether.

Max's stomach rumbled, but he put the pizza aside. He'd puked more today than he thought possible and didn't feel like doing it again.

He went over to the front door and checked the locks for the fourth time. Horror movies and splatter films had never bothered him. He'd already watched *Saw* eleven times. Really sick stuff happened in that one—but the screams of that woman today had been real, and so had her death. He was afraid now. Actually afraid. Not the pleasant skin crawl you got watching horror films, but rather that kind of fear you felt as a kid. The fear that made you claw your fingers at the pillow, weeping. But his mommy wasn't here now, and there'd be no hiding under her covers. No daddy to comfort him.

Max tossed the pizza in the trash. He'd had so much fun helping Jan at first. The guy was his only friend. But today they had crossed a line. There was a psychopath running around out there, one who enjoyed slaughtering people. Being that close to a murder had shaken every fiber of Max's body. How could a person handle such a thing? How could someone work as a detective and confront such horrors every day, without going mad?

He had to give it all up. Forget the whole thing, go play *World of Warcraft* all night and try out the latest creations from his pizza delivery service. At some point the screams in his head would go away.

Then he thought about Jan again. How shocked the detective had been when he'd become a murder suspect, and how strongly he'd been affected by Betty's suicide. When Max and Jan had first met, the guy had been the life of every party. No one was more easygoing. But Max had seen a change in him. Jan's up-for-anything grin and his let's-grab-one-more-beer state of mind had vanished.

Jan had always treated him with respect, and it had been a great feeling helping his friend, but he couldn't do it anymore. One more murder just might cost him his sanity.

Without him, though, Jan wouldn't get at any more data, and Patrick would be able to manipulate the evidence to convict Jan. "Shit," Max spat out.

In a rage, he swept his laptop with its smiley-face sticker right off the table. He went into the bedroom, with its narrow bed and wardrobe. Old pants and T-shirts lay on the floor. A case of Coca-Cola stood on a stool. Max threw himself onto the bed and pulled a blanket over his head. He'd had more than enough of the world. He only wanted to sleep and forget everything. No more murders. No screams.

·   ·

Jan was on the way to the church when his cell rang. He yanked it out of his bag.

"Yeah?"

Zoe dived right in without saying hello. "My coworker is working on the corpses right now. I've seen the crime-scene photos, so I wanted to give you a brief status report. The victims are Sarah and Horst Esel. Who would have thought?

"Someone really worked him over good. On top of fractures to the legs and arms, his kneecaps were broken. As he lay there tied up on the couch, toy swords, the kind made of wood, were driven into his internal organs. By the way, the swords had clearly been sharpened. From the amount of blood on the couch, we've determined that he was still alive at that point."

"Zoe, I—"

191

"Don't interrupt," the medical examiner snapped at him. "He died of the wounds, though the attacker was careful not to pierce heart or lungs, which prolonged the dying."

"So the murderer has a good idea of human anatomy," Jan said.

"You don't say."

"What about Sarah Esel?"

"Oh, she won the jackpot," Zoe snarled. "Her bones were broken until she couldn't move anymore. Then her hands were bound behind her back, her eyes carved out and the eyeballs replaced with flashy rings, the cheap costume-jewelry kind. Then the murderer sliced her arteries and watched as she slowly croaked."

"Why did he do that with her eye sockets?"

"Because he's a sick fucker," she barked at him. "How should I know? You're the one who's the brilliant investigator."

"In my whole time with detectives? I've never seen anything like—"

"Don't babble on with your sappy stories," Zoe cut in. "You know who did it and still you don't want to put a bullet in his head. Even though killing him quickly would be showing more mercy than that bastard deserves."

"I, I can't think straight—"

"Spare me your excuses. This is the last time I help you. When you're ready to take out Patrick for good, give me a call. Otherwise go find yourself a new chump."

The call disconnected.

Jan rubbed at his eyes. He could understand where Zoe was coming from. The perpetrator had to be punished. But he wouldn't let himself get carried away and commit an act driven by rage. If he only had more than just circumstantial evidence, some irrefutable proof or a confession, then maybe he'd be able to fulfill Zoe's wishes. Because he wanted justice. Not for himself. For Betty.

．　．

The time Chandu spent with his mother was a wonderful retreat from his daily world. She was the most important person in his life, as well as his only living relative. Memories of his brother and sister and of the old country did hurt, and yet recalling them let Chandu immerse himself in those days before they'd had to flee. Even though it had left him with horrible scars, he remained bound to the place where he'd grown up. Rwanda was in his blood, his homeland. But Berlin was his home.

Driving back home, he felt a guilty conscience stirring. Jan was his friend. One of the few people he trusted. He shouldn't be leaving him all alone, but that woman's screams had awakened experiences that he had buried deep in the farthest reaches of his memory. He was not some defenseless child any more, no, but the murder had taken him back to a time full of unimaginable atrocities. That fear of dying. Corpses in the streets, and the stench of bodies rotting.

Seeing a corpse, back then, most people had turned their heads away in terror. But Chandu hardly had a shrug left for it now. He had been in the darkest place imaginable. There, people had done things that couldn't be explained with even a million words, the horrors robbing you of sleep forever. Yet the nightmares had made him stronger. It was like taking a "steel bath," soaking in chalybeate springs. A harsh yet sacred thing. He'd kept his nerve in even the wildest shootouts.

And yet, that woman's death cries had really hit him hard.

Tonight they would return to stalk him: the nightmares. The rot stench. Like old friends. But he would not allow that to deter him from aiding Jan. He would always be in his debt.

Chandu stepped on the gas, speeding onward.

．　．

Seeing Father Anberger made Jan smile. His easygoing ways and his friendly expression gave Jan a sense that all would be made right again. The burden on his soul would lighten, and the murder would be solved.

"Thanks a lot for taking the time for me," Jan said, shaking the priest's hand. "I'm sorry that I asked you here so late, but I didn't know of any other way."

Father Anberger waved aside the thought. "It's all right. At my age you don't need much sleep, so if I'm able to bring a tortured soul some relief, then it's my duty to do so."

Jan wrung his hands. "I guess I don't know where I should begin. The last few days have been the worst of my entire life."

"Perhaps you should start at the beginning and tell me all about it. It helps if one gets all his worries off his chest."

"I'm suspected of murder."

"The judge, I remember. Your fingerprints and your DNA were found, and you had to go on the run. Then there was a second murder."

"They found my fingerprints there too. I was with friends at the time and I didn't know the victim, so clearly I couldn't have been the killer. Someone's trying to pin the whole thing on me. I've relied on help from my friends to find out more, but none of the three has ever done any police investigating."

"You're afraid that they might not handle the pressure well?"

Jan nodded. "I roped them into this without realizing I could put them in danger."

"Are they in danger?"

"Physically, no, but I think their psyches have taken some hits."

"What happened?"

"I recently gave a possible source my phone number. Tonight someone called it, frantic. It was a woman—and her husband was being murdered in the next room."

"My God." Father Anberger crossed himself.

"Hearing the man scream was already tough to take, but then the murderer went after the woman and tortured her to death. The phone transmitted every moment of her torment. You can't imagine it if you've never experienced it," Jan said, his voice straining with despair. "The screams of someone tortured to death, they're horrific. They bring out a primal fear, and you get wise to your own mortality. It's pulled me down too, so I can't even imagine what it's doing to the others."

"So you consider yourself guilty in some way?"

"I *am* guilty," Jan insisted. "Without me, they wouldn't be going through this."

Father Anberger leaned back on the pew, deep in thought.

"I've known you some years now, Herr Tommen. You've never given me the impression you would ever force a person into anything."

"No, not really."

"So, from that, I'm going to assume that you haven't *made* your friends come help you."

"I didn't make them, no, but I should have kept them out of it. I work in Homicide. I should have known what could become of a case like this."

"Perhaps your very despair induced your friends to help you."

"I should not have accepted their help. Now I'm to blame for them not being able to sleep at night."

"I understand now."

"You do?"

"You're suffering from too much protector instinct. You're like the mother of children who shields her offspring from all adversity over the years, but forgets that the children will have to grow up."

"I don't understand."

"You're afraid that you've robbed your friends of their spiritual innocence."

"That's what it amounts to."

"It's not as bad as you think."

"Not so bad?" Jan said, surprised. "It's not bad that my friends need psychological help?"

"Give people more credit for their internal fortitude," the priest urged. "You've seen many horrible things in your job, all without perishing yourself. You, too, experienced a shock, one that would have driven many out of their minds. And yet it didn't break you. Do you remember what I'm talking about?"

Jan sighed. "The murdered child. You cannot imagine what was done to that nine-year-old girl."

"And how did that case make you feel?"

"I was delirious for two days. I couldn't sleep, didn't eat a thing, was wandering the corridors of Homicide like the walking dead."

"And then?"

"My boss, Klaus Bergman, he chewed me out. And when we got a new lead, my lethargy disappeared. The chance of nabbing the guy gave me my strength back. Four days later, we caught him. That was when I first started sleeping again."

"So, you know firsthand that a person can gain strength from a terrifying experience."

"My friends will come out of this stronger?" Jan asked him, uncertain.

Father Anberger placed a hand on Jan's shoulder. "God is our refuge and our strength. There to help us in times of the great troubles that afflict us," he cited. "Have faith. Others can bear pain too. You must not stanch it all on your own. Share your sorrows."

Father Anberger stood. "I'll leave you now, to be alone with God. Have faith in Him, and He will soothe your soul."

Jan closed his eyes. "Thanks," he said, full of emotion. "I will pray for the slain Herr and Frau Esel."

Father Anberger looked shaken for a moment. It was little more than a flash in his eyes, a brief warping of the corners of his mouth.

"Did you know the couple?" Jan asked in surprise.

"No," he was quick to reply. "How could I?" His smile had returned.

Jan squinted. The man was old. Jan was probably just delirious again.

The priest hurried out of the church. The door closed with a loud bang. Jan stood and went over to the offering box. There he chose three candles. Two for Herr and Frau Esel. One for Betty.

He sought peace in prayer, but he couldn't get the priest's expression out of his head. When he'd heard about the Esels dying, fear had clearly run right through him, down to his marrow.

• •

It was midnight by the time Jan emerged from the subway station and headed toward Chandu's apartment. He was still scared someone could recognize him. It didn't have to be a fellow cop. Even just an old acquaintance could make things dangerous. One accidental run-in and his noose would pull even tighter.

He squeezed between two parked cars and crossed the empty Oranienburger Strasse. A few pubs were still open, but they were nearly vacant.

He was heading into the inner courtyard of Chandu's building when someone called his name. He turned but could see only a dark figure, freeing itself from the shadows. He tried to make out a face.

"Do I know—" Jan started to say, but his words gave way to a scream of pain as a knife rammed into his stomach. He doubled over, gasping. The figure pulled out the knife and went to stab again, but Jan, using every last bit of his strength, ran headlong for the street. Instinct made him flee his attacker despite the staggering pain. He pressed a hand to the wound. Blood leaked out around his fingers and soaked his shirt.

The figure followed him. It was dressed in black, wearing a ski mask and mirrored sunglasses. In its gloved hand, it held a small, blood-smeared scalpel.

Jan wanted to keep running, but everything was spinning around him. He didn't know up or down. He wouldn't get away like this, so he yelled out for help. Then his strength drained away and his legs buckled under him. His head slammed against the road. The figure stood over him, raising the scalpel. Jan tried to crawl away. Blood ran through his fingers onto the asphalt.

As the blade came down again, he heard the loud squeal of a car braking. Then came nothing more. Only darkness.

Chapter 14

Jan had trouble opening his eyes. He felt sluggish and heavy. His mouth was dry and his throat felt raw. He lay in a bed, in a room he didn't know. The ceiling was covered with white squares of gypsum board. A fluorescent tube illuminated the whitewashed wall. He turned his head toward an assortment of flashing machines. A metal stand held a bag of transparent liquid that flowed through a tube into his left arm. He raised his head. A sharp pain made him yelp. The room spun around him, and he threw up on the bedspread. A woman in a white coat came running into the room. And he fainted again.

· ·

Patrick, yawning, pulled down the shades. The rising sun was blinding him. Here he was, on the job. While his fellow officers were at home sleeping, he had kept at it on through the night. And now, before their investigations of Judge Holoch and Michael Josseck were even solved, a new case had landed on top of them. The murders of the Esel couple had forced Bergman to expand the homicide staff, yet the files were already piling up to the ceiling.

Patrick was pouring himself a cup of coffee when the phone rang. It was half past six in the morning. Who could be calling this early?

"Stein, Homicide," he snapped.

"My name's Niedermayer," a woman's voice said. "Good day."

"What can I do for you?" Probably another of those do-gooders who thought they'd seen something. He'd had it up to here with leads coming from the general population. They constantly led to nothing.

"I'm a nurse at Charité Hospital. Yesterday we had a seriously wounded man brought in who needed emergency surgery. He is doing better, but not yet responsive. He was discovered out on the street, without ID. It wasn't till this morning that we found a detective's badge in his jacket."

Patrick listened, poised, electrified. His fatigue had evaporated. "Who we talking about?" he panted.

"We didn't find any other ID."

"Can you describe the man?"

"I'd put him at early thirties. Six foot. Light-brown hair, cut short, green eyes. Sturdily built and wearing a dark leather jacket—"

"Don't let him go!" Patrick barked into the receiver and slammed down the phone. He grabbed his jacket and fumbled in his pockets for his car keys. Then he ran down the hall for the exit. His harried face showed the hint of a smile. He had Jan, finally. He just had to go collect him.

•   •

When Jan woke up his pain was gone, but he felt weaker than before. He could hardly lift his arm. Someone was talking next to his bed, disturbing his sleepy trance.

"Are you sure he's not feeling any pain?" a deep male voice was asking.

"All that morphine in his blood would put a herd of camels to sleep," a woman replied.

"So how's the wound?"

"The incision is stitched and all covered up. The wound won't rip open if you carry him gently."

"What about internal injuries?"

"According to his chart, he's out of the woods."

Jan opened his eyes and tried to recognize who was speaking. The voices sounded familiar, but he couldn't attach any names to them.

"I think he's waking up," the man said.

"Won't matter much," the woman replied. "He's sedated."

Someone lifted him out of bed. Ceiling lights drifted by him. He was being carried down a hall.

"Hurry," the woman urged. "They notice he's not in the ward, all hell will break loose."

"Don't you think I know that?" the man shot back, annoyed. "Jan isn't exactly a lightweight. You wanted to take the stairs."

"We're in a hospital, Mr. T." The woman was bossing him now. "Here? Patients are transported on beds, not carried. If just one nurse got in the elevator with us, this would be a real short getaway."

"So why aren't we using a bed or a wheelchair again?"

"Because we can't be rolling out onto the parking lot like this."

The man grumbled something, but Jan was too tired to follow the conversation. He let himself glide back into sleep.

•   •

Bergman looked over the photos. The air was stale, and the low-ered blinds had dimmed the investigations room. The photos on the walls created a depressing atmosphere. Their classification system was easy to figure out. The photos on the left were devoted to Jan's possible hiding places. In the middle were photos and notes for Judge Holoch's murder. On the right was the Josseck case. Over near the door, Patrick Stein was pinning images of the Esel murder to the wall.

Patrick had always been the paragon of correctness, of reliability. Normally he wore a suit and tie, his shoes were clean, and he paid attention to his personal hygiene. All that had disappeared during this case. Patrick's dark suit was bedraggled, his tie lay on the table, and he had opened the top three buttons of his shirt. He hadn't shaved in ages, and his unkempt hair stuck up on his head.

"We've beefed up surveillance all around the hospital," Patrick said, turning to Bergman, who fought the urge to step back from his bad breath. "Jan won't be able to slip through."

"Not from the front," Bergman suggested.

Patrick, edgy, ran fingers through his hair. "Jan was brought to the hospital last night, seriously injured. The emergency surgery went well."

"So what happened?"

"The doctors are calling it a severe stab wound to the spleen."

"Someone tried to stab him to death?"

"That attack on Jan occurred on the same day the Esels were murdered. Maybe they had put up some kind of a fight."

"Was a knife found at the crime scene?"

"No. But not all the blood samples have been checked yet."

"Why are we only being informed of this now?"

"During the night, several injured were brought in because of a gang fight, so no one had time to identify. They only just found a faked detective badge in Jan's clothes three hours ago. Which was when the hospital called. But by then Jan had already disappeared."

"He fled the hospital? After a procedure like that?"

"The doctors are saying that he couldn't have acted alone. He was so sedated he wouldn't have been able to get out of bed without help."

"Any ideas on who got him out of there?'

"We have two officers on it at the hospital. They're questioning possible witnesses and checking surveillance cameras. All patrols are looking for him."

Bergman swatted at air. "You can call it off."

"I don't understand."

"Let's suppose Jan was able to drag himself out of the hospital on his own. He'd still be in the vicinity. But if he had helpers, they didn't come by foot."

"But what if he really still is in the vicinity—"

"Did you check out Jan's friends?" Bergman interrupted.

"Every last one. For most of them, we were even in their homes."

"Well?"

"Nothing. No leads as to Jan's whereabouts."

"What about the Esel case?"

"Just about done securing evidence. The corpses are autopsied. Based on the brutal manner of killing and a connection to Judge Holoch and Michael Josseck, we're going on the assumption that it's the same perpetrator. The report will be ready in an hour."

"There any evidence pointing to Jan's involvement?"

"Well, since we've found his fingerprints at the first victims' crime scenes, we're also going on the—"

"No speculating, Patrick. Do you possess evidence of Jan's involvement in the most recent murders?"

"Not yet."

"Is there a link between the Esels and Jan?"

Patrick hesitated. "So far, no clues."

"And the building contractor?"

"There is no link to Michael Josseck either."

Bergman sighed. Too little sleep and too much stress—his job just wasn't much fun anymore. "So, we got nothing."

"Why nothing?" Patrick replied. "For the first two murders, the evidence is conclusive."

"But a motive was already missing for the second murder. It's not going to be any different now."

"I don't understand."

"Look at the case objectively," Bergman began. "Jan murders Judge Holoch and acts like a beginner doing so. The judge had delivered a harsh verdict against him, so he's got the motive there, but we don't have any clue why he'd commit the second murder."

"But we have his fingerprints on the murder weapon—"

"An idiotic mistake that not even a twelve-year-old would make. And Jan is an experienced homicide detective."

"Just because we haven't found anything linking him to Michael Josseck doesn't mean there isn't any connection."

"The third murder, of the Esels, it's unrelated to him too."

"We're checking on that, though—"

"You've been looking into Jan's history for days, Patrick. If there was any connection to Josseck or the Esels, you would have found it."

"Maybe we'll find it at their—"

"Maybe you stop and listen," Bergman fumed. "The media have been wallowing for days now in this story, and the chief of police is demanding a report from me twice a day. Not to mention all the politicians farting in their comfy chairs. All I have to show is a possible suspect on the run, whose motive becomes more implausible by the day."

"Though in the first two cases the evidence looks—"

"Go get some sleep."

"Excuse me?" Patrick asked, surprised.

"You look terrible. Your dedication to this case has been exemplary, but you've sunk your teeth too far into Jan. Get some rest and leave the investigation to your colleagues for a few hours."

"I'm fine. Tonight I can get—"

"That was not a suggestion," Bergman declared. "You're going to go into the storage room right now, the one with the old couch. You're going to shut the door and sleep at least eight hours. Then you're going to go home, to have a shower and change. After that, you can start giving some thought as to who could have committed these murders."

"Can't I sleep at home?"

"No, because there you won't go to bed. You'll just keep working on the case."

Patrick wanted to keep arguing, but Bergman cut him off with a severe sweep of his hand. "Go, do it now!"

Patrick bristled at such an order, but he complied. He trudged into the storage room and lay down on the couch.

Bergman sighed. The fixation on Jan had cost too much valuable time. They weren't getting any closer to the real murderer. Patrick was a diligent investigator, but he clearly wasn't able to veer off the one path he'd beaten for himself. Bergman missed Jan.

• •

"Jan," a voice said, wresting him from sleep. "Wake up."

He turned over in bed, groaning, and tried to keep sleeping. Someone was shaking him. He opened his eyes, scowling. Before him stood a vaguely familiar attractive blonde woman, looking him over, taking stock.

"Hi, baby." Jan grinned wide.

"Evidently the morphine's still working," the woman said. "I'll speed up the wake-up process." She took a glass of water and poured it on Jan's face.

All at once, his elated feeling dropped away.

He blinked away moisture and looked around, feeling more alert. Either he was in the world's oddest hospital room or someone had returned him to Chandu's place. A faint throb in his gut brought back his memory of being attacked.

The next moment, Chandu loomed in front of him. "Welcome back," the big man said. "How are you feeling?"

"Not too bad," Jan said in a hoarse voice, wiping water off his face. "Like I spent a night out carousing and then ran a marathon after." He wanted to sit up, but his arms buckled under him.

"I would take it slowly at first," Zoe said and lit up a cigarette. "I sedated you real good, so that's why you can hardly move or think clearly."

"What happened?"

"You got knifed," Chandu explained. "What do you remember about it?"

"I was on my way into your building. Someone was waiting for me in the inside courtyard."

"Who?"

"The attacker was wearing a ski mask and dressed all in black. But he called my name."

"*Called your name?*" Zoe and Chandu replied at the same time. Jan nodded.

"Oh, man," Chandu said. "Someone wants you out of the way. That was no mugging."

"It all went down so fast. Before I knew what was happening to me, I had a knife in my gut."

"A scalpel," Zoe corrected him. "And to be more precise, it was your spleen."

Jan lifted the covers and looked over himself, feeling uneasy. He was still dressed in a hospital gown. His stomach was wrapped with a thick bandage.

"What happened after the attack?"

"You were really lucky," Chandu told him. "After that first stab you ran out into the street. A car almost ran you over there, which saved your life. Your attacker was thrown off by the headlights. He backed off and then ran away. The driver got out, saw all the blood, and called an ambulance."

"They did emergency surgery on you in the middle of the night," Zoe added. "Chandu got to the scene a couple minutes after the assault and followed the ambulance. That's how we knew where they were taking you. We got you out when they were changing shifts. They went through your things and found your fake badge and called the department. If you'd stayed put, you would have been done for."

"How long since we got back here?"

"Twenty-four hours," Chandu said. "Zoe has been keeping you sedated and watching over your recovery."

Jan turned his head to her. "I thought you were a medical examiner."

"I worked in a hospital while studying, and I did paramedic training along the way. As long as there's no complications, it's really no worse for you here than at the hospital."

"Thanks," Jan said, touched. "I thought you weren't going to—"

"Don't go flattering yourself," Zoe cut him off. "I still think you're a dumbshit. But Mr. T here kept bugging me until I came over. Once you're healthy again, my sweet ass is outta here. Also, you owe me two days' vacation."

Jan blinked at her, baffled. Zoe had a unique way of showing she cared.

"She's quite the charmer, our little Zoe," Chandu said, heading into the kitchen.

"I'm not your little Zoe," she shouted after him. "Say that again and I'll show you 'little.'"

Chandu waved in apology and turned on the coffeemaker. Soon the scent of those pungent African coffee beans filled the whole apartment. Jan felt a huge craving for a cup, with a croissant. Yet before he could get out his request, fatigue overcame him again. He fell asleep, feeling at ease.

• •

The aroma of frying meat woke Jan. Chandu stood in the kitchen, messing around with a pan. Closer to him, Max sat tapping away on his laptop. The young hacker stuck his head up.

"Hey, Jan," he said smiling. "Welcome to the living."

"Hi, Max," Jan answered, his mouth dry. He still felt tired and wrung out. He reached for a glass of water, allowing himself a drink, but had trouble getting his trembling hands under control.

"You'll get better soon," Max told him. "Zoe says you'll be able to stand up again tomorrow."

"Good to hear."

Chandu came out from the kitchen, pan in hand. "So you're up and awake," the big man said cheerfully. "We're eating in ten minutes."

At the thought of food, Jan's stomach growled. He drank the whole glass of water and leaned back against the pillows, sighing. The sun sent its last evening rays into the living room. Chandu had already turned lights on.

Jan turned to Max. "How many days have gone by since I left the hospital? I keep falling asleep."

"Zoe and Chandu brought you back here two days ago. This morning was the first time you were able to eat anything. Now? It's nine in the evening."

"So, what are you doing here?" Jan said.

"I have my reasons," Max said. "First, I wanted to see you, since Chandu told me you got knifed. Second, Zoe threatened to cut off my fingers if I didn't keep watch by your bedside. Said she didn't want to leave you alone with a meathead like him," he said, nodding at Chandu, "while she tried to catch up on her sleep."

"She was here the whole time?"

"Two days."

"And third, I want be working the case again," Max added.

"That's kind of you, Max, but I know the effect the Esels' death had on you. You may never fully get over what you heard. I didn't want to drag you into this. If you pack up your stuff and head out, I will understand."

Max waved the thought aside. "It wasn't that bad. After one sleepless night, I started realizing that you guys wouldn't get very far without me. You'd end up in the slammer and Patrick Stein would get away with it. That would eat at me so I'd never be able to let it all go."

Someone pounded on the door. Jan started. Max went to the door and opened up. Zoe came storming in. He could tell she hadn't slept, but her appearance was perfect. Her carefully combed hair ran down her back. She was wearing a form-fitting suit and high-heeled boots that would probably bring tears to the eyes of any shoe fetishist.

"Ah, our patient's awake," she said to Jan. "How's it going?"

"Well, since you asked, I—"

"Quit babbling," she interrupted. "It was just a rhetorical question. I'll take a look myself." She shoved him back onto the couch. She took his pulse, looked over the wound, and peered into his eyes with a flashlight. Jan felt more like a guinea pig than a patient. Thank God Zoe was a medical examiner. As a doctor, her bedside manner wouldn't bring her many patients.

She finished her checkup. "Looking good. The docs at Charité did their job. You'll have some pain for a while, but you'll live."

She set her flashlight aside. "And now I'm hungry." She turned toward the kitchen. "Living room to Chandu: How's dinner doing?"

"The tortillas need another minute, but you can go sit down."

"Tortillas?" Jan said. "That doesn't sound very African."

"African food? You nuts? I did not come all the way over here just to have some insect stew put in front of me. I told Mr. T here to either cook something proper or order pizza."

She sat at the table and then turned to Max. "Hey, Maximum Couch Potato, hoist your sorry ass from the sofa and get it over to the table. Eating something will do you good."

Max set his laptop aside and helped Jan up. Jan had to hold onto Max to walk, but it was a nice feeling being able to stand again.

Chandu put a tray of heated corn tortillas on the table. After that came a big bowl of ground beef, a plate of veggies, toasted tortilla chips, and a bottle of Tabasco. Then a salad of sliced tomatoes, beans, corn, and grated cheese. Like always when Chandu cooked, it was enough for a whole soccer team.

Jan, starving, loaded up a tortilla and bit into it. The spicy heat brought tears to his eyes, but it was a joy to eat real food again. Even Zoe must have been happy with Chandu's cooking skills, because she ate without commenting at all.

After satisfying their initial hunger, they talked about all that had happened the last couple of days. Chandu began with an anecdote about Zoe and an orderly who hadn't gotten out of the way fast enough. As the first shots of tequila were poured, the murders were left behind and they chatted away, as if they had been the best of friends for many years now.

.   .

While Chandu puttered around in the kitchen, Zoe leaned back, satisfied, and blew clouds of smoke into the room.

"What's for dessert?" she asked.

"Flan," the big man answered.

"What the hell is that?"

"A Mexican vanilla pudding."

"All right, fine." She sounded unconvinced.

"You'll like it."

"Well then, ladies," Zoe began. "While we wait for our dessert, I'll recap what we've learned about the Esels. I'll forgo the photos, because I don't want anyone barfing again," she said, one eye on Max. "The first victim was Horst Esel, the very same who was employed by Michael Josseck and sent to jail by Judge Holoch. Our initial guess is that the murderer broke into the Esels' in secret and surprised them as they watched TV. Old Horst got the special treatment from a stun gun, which made him unconscious a while. After that, he got pummeled in the worst way. While we did identify twenty bone fractures, the actual cause of death was three wooden toy swords rammed into his organs."

"Toy swords?" Chandu said from the kitchen.

"The things would normally be too blunt to penetrate the body cavity, but the murderer had sharpened them up. Horst Esel was pretty much nailed to his own couch."

Zoe took a drag of her cigarette.

"Sarah Esel was killed in the neighboring bedroom. She had countless contusions, internal bleeding, and bone breaks. The real nasty part was her eyes. The murderer cut them out and replaced them with those cheap, tacky, costume rings. The incision was done with expert precision. Most likely with a scalpel."

"Pretty sick," Max said.

"Yeah," Zoe replied. "Especially since Sarah Esel was still alive when the murderer cut out her eyes. Which brings me, once again, to the discussion we had before Jan ended up in the hospital. When do we go take out Patrick? Now that he's almost stabbed you to death, don't you think a bullet to his head would be about justified?"

"He didn't attack me."

"Ah, man," Zoe said. "How much more proof do you need?"

"I didn't see his face, plus the person spoke to me—and it wasn't his voice. What makes you think it was Patrick?"

"Who else could it be? Patrick had set out in search of Chandu. He didn't find him at his official residence. So he put the screws on Chandu's renter and trailed him to his local bar. It only makes sense he finally discovered our cook's little hideout. A man with Chandu's build can be followed pretty easily. Patrick probably just waited till it got dark and you showed up."

"It had to be Patrick," Max added. "It makes sense."

"No," Jan said. "Too much work. He could have just stormed the apartment with a special unit and taken me in. That would have been all official too. Why should he take the risk of attacking me on his own?"

"Because you know things that could get him into trouble," Chandu said, drying a big bowl with a kitchen towel.

"What would that be? I highly doubt he's even noticed we found his drugs. We were too careful about it."

"Maybe he thinks that you know something, something that you actually don't know at all," Max said.

All three heads turned to him.

"I told you not to give the little one tequila," Zoe said.

"What if you, on the Saturday Judge Holoch was murdered, saw something that could either incriminate Patrick or clear you of suspicion?"

"I still don't know what happened, though," Jan told them.

"That's not important," Max said. "Just the possibility that you could remember, it could be making Patrick nervous."

"I have a hard time believing it. Patrick was always the good cop. He was always so meticulous in sticking to the rules that it drove me nuts."

"Maybe the Patrick that you used to know," Chandu said. "But something made him snap, right? Maybe something to do with his sister. Who knows? So he starts in with Judge Holoch and turns into a psycho serial killer."

"Goddamn it," Jan said. "Why can I not remember?" He turned to Zoe. "Is there no kind of treatment for this?"

"Jesus, Jan. I'd first have to determine what sort of amnesia we're talking about and then discover what triggered it. That could range from meds like morphine or knockout drops to things like stroke, poisoning, drugs, alcohol, or some traumatic experience. There is no treatment. Most quacks, they lure people in with promises that electroshock or drug cocktails will help them regain their memories. Nothing works. Your only hope is getting a flashback."

"Okay, fine. So how do I get one?"

"By accident. It has to be released, through a trigger that awakens parts of your memory. It can be a smell, a sound, a place, or just a certain touch. It can't be controlled. But it's most likely that your memories will stay submerged forever."

"So we have a talk with Patrick," Chandu said. "Though I really would like to put him down, we should talk to him first."

"Talk with a serial killer?"

"I understand what you're feeling, Zoe. But look at it matter-of-factly. Jan is a veteran detective. We should trust his instincts."

Zoe, sulking, lit another cigarette.

"And what if we actually are wrong? Bumping off a police officer is not a good idea."

"How are we supposed to pull that off?" Max asked. "We can't just invite him to talk."

"We'll have to catch him at home," Jan said.

"And why won't he just put a bullet in you?" Zoe responded.

"Because he'll get no chance to draw his weapon."

"There's only one way to do that," Chandu said.

"He'll be looking into the barrel of a gun," Jan added.

"I don't hate the idea," Zoe said, "but how do we get him to confess?"

"Interrogating is improvising. His first reactions alone will tell us a lot."

"We don't need a reaction, we need a confession," Zoe said.

"He's not that stupid," Jan said. "Even if he is the murderer, he's not going to stand there with a grin and confess." He turned to Max. "I think I might like a camera on me no matter what. Can you set me up something, one that can take shots in the dark?"

"Sure," Max said. "With a sensitive enough lens, I don't need much light."

"Good," Jan said. "We'll go wait for him tonight."

"You did notice you had trouble making it all the way from the table to the couch?" Chandu asked him. "You won't even make it out to the car in this condition."

"I'm betting that Zoe has a knack for miracle cures."

"It's got nothing to do with miracle cures," she replied. "It's way too soon for much physical activity, but I can give you some nifty painkillers. If that wound of yours rips open, though, you'll bleed to death before we can get you to a hospital."

"I'll take the risk. There could still be more victims, so every day we wait just puts them in danger."

Zoe shrugged. "Just wanted to warn you."

"Thanks." Jan's wound did hurt. Just the thought of walking more than five yards made him cringe, but he had no other choice. He had to be certain.

Chapter 15

Zoe's painkillers were working. Apart from a little twitch in his gut, Jan couldn't feel anything. But the meds made him lethargic and he had trouble concentrating.

At 10:00 p.m., Jan and Chandu drove to the station in an inconspicuous Ford that Chandu had borrowed from his neighbor. Jan had never been afraid of facing a murderer or a violent nutcase, but this time, he felt torn. The police officer in him really wanted to get out of the car, head inside, and tell Bergman all he knew. Yet the last few days had left him doubting. If Patrick was behind it all, then the system wasn't working. He wanted nothing more than to put an end to the murders. On the other hand, he was hoping he'd gotten it wrong. He hated to think that a homicide detective was committing such beastly crimes.

"Here he comes," Chandu said, jerking him from this thoughts.

Patrick looked overworked, tired. He dragged his feet, his shoulders hunched forward. His hair was disheveled and his suit crumpled.

He went to his car, started it up, and merged into traffic. Chandu followed at a safe distance.

"How do you want to do this?" he asked. "Want to wait for him right inside his place?"

"That's too tricky for me. The underground parking garage should work. We only have to get in before the garage gate comes back down."

"You think he'll listen?"

"I'm not fooling myself. He'll only talk to me if he's looking into the barrel of a piece. You bring your peashooter?"

Without replying, Chandu pulled a pistol out from under his seat. Jan let out a little whistle.

"Heckler & Koch USP40, Smith & Wesson slugs," Chandu said. "Hey, you wanted to bring it. And this is just the warm-up act. I got big brother in my holster. If that bastard makes one false move, I take him out."

"I want to talk first."

"Be careful. If Patrick is the killer, he could take you out and claim it was self-defense. Plus, you're on painkillers. Slows your reactions."

"I'll be on guard." Jan worked the slide on the pistol, trying to not to notice his hands shaking.

Ten minutes later, they still had their target. Patrick's car waited in front of them at the entrance to the underground parking lot as the gate slowly lifted. Once the car was inside and out of view, Chandu sped under before the door lowered again. He parked in the first space they saw, turned off the lights.

Jan got out and hid behind an SUV. Patrick had parked only ten yards away and was just locking his car. He hadn't seemed to notice them coming in.

"Hello, partner," Jan said, raising his weapon.

Patrick turned around in surprise.

"I should have known," he said.

"That I'd be on your trail?"

"What trail?"

"Don't lie to me, asshole," Jan barked. "I know you're behind the murders."

"Have you completely lost your mind?" Patrick shouted back. "Evidence puts you at two crime scenes and you're calling *me* guilty?"

"Someone's pinning it on me."

"Who, then?"

"You are."

"Me?" Patrick flared up. "You really have lost it."

"You never liked me. You resented me, my career."

"I think you're a Rambo wannabe who should have his weapon taken away, but that's no reason to pin a murder on you."

"We know about your sister."

Patrick pinched his eyes together. "What does my sister have to do with it?"

"George Holoch and Michael Josseck were clients of Nathan Lefort. Apparently the Frenchman sold her to them, as his whore."

Patrick neared Jan a step. "My sister had a ton of johns," he snarled. "If I was to take out every one of them, the cemeteries would have to shut down because of overcrowding. And how does the Esels' murder fit in? Did they procure my sister through Nathan too?"

Jan hesitated, just a split second. Patrick used it to attack. Normally Jan could ward off such a move, but the meds made him slow. A kick caught him in the stomach, knocking the air out of him. Patrick grabbed his hand and tried to wrest his gun away. Jan had always been better than Patrick in hand-to-hand combat, but this time Patrick disarmed him like he was some schoolboy.

Holding Jan's weapon, Patrick took a step backward.

"Put down the gun, dipshit, or I'll blow your brains out," Chandu's voice echoed through the garage.

"I could give a shit," Patrick shouted back. He held the pistol to Jan's head. "You better toss your gun over to me, or you'll be scraping what little brain this idiot's got off the walls."

"Jan gets even a scratch, they'll find *your* brains on the wall," the big man growled back.

Jan held his stomach. The kick had missed the sutures, but still it hurt.

"My God, Patrick. Why did you have to slaughter all those people? It won't bring your sister back."

"I told you. I did not murder anyone."

"We were in your apartment. We found drugs. There were knockout drops and ecstasy, which is what I think someone put into me."

"You're wrong." Patrick stepped back, hesitating. "I'm looking out for a kid in the neighborhood who has the wrong friends. He lifted it off a dealer and thought he could sell the stuff. So I took it away from him."

"So why didn't you toss it?"

"I was going to hand it over to drug squad, to secure the evidence."

"What were you waiting for?"

"I'd get asked where I got the stuff, and I didn't exactly have a great excuse."

Patrick had lowered the weapon. They stood face-to-face.

Jan broke the silence. "So what now?"

"You come down to the station with me," Patrick told him.

"Never," Jan said.

"I have your gun."

"And I have a friend with a bigger gun."

"This is crazy, Jan. You're digging yourself a deeper hole."

"Which is your fault. If you would have ruled me out as the main suspect, you'd have the real killer by now."

"That's bullshit! We have a binder full of evidence on you. What was I supposed to do?"

"Believe me, I'm not behind this."

"That's not a hell of a lot to go on."

"But it's true. Once the Esels died, you must have realized you were on the wrong track."

"So, what are we supposed to tell the police chief, and all those snooping politicians? Much less the reporters. I'm supposed to go to Bergman and say, 'Sure, we know the first two murders have conclusive evidence. But it was someone else, a guy we got no clues on'?"

"What you guys have been telling the public doesn't matter. Internally, you could have been tracking down other suspects."

"Why? We have no evidence on other suspects. It all fits, and the evidence clearly convicts you."

"My word will have to be enough for now. It was not me. The psycho is still running around out there."

"I'm still not going to let you walk."

"But you will," Jan stated. "I'm not going to the pen and put my fate in your hands. I'm going to march on out of here and go underground again."

Jan eyed Patrick. A hint of uncertainty had crept into his eyes.

"Tomorrow morning? You'll get an e-mail with all I've found out. Maybe it will help." Jan turned around and went back to the car. It was the longest walk of his life. If he was wrong, Patrick would shoot him down right there and come up with a story.

Behind him, Patrick cocked the weapon. Jan clenched his teeth. Every step was torture. His knees trembled, and he had trouble keeping his hands steady. After an eternity, he was at the car. He opened the door and sat down inside.

The gate moved up, clattering. Chandu jumped in, started the motor, and raced off.

Jan looked in the rearview mirror. Patrick had disappeared.

•   •

"I would've shot him in the knee."

"Zoe, for the third time," Jan said. "He's not the murderer."

"Why not? Because he told you so?"

"It's hard to explain. When you've interrogated actual murderers, you come to know when someone's lying or hiding something. You develop an instinct."

"And you've never made a mistake?"

"I have. But it's not about what he said, but rather what he did."

"So what did he do?"

"Not shoot me."

"And that's why he's not the murderer?"

"Disarming me was his perfect chance. If I'd died, investigations into the first two murders would have been shelved. It would have taken all of the pressure off him."

"Huh," Zoe said, sucking on her cigarette. "He still remains an asshole."

"I hate to spoil the mood," Max cut in, "but did we just lose our one and only suspect?"

"Maybe Patrick can get something going with what we've found out," Jan said.

"I can't believe you're helping the piece of shit."

"This is about solving the case, Zoe. When that happens, not only is the murderer caught, but I'll also get my old life back."

"Isn't it a little lame to just sit here and hope Patrick succeeds?" Chandu remarked.

"That's not exactly my plan."

"So what then?"

"We have no all-encompassing motive. With Judge Holoch and Michael Josseck, it could have been a hooker. You could throw Horst Esel in there too, on a hunch. But when it comes to Sarah Esel? It doesn't fit anymore."

"What if she was into some kind of perverted sex acts?" Zoe said.

"Possible. But we can't even prove that for Horst Esel."

"We should take another look at the construction angle," Chandu proposed. "If the murder of Judge Holoch has nothing to do with those hookers getting beat up, then Michael Josseck's concrete comes back into the picture."

"Fine, but toy swords and costume rings?" Jan asked.

"Sarah Esel could have just been in the wrong place at the wrong time," Max said. "So the murderer turns it into a killing spree."

"The thing is, Sarah Esel's murder was too personal. Someone cut out her eyes with surgical precision and replaced them with cheap rings. Those baubles weren't just lying around. The murderer brought them, which means her murder was planned out too."

"But how does it all add up?" Chandu said. "The way she was killed, it's supposed to say something. Judge Holoch, he beat up women. That's probably why he was beaten to death with a hammer. Michael Josseck was a building contractor. Not hard to make the connection to concrete. But when it comes to jewelry in the victim's carved-out eyeball sockets? Me, I pass. And I don't even want to talk about those toy swords in Horst Esel's organs."

Jan scratched his head, uneasy. "That one's a mystery to me too. Costume jewelry, toy swords? Doesn't bring any sexual deviation to mind."

"Maybe you lack imagination," Zoe said, adding a grin.

"Oh, wise medical examiner, do enlighten us," Chandu scoffed at her.

"I don't know either," she snapped at the big man. "But why aren't we looking in the Esels' house? We might find something there."

"Judging from the report, the crime scene was thoroughly combed over. The apartment was pretty small, so I wouldn't count on striking gold, not like with Judge Holoch."

"Not their hideaway, Janni," Zoe said, "but their actual home."

"That's where we're supposed to find clues?" Chandu said.

"We're not looking for the clues, but rather a motive," Zoe explained.

Jan thought over the plan. It was possible that the place hadn't been checked out yet.

"It doesn't please me to say this," Chandu added, "but Blondie here might just be right."

"Thanks. And since I am so brilliant, you can go top off my coffee."

Chandu yanked the cup from her and went into the kitchen.

"Okay, then," Jan said. "It's late, and I want to be rested up for this operation of ours. Chandu and I will head over there tomorrow evening and—"

"Me too," Zoe interjected.

"Zoe, I thought we'd made it clear that—"

"Oh, quit babbling. I'm coming along, if only to see how Mr. T here cracks the lock. That counts as one of those things you can always use later. Plus, it's not like the place is a sealed-up crime scene."

She turned toward the kitchen. "What, you have to go harvest that coffee? Move it!" She pulled a Gauloise from her pack and lit it up, grinning. "When we going?"

Jan sighed. "Tomorrow, ten p.m. Wear something low-key. Preferably no high heels."

Chapter 16

Patrick sat between stacks of files, wearily stirring his coffee. He just wanted to go home and sleep for a week. His run-in with Jan had not given him peace. At first he'd wanted to laugh at Jan's accusations, and yet the way Jan had laid them out did make them sound convincing. He didn't know what to think. It was no different from his own speculations about Jan being the serial killer. Once the evidence gets interpreted another way, every theory disintegrates into nothing.

He did not like Jan. That, combined with his shot at solving a big case as head of Team Judge, had blinded him to everything else. He was realizing his mistake too late.

He looked around the office. At this early hour, only Jan's friend Andreas Emmert was at his desk. The man's typing was the sole sound on the floor. Andreas had doubted Patrick's theory from the beginning. He'd never bought the idea that Jan had murdered Judge Holoch. Patrick should've listened to the guy.

"Morning, Andreas."

"Nothing new on Jan's hideout," Andreas said without taking his eyes off the screen.

"It's not necessary."

Andreas stopped typing.

"Maybe we should be investigating other angles," Patrick suggested.

"Other angles?"

"Such as ruling out Jan as the serial killer, and coming up with new suspects."

"Uh . . ." Andreas scratched at his head, confused.

"It's a long story," Patrick told him. "It all started yesterday, when I was just getting home . . ."

•   •

It was one of those middle-class housing developments near a subway station. Row houses with little yards set close to schools and a daycare. Every half hour a bus passed through the street, which was lined with midrange cars.

It was 11:00 p.m. Jan had waited till all the lights in the neighboring houses had been extinguished. He still felt wiped out, but the painkillers were working their magic. Chandu fiddled with the lock while Zoe tapped her foot, impatient as usual. Not being allowed to light up a cigarette was really wearing on her nerves. She had dyed her hair black, and she wore dark pants and a thick, warm black-leather jacket. With the huge flashlight in her hand, she looked like the perfect cliché of a burglar. All that was missing was the black mask.

Jan finally heard that welcome click. Chandu shouldered the door open and they darted inside. The air was stagnant. The burglar gods were looking out for them, though, because the shutters were rolled down and the blinds pulled shut. In here their flashlight beams would not give them away.

"What now?" Zoe whispered.

"You can talk normal," Jan replied. "As long as we don't knock over any furniture, no one's going to hear us."

"Oh," she said. She shone her light around as if expecting an ax murderer around every corner, but she didn't seem nervous. He'd never seen her so steely.

"We should split up," Jan said. "Zoe searches the basement, I stay here, and Chandu goes upstairs."

The medical examiner headed to the basement stairway while the big man made his way upstairs. Jan stood in the middle of the living room and circled his flashlight beam, trying to form an initial impression. The Esels' house was a typical single-family home. Bland from the outside and even more so inside. Shelves full of items found in a million similar homes. A handful of CDs, a few books, souvenirs from vacations, cheap prints from furniture stores. The leather couch, which had clearly served its time, was set in front of a flat-screen TV and DVD player. The half-open kitchen was small and not especially well equipped.

Jan took books from the shelf, searching for any hidden notes. He opened CD cases and confirmed that the silver discs inside matched. Then he looked under the couch and was just scanning his light along the floor when a loud clang made him jolt.

"My bad," Zoe shouted up from the basement.

Jan closed his eyes, sighing. What he'd give for his old investigations team. He went into the kitchen, set dishes aside, and checked the cabinets, then opened the washing machine, but nothing caught his eye in any way. He scrutinized every inch of the ground floor for an hour. Then he dropped onto the couch. He needed to rest a moment. His injury was bothering him. He felt ten years older. Just as he was shutting his eyes, he heard Zoe coming up the basement stairs. She stood behind him.

"I'm not certain," she said, "but I might have found something."

Jan got up. "What exactly?"

"It's hard to say. Call Mr. T and come down to the basement." With that, she went back downstairs.

"I can hear you guys." Chandu was coming down his stairs. He and Jan followed Zoe to the basement.

"What's up, Lady Cadaver?"

"Check this out," she said, her voice clearly excited. "I went about my search down here systematically. From rear to front. Then right to left. The walls are spaced evenly. Over there is a little storage room." Her head jerked to the right. "On the other side, there's nothing. Except for the wall."

"What if they needed room for pipes, something else like that?" Jan said.

"The shaft for pipes and wiring, it's back there behind us."

"Maybe they didn't include that area in the foundation, for structural reasons."

Zoe shook her head. "There's something behind the wall. One part of it is made from stagrock."

"It's called sheetrock," Chandu corrected her.

"Whatever."

Jan studied the wall. "Could be possible, but I don't see any way in. Whoever was hiding something back here would have to break through the wall to retrieve it."

"What I thought at first too, but check out that wallpaper."

Jan felt along the wall. "Thick, lots of fibers. What's so weird about that?"

"Only this stretch of wall is covered with wallpaper."

"Why just cover one part of a basement wall?"

"That's what I'm wondering," Zoe replied.

"Well, then . . ." Jan ripped down wallpaper. A bare wall appeared behind it. A person had to look closely to make out two hinges and a small finger hole. Jan stuck his finger in and pulled. The door opened with a faint creak.

"Holy shit," Zoe said as their three flashlights lit up the room.

Jan's mouth dropped open. No words came out.

The room was lined with narrow shelving holding countless movies. Most of them were older movies, copied from VHS onto CD or DVD. All had one thing in common: they were child porn. The room was every pedophile's dream.

"Fucking bastard," Chandu said.

"Who can even watch sicko shit like this?" Zoe remarked.

"I don't think the Esels were the ones watching it," Jan said.

"What?"

"Every movie here has at least five copies. I'm thinking the Esels had a thriving little racket selling child porn."

"And to think I felt sorry for the woman," Chandu said. "They got what they deserved, at least."

"Let's start going through this," Jan said. "We have to be done before it gets light out. Later, at home, we can speculate on how it all fits." He turned to Chandu. "Are you done upstairs?"

"Not completely," he replied. "I found a couple photo albums in some kind of den. I was about to go through them when Zoe called us."

"This room's too small for three," Jan said. "I'll keep looking upstairs. Take photos of all of it. Keep an eye out for names of possible clients, but don't take anything. Put everything back in its place. Tomorrow I'll be tipping off Homicide, so get those gloves on."

On the way upstairs, Jan looked at the clock. It was after two. In three hours they had to be out of here so they wouldn't run into any early risers, bread trucks, or paperboys. Still, there was a chance the Esels had done him the favor of taking photos of some of their clients.

Jan held a photo album and paged through it. "Construction 2001," it read on the front. The first shots showed the excavating. Then came the basement, walls, ceiling, and the roof. The topping-out ceremony was one big party. The beer-garden tables were practically bowing under all the food and drink. They had maybe forty guests there. Children frolicked around, and two dogs were tussling over an old cable. Horst and Sarah Esel looked happy.

Jan turned pages. By evening, the guests were clearly on their way to getting drunk. The next photo had been cut out in the middle, the lower part removed. Only five faces could be seen. Standing before the celebration wreath, all friends in complete harmony, were Horst and Sarah Esel, Judge George Holoch, and Michael Josseck. Jan had always guessed a connection between the four, but the fifth person shocked the breath out of him.

It was Father Anberger.

He had more hair on his head and looked younger, but that was his neighbor in the picture, unmistakably.

"Goddamn it," Jan said. Now everything was clear. The priest's interest in the case. His willingness to help. Jan felt like he'd been slapped. He had trusted the old man, but it turned out he'd only wanted to spy on Jan. He set the album down and ran down the stairs.

"Chandu, Zoe!" he shouted through the house. "Drop everything. We have to go."

Zoe appeared at the basement steps. "We're not done yet."

"We got what we need," Jan told her. "I'll tell you all about it in the car."

• •

"Father Anberger?" Chandu couldn't believe it. He drove them down the empty city highway. "I never would've guessed."

"It fits," Zoe said. "Now we have the connection to Jan."

"But we're missing a motive," Jan said.

"It's obvious," Zoe explained. "Father Anberger found out what kind of sick bastards his friends were. Then he found a passage in the Bible that justified brutal vengeance for the sins, and he went off."

"But why frame me for it?"

"So he'd be left alone," Zoe replied. "While the police are focused on you, he's spying out his next victim. He was friends with all of them, so he could easily get into their homes. Then he either shocks them with the stun gun or mixes drugs into their drink, and then he can do with them what he wants."

"I don't believe this." Jan buried his face in his hands. "Father Anberger, a psycho serial killer? I cannot have been that wrong about a person."

"Don't act so surprised," Zoe said. "There are hundreds of psychopaths who've used religion to justify brutal killings."

"People like that were nuts from the time they were born, though," Jan said. "Father Anberger is a considerate man, admired in his congregation. No religious maniac could keep up a masquerade for so long."

"Sometimes we don't know people as well as we think."

"What's the plan?" Chandu asked.

"We go over to Father Anberger's."

"At three in the morning?"

"All the better. Then he'll be at home."

"You do know that police are still observing the building," Chandu reminded him. "Even if Patrick did let you go, they haven't lifted the manhunt for you."

"There's a little hidden path around my building that leads to the rear entrance. At this hour we'll be able to get in without being seen."

"So what do we do then?" Zoe asked. "Shoot the priest?"

"I'll confront him with all the facts. Then we'll see what drove him into doing this, why he picked me to be the fall guy. I trusted him and confessed it all to him, but he only used the knowledge to throw me to the vultures." Jan pounded on the seat in rage. He felt so damn betrayed.

"When do we get there?" he said.

"Ten minutes."

"Good," Jan said. It was about time he put an end to all this.

•   •

It was a strange feeling being home again. Jan had dreamed of this day again and again, yet his return was not like he'd hoped. He tiptoed up the stairs, Zoe and Chandu in tow. It was dark, the halls empty. He cursed at how loud the stairwell was, his soft footsteps echoing like thunder. Even so, all remained calm. No door opened and no lights turned on to give them away.

At the door to Father Anberger's apartment, Jan gave Chandu the signal, and he went to work on opening the door. They would surprise Father Anberger inside his apartment. The more unprepared someone was, the more you could find out. So if the three of them had to pull the old man out of bed, that was a good thing.

Jan felt torn between rage and betrayal. He had believed that Father Anberger was his friend, and even more than that, his confidant. But the priest had not only lied to him, he had used Jan's confessions against him.

Chandu bumped at the blank key in the lock. He needed only two attempts and the door came open. As if on silent command, the three hurried inside and paused in the foyer, which led to the living room. Jan switched on his flashlight. And stopped himself from swearing out loud. This, he had not expected.

• •

Jan had been in the old priest's apartment only once before, when he'd helped the man with his groceries. At the time he'd noticed the spartan furnishings and the clinical order of things. Now the furniture was the same, but there was no more order. The kitchen floor was covered in the shards of a broken ceramic flower pot. Dirt and water had blended into a brown, pulpy puddle. The little table in the middle of the room was tipped on its side. A wooden chair with a busted backrest lay against it.

Chandu went into the bedroom and shone his flashlight around. Zoe checked the bathroom.

"No one here," the big man said. The medical examiner shook her head. Jan inspected the furniture and discovered a small drop of blood on the chair. Zoe bent down and examined the sticky glop.

"Not too old," she said. "From a few hours ago."

"What went on here?" Jan said, wracking his brain. "I just don't get it."

"If it wasn't for that blood? I'd guess a break-in," Zoe said.

"This looks like a struggle," Chandu remarked.

"But who was struggling, exactly?" Jan asked.

"Maybe it was the father and his next victim," Zoe said.

"All the victims were killed in their homes," Jan said. "Why would he bring someone here?"

"Who knows what a serial killer's thinking?" Zoe replied.

"I'm going with an abduction," Chandu said, shining his light over a house key and wallet left on a side table. "Someone nabbed the priest."

"Then there must be a third party. Judge Holoch, Michael Josseck, the Esels, and Father Anberger knew each other. With the first three, it's not hard to imagine them up to some disgusting shit, but how does a priest fit into this?"

232

"They got child abuse in the church too," Zoe said.

"We've just happened upon a child-porn ring," Chandu said. "What if the murderer is an abused child? When I think of all those DVDs at the Esels', there's a ton of suspects."

"They don't just have to be abused children," Zoe added. "Have to consider parents or friends too."

"So where's the connection to me?" Jan asked them.

"Maybe it was just bad luck," Chandu said. "The murderer sought you out as a scapegoat. Could be that you didn't even know him."

Jan cursed under his breath. Every time he thought he'd found the murderer, his hunch dissolved into nothing. He was relieved Father Anberger was only a victim, but it set him back. They still had nothing.

"The priest could still be alive," Jan began, "and if I call the police, my fellow cops will show up here at the door any minute. But every second I wait, his chance of survival keeps dropping. So. Check out everything. The apartment is small. I'll give us five minutes. Then we clear out and I'll report an abduction."

Zoe rushed into the bathroom as Chandu hurried into the bedroom. Jan started on the living-room cabinet. Two minutes later, he had found their clue.

Chapter 17

Jan stared at the picture in his hands. It was the same one he'd seen in Sarah and Horst Esel's photo album. But on this copy, the bottom area was not cut off. It showed a girl, sitting in the meadow and dreamily smelling a flower in her hand. The photo was about ten years old, but Jan knew that face like no other.

"Betty," he whispered.

"You find something?" Chandu shouted.

Jan started, stuck the picture in his bag.

"Yes. I don't know how it helps, but I'll tell you in a second. Let's get out of here quick."

A minute later they were back out in the open air, sneaking through the rear courtyard to the car. Jan started dialing on his cell before Chandu could drive off.

"Max," he said into the phone, "look and see if the Esels had any children."

"Just a sec," Max said. The sound of typing on the keyboard clattered in the background.

"They did," he confirmed. "Bettina and Johann."

"Goddamn it." Jan had suspected it. But finding out for sure was horrific. He felt like throwing up.

"You going to tell us?" Zoe asked him.

Jan sighed. Something inside made him want to resist sharing the news, as if he'd be sharing some private, intimate secret about Betty. But he had to start talking.

"Betty was the daughter of Sarah and Horst Esel."

"Oh, man," Zoe said.

"How do you know?" Chandu asked him.

"I found an old photo."

"I guess she changed her name? She wasn't Esel."

"Her last name was Windsten, but I never saw her ID. She must have changed it."

"I hate to reopen old wounds," Zoe began, "but this could be the reason your girlfriend killed herself."

Jan nodded. "Judge Holoch getting murdered brought it all back to her. Doesn't take much to guess she was abused for child porn too."

"My God," Chandu said. "Who does such a thing to a child?"

"At least we have a new suspect," Zoe said.

"Who you mean?" Chandu asked her.

"Well, the brother, right?" Zoe said to Jan, "Did you know him?"

"No. Her parents supposedly moved to Bavaria and had little contact with her. She never mentioned siblings."

"I hate to spoil your fun," Max's voice clanged through the phone, "but we can cancel the idea of Johann Esel as the murderer."

"How come?" Jan asked him.

"You can thank your fellow officers in Homicide for that. They went searching for any kids of Sarah and Horst Esel. They never found Betty—they lost her trail after she was nineteen years old. But Johann, he has been in a clinic since he was fourteen. He's got a whole range of mental disorders, the kind that keep you living in a closed institution for a long, long time."

"That's perfect," Zoe said. "Now we have our psycho."

"Actually not," Max remarked. "According to the notes, Johann is catatonic and can't move a finger. Jan's fellow cops followed up. He hasn't left his room for months. Surveillance camera recordings in his psychiatric ward confirm it."

"So we still got nothing," Jan said. "What we do is, we find Father Anberger and hopefully catch the killer in the act."

"Where are we supposed to look for him?" Chandu said.

"Normally, the murderer kills the victims at their homes," Jan observed. "Abducting him like this, it doesn't fit the normal picture."

"Father Anberger could have faked his abduction with the idea of trying to bolt," Chandu said.

"He didn't need to trash his apartment for that. He had enough time to take off. Pack a suitcase, buy the plane tickets, done. No, he was abducted."

"Maybe the murderer dragged him to some place with special meaning," Zoe said.

"Since we don't know who the murderer is, we can't know that," Jan replied.

"Well, it could also be a place that's important to Father Anberger," Chandu said.

"Meaning where?"

"That church, his old congregation."

"It's a possibility," Jan said. "The church is not even two minutes from here."

"We don't have anything better," Zoe said, lighting up a cigarette. "Let's head over."

Chandu made a breakneck maneuver changing lanes and stepped on the gas.

Jan pounded on the seat again in frustration. They should have broken into the Esels' house sooner. Then they would've found Father Anberger alive and would know who was behind all this.

"What's eating you, Jan?" Chandu asked him. "We're almost there."

"I'm pissed off, that's what, that the murderer's always one step ahead of us, that my instincts have totally failed me. First I suspect Horst Esel, then my coworker Patrick, and even Father Anberger. Each one of them was the perfect suspect—and now we still have no idea who's doing it."

"Don't jump to conclusions," Zoe warned him. "Apart from the Esels, who are certifiably dead, we can't rule anyone out. Patrick might be a terrific actor, or maybe you didn't know the old priest as well as you thought."

"Anything's possible," Jan said. "But we're talking about four murders at least. Judge Holoch, Michael Josseck, and the Esels. Maybe Betty's death was no suicide. And now, Father Anberger." He raised six fingers. "That would make six dead, and we're still stumbling around in the dark."

"We're closer to him than we've ever been," Chandu said. "If the killer took the priest into that church? We'll get him."

"Let's hope," Jan said.

Chandu drove past the church and parked the car on a side street. Then he reached under the seat and handed Jan a pistol.

"Please don't lose it this time."

Jan checked the ammo. He turned to Zoe. "Stay here."

"No way."

"Zoe," Jan said, on edge. "There might be a psychotic serial killer in there. This isn't a game. I'm not going to discuss it anymore."

"Then don't. I'm going in with you."

"You don't even have a weapon," Chandu said.

Zoe reached into her pants pocket and pulled out a silver surgical knife. She sprung open the scalpel blade with a little click. "Damascus steel with a special cutting edge," she explained. "Custom-made for my specific needs. Cost three thousand euros, but worth every cent. Compared to this, those scalpels from Forensics are just butter knives."

Zoe folded up the blade and sprang from the car. Jan released the safety on his gun and followed after her.

"So what's the plan, Mister Homicide Squad?"

"The church is closed at this hour," Jan said. "Let's check the doors anyway and see if we can get in somehow."

He pointed at Chandu and himself. "We will go first and you stay right behind us. Don't talk. If we say take cover, then jump for cover. We say get down, you're down on the ground a second later."

Zoe saluted.

"We'll start with the side entrance on the left," he said to Chandu.

All Jan's senses were keyed up. They had the element of surprise. If the murderer was inside there, they had to get as close as possible to him before he noticed. The church was vast and offered a lot of ways to escape. This psycho could not be allowed to slip out. He owed Betty that.

They made their way around the church, but every door was locked shut.

"Goddamn it," Jan whispered. Either the murderer didn't want to be interrupted, or they were simply all out of luck.

"Can you crack one of these locks?" he asked Chandu.

The big man shook his head. "These must be a hundred years old. We'd need a bigger key. I can't do a thing here with a little tool like this."

"We've wasted too much time looking for a way in. We'll have to bust in. No more element of surprise."

Jan took off his jacket, wrapped it around his hand, and punched through a window. The shards hitting the floor made a loud clang. He laid his jacket over the frame and climbed in. Once he'd made it, he guarded the window and waited for Chandu and Zoe to come inside.

The light in the church was dusky. Burning candles prevented utter darkness. They stood in a side aisle of the nave. Two banks of pews stood facing the altar. A small Maria figure glowed golden in a niche.

"Stay together," Jan whispered. He went out into the middle of the nave. After three steps, he stopped. He couldn't believe his eyes.

Up at the altar lay a huge crucifix. But instead of a wooden Jesus, Father Anberger lay on it. He was naked. His hands and feet were nailed to the wood. Blood was running out a gash on his right side. Apart from the priest, no one could be seen around. It was a ghostly stillness.

Jan had to see if Father Anberger was still alive, so he kept creeping along, ducking down. The cross lay a couple yards from the closest pew. He would have to give up his cover. He'd make a perfect target at the altar. Still, Chandu and Zoe could keep an eye out.

"You two stay here and cover me," he whispered. "I'll get closer." They both nodded.

Jan kneeled next to the cross and placed a hand on the priest's neck. The man's glassy pupils and lack of pulse told him Father Anberger was dead. The lifeless eyes stared at the ceiling. His mouth was stuffed with pages from a Bible; its empty binding lay next to the crucifix.

"We're too late," Jan said.

"The murderer can't be far," Zoe said. "The blood is barely clotted."

Zoe checked the body as Chandu stood guard next to her with his gun drawn. Jan went over to the top end of the crucifix. His eye caught, at the altar, a ring of intertwined twigs. He lifted it and almost cut himself.

"Crown of thorns," he muttered under his breath. "Didn't Jesus wear the crown on his head?" he asked them.

Zoe straightened up. "Yes. Why you asking?"

Jan's eyes widened. This scene was not finished yet. They'd disrupted the murderer.

"Goddamn it." He reached for his gun.

A bang pierced their ears, echoing through the nave. Zoe was thrown backward and Chandu doubled over, screaming. Jan lunged to his side as a second shot struck the altar just behind him. Splinters of stone scattered over them. He crawled behind a column while Chandu, wounded, pulled the motionless Zoe to the pews. If she'd taken a direct hit from the shotgun shell, she wouldn't survive more than a minute.

Another shot hammered into the columns. A splinter of stone grazed Jan's forehead.

"Bastard!" he yelled, getting out all his rage. A thin trickle of blood ran down his forehead. "Show yourself. Then we'll end this."

Chandu had squeezed in between two pews. The trail of blood along the floor was not a good sign. The big man shielded Zoe's body, aiming his gun in the shooter's direction.

Jan cursed himself for having left his cell in the car. It was routine not to carry a phone when called into action like this—a phone ringing at the wrong moment could pose a danger, and in the heat of action it was easy to forget to turn off the ringer. Now he'd give everything for his cell phone. He'd call Homicide, send all available units over here. Shootouts were a risky part of his job. But he'd brought his friends into it this time. And he didn't want to be responsible for their deaths.

He pressed against the column and rose up. This was no time for tactical maneuvers. Chandu was shot and Zoe was probably dying. He had to locate the killer. *Right now.* Every second counted.

"You're not getting out of here," he shouted. His voice echoed loudly through the church. He was hoping the murderer would reply so he could get a better fix on him.

Silence. Only the crackling of broken stone and wood disturbed the calm. Chandu ripped apart his shirt and wound it around his leg, his face twisting with pain. Zoe still lay on the floor, not moving.

"I called the homicide squad," Jan called out. He had to try. "In two minutes they'll be storming the place. Throw down your weapon and you'll come out of this alive."

Still no answer. Jan thought he heard candle wax dripping onto the floor. Then a voice spoke out. It left him speechless.

"You never were a good liar," said Betty.

Chapter 18

Jan's heart skipped a beat. He had to be hallucinating. Betty. He had seen the photos of her corpse. With that melted chain around her neck.

"It can't be," he gasped.

"You really didn't know?" A giggle echoed through the church. "Super Detective got conned by the girlfriend. That has to bruise a guy's ego."

"How did you . . . ?"

"A cadaver from the Charité," she said. "There was a fire in an apartment building. The dead woman fit my build. So I faked my death."

Her internship at the hospital. She had told him about it. She probably took the dead woman from Pathology. The theft was surely reported, but no connection would ever have occurred to him.

"It was all just pretend?" he asked her. "All those happy times together."

"Poor Janni," she taunted. "It wasn't your good looks that attracted me to you."

It all fit. The lengthy evenings spent telling her about his work. The way she had listened so attentively. Sometimes she'd even had follow-up questions.

"So I was just the fall guy?"

"Don't act so hurt," she said. "You had your fun."

Jan was trying to place Betty's voice inside the church. She was somewhere out in front of him. In an alcove, beyond the column. She had to be aiming her shotgun, waiting for him.

"So where do we go from here?" he said, trying to keep the conversation going.

"Stupid question," she replied coldly. "I'm going to kill all of you. By the time your fellow cops find out, I'll be lying on a beach in the sunshine."

"You're not going to get out of this."

She gave a loud sigh. "I've been planning this for years, Janni. If I hadn't decided to kill the good Father Anberger here at church, I'd be on a plane and you'd be dealing with his corpse right now. But I found this place somehow . . . fitting. He was actually supposed to choke on that Bible of his, the one he used to chastise me with before he did the deed on me. But then I saw that crucifix."

A bright light flashed through the church.

"Just a little souvenir photo," Betty said.

He heard her cocking the shotgun.

"It was fun."

Something hit the floor next to him. Jan turned, aiming his pistol. A bent candlestick.

He cursed at himself. The oldest trick in the world. He dropped to the floor. The same moment, a shot rang out. He felt the hot draft of small shot whizzing by his face. She'd missed. He raised his gun, shooting blindly in Betty's direction. After the third bullet, he heard moaning. He rolled onto his side, turning to look and aiming his gun.

Betty fell to the floor. She was pressing a hand to her neck. Blood flowed through her fingers. His shot had struck the carotid artery. The shotgun lay next to her. He dropped his gun, ran to her. He pulled off his jacket and pressed it to her wound, but the stream of blood would not stop.

"No, goddamn it!" he said, frantic.

Betty's eyes raised up to him. She appeared to want to say something, but nothing came from her mouth except a gurgle. Then she smiled. She squeezed his hand. And it was over.

•   •

Jan experienced the next few hours like some silent observer hovering above the chaos. When the police reached the crime scene, he was still sitting next to Betty's corpse. Someone put handcuffs on him and led him out of the church. Outside, a sea of lights met him. Countless police vehicles and ambulances blocked the street. Sirens pierced the night's silence. Men in uniforms and paramedics in white coats ran back and forth. Two people were loaded into an ambulance. Someone put him in the rear seat of a car. Then they drove off, away from the noise and the lights.

He spent the ride in total silence. He didn't know how long it lasted, had no idea where they were going. The car stopped in front of a large building, and he was pulled inside and into a stark room. A man spoke to him, but he didn't understand the words. Another man set a glass of water on the table in front of him. But Jan could not move. He felt nothing. No thirst, no hunger, no pain, no sorrow. His head was a vacuum, aside from one word that repeated relentlessly.

"Betty."

•   •

Around noon, Jan emerged from his stupor long enough to recognize his former boss, Klaus Bergman. The man brought him a cup of coffee, and its aroma pulled him further into the present. For the first time, Jan noticed how tired and hungry he was. He reached for the cup, drank, and contorted his face in disgust. The coffee tasted terrible. He had grown too accustomed to his friend's finer blend.

He dropped the cup in horror. Coffee flowed across the table, dousing Bergman's jacket. Chandu. The last time he'd seen him, he lay bleeding in the church.

"What about—"

"They're doing okay," Bergman reassured him, wiping the coffee off his suit. "Your friend and that lunatic from Forensics are both alive. I don't have the details on their injuries, but the bullet wounds weren't critical."

"Zoe took a full load of shot. People don't survive that—"

"What part of 'wounds not critical' do you not understand?" Bergman cut in.

Jan stood. "I have to get to them."

"The fuck you do. Just sit there on your butt and tell me a few things."

"You don't understand," Jan told him. "The two of them got shot because of me."

"I understand one thing: you're not a doctor, and you can't do anything for them at the hospital. I've given instructions that I be told of any change in their condition. They survived, so until I hear otherwise, they are not dead."

Jan needed to see for himself that Chandu and Zoe were doing fine—but Bergman would not let him go. He had a tough time sitting down again. He rubbed at his face, weary. The last few days had taken all his strength. He was slowly perceiving the magnitude of what had taken place the previous night. He had shot his girlfriend dead. The fact that she was insane did not make it any better. He just wanted to get into bed and sleep for the next hundred years.

"Can I have something to eat?" he asked. "Otherwise I won't be able to get out a clear sentence."

Bergman, clearly irritated, stood and yanked the door open.

"You guys head over to the donut shop and grab a dozen," he bellowed into the corridor. "Two vanilla for me."

He slammed the door shut, sat back down.

"Okay, Jan," he said gently. "Just start from the beginning."

Jan started talking. About his escape. How Chandu had put him up. How Zoe and Max had teamed up with him. How they had tracked down the serial killer. He left out no details.

In the meantime, a coworker came in with a box of donuts. Jan scarfed down several without pausing his story. His stomach and his circulation thanked him. His account ended with the death of his former girlfriend. Then he turned to Bergman.

"I have a hunch, but it would be nice to know why Betty did it all."

The chief of detectives sighed and laid a stack of notebooks on the table, all inscribed with the word "Diary." Jan recognized Betty's handwriting.

"We found them in her car," Bergman said. "We've been analyzing the passages the whole night. In these journals, we found a life of misery for one Bettina Esel, who you knew as Betty Windsten. Many of the entries are horrifying. One of your coworkers puked his guts out after reading it."

Bergman ran his fingers through his hair, as if he didn't know where to begin.

"The sexual abuse started at thirteen. At first, only Bettina's father was assaulting her. The mother knew about the rape but was too weak to get Horst Esel to stop.

"At fourteen, Bettina was sold for the first time. The client was Judge Holoch, who was into little girls. Her description of the rape is hard enough to bear, but it also gives some insight into Holoch's true character. He had a great time beating her up. What started with a few slaps in the face turned into this orgy of beatings. Holoch let himself loose a little more with each visit, eventually putting her into the hospital. The parents, they just called the injuries an accident and got away with it.

"Then the writing style started to change. It became dry, almost matter-of-fact, as if she was some impartial third party, observing events from a distance.

"She had barely recovered when a new client came to her bed."

"Michael Josseck," Jan said.

"She described the building contractor as a fat stinking swine, though he didn't hit her. Compared to Holoch, he was bearable."

"So Holoch wasn't coming to her anymore?"

"No. Our guess is that around this time he was taking it out on other girls, the ones you found in his photo album."

"Did anyone find out who the girls were?"

"It's still too early for that. I've formed an investigations team to find the women. I'm not too confident, though, since some of the photos are ten years old. Also, the facial injuries in the pictures are going to make it tough for any recognition software."

"That explains why she beat Holoch to death, but why did she choose concrete down the throat for Josseck's murder?"

Bergman hesitated again. Their discussion was clearly putting a strain on him. "The builder, he was into oral sex."

"What was with those wood swords in her dad's body, and flashy costume rings in her mother's eyes?"

"Playthings."

"Playthings?"

"When Josseck was satisfied with her, Bettina got a present. After one especially nasty rape, Bettina's father gave her a wooden sword and her mother gave her some cheap rings."

Jan shuddered. He was having a tough time keeping the donuts down. Who treats their own daughter like that?

"A year later, another client came," Bergman continued. "Father Anberger."

Jan groaned. He knew it.

"Father Anberger had been a friend of the Esels. He'd even baptized Bettina. But at some point he lost control of his sex drive and started doing things to her regularly. The really sick part was that he blamed Bettina for her sins. She was this devil in the flesh, come into the world to seduce him. What religious bullshit. Before getting raped, she would have to pray with him. After the rapes, he'd read from the Psalms."

"What a life," Jan said, shaken.

"A life is not what I'd call it," Bergman added.

"How did she escape this living hell?"

"Thanks to her superior intelligence. Despite being sexually abused, she was an outstanding student. As the head of her class, she received a stipend to study medicine."

"And her parents just let her go?"

"The journals don't say exactly. But once she'd reached legal age, Holoch, Josseck, and Father Anberger lost interest in her. She was probably too old for them by then. If I had to guess, I'd go with her taking off for good in the dead of night. One day she was gone, and then she began her studies. By then her name was Bettina Windsten, though she doesn't mention why she chose that last name."

Bergman paged through his records.

"Over the next few years, she lived the life of a medical student and, in her free time, worked on planning the murders. She was going to make her rapists and her parents pay for her suffering. She went about it with mechanical precision. She made a list of subjects and skills she needed to learn in order to commit the perfect murder. These included certain medical techniques, and also criminal skills like scoping out weak spots in secure homes and opening locks.

"She picked out her male lovers for their usefulness to her. These included doctors and police officers but also small-time criminals, anyone she could learn something from.

"You shouldn't blame yourself, Jan. She could act the part perfectly. Before you, countless men fell for her charms, and not one doubted she loved them."

"Cold comfort." Jan still couldn't believe that it was all pretend. "So, I was just another thing on her list."

Bergman paused. "Yes. With all you know about homicide investigations, you filled in one last blank."

"Did she choose me because of Judge Holoch's ruling as well?"

"She describes it as an 'unexpected bonus.' She hadn't dared hope to get so lucky. With her homicide detective having a possible motive, she killed two birds with one stone."

"That's why she was so interested. The girlfriends I had up till then? Didn't want to know a thing about what I did—but Betty used to ask me about it every night. One time I even gave her a tour of the Homicide offices."

"According to the list in her journal, she had compiled everything she needed for the perfect murder before she got started."

"Faking her death with a farewell note—was that part of the plan too?"

Bergman nodded. "She was waiting for a burn victim to be delivered to Pathology, one roughly her size. Then she stole the corpse from the Charité and brought it home."

"It's that easy?"

"Actually, no, but Bettina was working it out for a long time. She had reconned a way of stowing the body into her car without getting caught. She had factored in security staff as well as the cameras. Falsified documents were perfect too."

"So how did she get the body into her apartment?"

"She had that figured out from way back. Her apartment had to have an underground garage without surveillance inside, along with an elevator."

"Unbelievable," Jan said. "How long did she work on her murder plans?"

"Three years."

"And once the corpse was in the apartment?"

"One of her first boyfriends was a gas-line fitter. She knew just what she needed to turn to make the apartment blow to pieces. Her knowledge of forensics helped her prepare the corpse in such a way that no one would ever doubt that Bettina Windsten had committed suicide. The piercing and your necklace were clear identifying features. Along with the suicide note, no one had any idea that she'd faked her death. So. From then on, she wasn't on the detectives' radar at all. The dead don't fit the criminal profile."

"Was I supposed to die in the explosion?"

"No. Apparently you were in the wrong place at the wrong time."

"Where was she hiding out the whole time?"

"At the home of a girlfriend who's studying abroad in South America for half a year. She was to water the flowers and feed the fish. The big building was impersonal enough that no one was surprised at seeing a new neighbor. At that point she knew everything about her victims. Their habits, the route they took to work, all their little everyday rituals.

"I'll spare you the gruesome details about George Holoch's death, but she describes murdering him as the first orgasm she ever had in her life. From then on, she wasn't of sound mind any more. Plenty of people dream of killing someone. Some plan it, but only the insane ones carry it out."

Jan felt a pang in his heart. He couldn't believe Betty was responsible for all of it.

"Does it say in her diary how she dragged me into the whole thing?"

"It was planned so perfectly," Bergman continued. "The body had to be stolen on a Sunday evening. At that time, there's fewer hospital staff. She calculated, based on your body weight, the amount of knockout drops and drugs to put you out for all of Saturday as well as rob you of your memory. According to her notes, you two took some aspirin after going out drinking Friday. The water she handed you had the first dose of knockout drops.

"She kept you drugged until that evening. Then she pressed your fingers to the murder weapon, took your blood, and removed your shirt—the one we later found to have Judge Holoch's blood on it. Then she gave you a major dose of ecstasy."

Bergman clutched his coffee. The long night had left its mark on him, too.

"Bettina wore black overalls that she'd outfitted with padding on the shoulders and chest. Together with military boots, she looked like an athletic male. An observer would never have taken her for the dainty woman that she was.

"She packed up her murder weapons, took your keys, and parked the car so that Holoch's neighbor would be bothered by it. She climbed over the balcony of Holoch's house and lay waiting for him. Then she paralyzed him with a stun gun and broke his leg, which made him more or less helpless. From there she proceeded quite methodically. She chose spots on Holoch's body that would not kill him before she bashed in his skull.

251

"She spotted your shirt with Holoch's blood, dispersed your blood around the scene, and drove your car to your apartment. Down in the basement, she tossed the main murder weapon into your neighbor's poorly locked storage room. She went back home, removing any clues, and waited till you woke up from your drugged-out delirium. That's where Patrick found you and brought you to the station."

"Did she ever consider that I'd bolt from custody?"

"Actually she didn't, but her faked suicide made her think she was clear of you, custody or no."

"For the most part, it was going perfectly," Jan said. "Until Michael Josseck died, I wasn't even sure myself whether I might have killed the judge."

"She used the time to observe her next victim, updating her notes as she went. A few days later came the chance to murder Michael Josseck.

"She broke into his apartment and spiked his cognac with drugs to put him under. The contractor came home and had a drink, just like he did every night. When he woke up, he found himself tied up tight down on the floor. She kept Josseck's mouth open with a spreader and poured the concrete down his throat.

"Even that, she didn't leave to chance. She'd tested different types of concrete beforehand, mixing them with various amounts of water until she had the ideal formula for carrying in her pack for the right length of time. When you were blacked out, she'd pressed your hand around that tube for pouring in the concrete. That's what set us on your trail once and for all."

"Which worked too," Jan said. "But that's when I was sure I wasn't the murderer."

Bergman shrugged. "Minor detail, from her point of view. The evidence alone for Judge Holoch was already so clear-cut that nothing you could have said would have helped you."

"And if I had ended up in custody? Then it would have been obvious I couldn't be the murderer, not once Michael Josseck was murdered."

"She didn't count on us connecting the dots so fast between the victims. Worst-case scenario, she would've just shot her parents and Father Anberger."

"But the Esels saw the link, so they went underground?"

"Betty didn't think her parents capable of that. It threw a wrench into her plans. But the Esels didn't know their own daughter was the murderer, so they fled to their vacation home. It wasn't registered in their name and was really the perfect hiding place. Except for the fact that Bettina knew about it."

"I had to listen to her parents dying. But what did she do, exactly?"

"Bettina's account reads like a lover's poem. From the way she confided in her diary, you can tell she felt joy in committing these murders.

"She took her parents by surprise. She immobilized her father with the stun gun and tied him up. Her mother panicked, fled into the bedroom. Bettina described her in the diary as a 'hysterical cow who goes into shock from the slightest strain.' She had expected Sarah Esel to go hiding under the bed. That she'd call you, she didn't expect that.

"While her mother was on the phone with you, Bettina went to work on her father. She had sharpened three wooden swords, and she drove them into his abdomen. Here again, she picked out spots that didn't cause immediate death, but rather let him die slowly.

"Then she pulled her mother out from under the bed, beat her, took her head between her legs, and carved out her eyes. It thrilled Bettina to see her crawling around the room blinded. When that stopped being fun, she killed her mother and inserted the costume

253

jewelry rings into her eye sockets. It was only then that she noticed the phone."

"Now I know who stabbed me outside of Chandu's building," Jan said.

"You had massive good luck. Seems you had told her about your friend's hideout."

"That's how she knew where I was."

"She was waiting for you, wanted to slit your stomach open."

"My leather jacket saved my life."

"Actually, it was you staggering out into the street before she could deal you the lethal blow—and luck. You almost got run over by a car, and being seen felt too risky for her, so she took off. She knew you weren't dead, but she'd neutralized you long enough for her to continue with her plans."

"It never would have entered my mind that she was the murderer. And if Chandu and Zoe hadn't carried me out of the hospital, I'd have ended up in police custody. Then we never would have caught her."

"It was the little things that brought her down in the end. We were lucky. Her plan was too good to go wrong."

"Where did it fail, then?"

"The fun she had tormenting them. If she'd just murdered the priest in his apartment and taken off, we never would've caught her. But she gave herself too much time with him."

"If Zoe hadn't found that secret room at the Esels, we never would've thought of it."

"Why she hauled him into the church is not clear to us. From earlier entries, we can conclude that she liked to go to church as a girl. After her father abused her for the first time, she stopped going altogether because she felt impure. From then on, her sheltered childhood was over. I guess you could say she wanted to put brackets around a whole life. There, at that very point where she'd experienced her last happy moment, she was going to close it off."

Bergman held up one of the journals and showed it to Jan. On the cover was a drawing of a woman, depicted like a white-marble statue, clad in a white toga. Cloth covered her hair. She cradled a little flame in her hands. The glowing light illuminated her face, contorted in sorrow. Tears ran down her cheeks, as if she carried some insufferable burden.

"Do you know who that is?" Bergman asked.

"It's Hestia," Jan replied. "The goddess of the family, home, and the hearth fire. Betty told me about her, about how significant she was in the Greek pantheon."

"So why is she crying?"

"She's mourning for lost innocence."

Chapter 19

Jan sat next to Zoe's hospital bed. She had a sling on one arm and was hooked up to a lot of blinking machines. She'd taken a direct hit of shotgun fire, but the bulletproof vest under her leather jacket had stopped the worst of it. Still, a broken rib had damaged her lung. After the operation they moved her to intensive care, but the doctor had reassured them that she was out of the woods.

In bed, the small woman looked fragile. Considering how self-confident she always acted, it was hard to imagine that anything at all could knock her over. She opened her eyes, weary, and turned to Jan.

"Shit," was her first word. "I almost bite the big one, and you're the first person I see?"

Jan laughed. A huge weight dropped from his shoulders. "I'm sorry, Zoe. I just needed to see for myself that you're still alive."

She looked around the room. "You seen my cigarettes?"

"I don't think you're supposed to smoke in intensive care."

"Don't care." She pressed and pressed at a button on a remote. A moment later a nurse came jogging into the room. Zoe started explaining to the woman, in her less-than-endearing way, that she needed something to smoke at once, otherwise she would pull all the tubes out of her arms and make a run for the nearest kiosk.

At first the nurse tried arguing reasonably. She explained to Zoe why smoking after surgery was not a great idea, but soon she saw how pointless this tactic was and resorted to Zoe's level. When two doctors came running in and Zoe threatened them with a horrible death if she could only get near a scalpel, Jan took the opportunity to exit the room. Zoe was back again. He wouldn't have to worry about her at all.

·   ·

It was a strange feeling, returning to Homicide. Jan stood a moment before the old building, looking over the facade. He absorbed every detail. That antique stonework that reminded him of an old castle, with its four statues carrying baskets on their shoulders. He'd always noticed how the modern, green police shield affixed to the building didn't really fit in.

Jan had needed a week to process everything. The first few nights he had woken up soaked in sweat, in fear that police were going to storm his apartment. Paranoia had become his permanent companion.

After he'd visited the hospital, he had confined himself to home, but memories were all around him. He only had to pass by Father Anberger's apartment, one story below his, for the images to come rushing back, beating on his head like a hammer.

Max had been the first to drag him out of it. Two days ago, he'd showed up at Jan's door with four bags of burgers and milkshakes and had kept pounding until Jan finally opened. They had watched Premier League football and stuffed themselves with junk food.

Jan didn't even know what they had talked about, but it had nothing to do with murder or rape. After the young hacker left, Jan had slept without nightmares for the first time.

The next morning he had informed Bergman that he wanted to start back at work again. He wouldn't be needing any more time. Bergman wasn't easy to convince, but eventually, he'd gotten the chief of detectives to at least consent to discussing his return.

Most likely there would be a horde of attentive psychologists waiting in Bergman's office to assess Jan, he realized. They'd want to weigh his each and every word like gold and make him interpret inkblots. But that wasn't going to stop him.

He took one last look at the front of the old building and headed for the front door.

"Off to battle," he said to himself. As he walked inside, the men at the entrance greeted him uneasily. Until very recently he had been the most wanted man in Berlin.

He stopped by his old office. Everything was still in its place. Andreas was sitting opposite his desk. They had survived countless cases together and just as many parties. Andreas waved to him with a big grin. Jan waved back—and almost ran right into Patrick. His colleague drew back a step and forced a smile. An awkward silence arose. Jan didn't know what to say, and Patrick just looked embarrassed.

"Hi, Jan," he said. "All healed up?"

"Getting there. Doing without the painkillers now."

"All right," Patrick said and drank a sip of coffee to mask his unease.

"I'm on my way to Bergman. Want to speak to him about my coming back."

"That's good. We have more than enough work."

"A new case?"

"Nasty stuff." Patrick waved away the thought. "We need all the help we can get."

"If Bergman will let me," Jan said, shrugging, "I'm there."

"Then I'll hope for the best."

Jan wrung his hands together, uneasy. "Guess I'll get going."

Patrick, nodding, went to shuffle on by him. He patted Jan on the shoulder like a friend would. "Good luck." Then he disappeared in his office.

Jan watched him go. Their talk was trivial, like all conversations with Patrick, but this time it had felt different. It had sounded something like *Welcome back*.

• •

Instead of psychologists, Bergman and the chief of police were waiting for him. Berlin's top brass had on the friendly-yet-opaque expression that Jan knew from so many photos. Jan wondered whether the chief being here was a good sign or not. He nodded politely to him as he sat next to Bergman at the desk, his hands relaxed flat over his stomach.

"You sure caused us a ton of trouble," Bergman began, getting right to it. True to form, his boss had no time for empty small talk. No "How you doing?" or "How's it going, getting over having shot your girlfriend dead?" Nope. Always right between the eyes. After all Jan had been through, this one invariable constant was somehow comforting.

"I'm sorry," Jan said, to be on the safe side. For what, exactly, he wasn't sure.

"All charges will be dropped, and your suspension is cancelled."

Jan shrugged a little. This was probably the least of it.

"There will still be an investigation into your exchanging fire with Bettina Esel, but I don't expect problems. The crime-scene investigators have confirmed what you've stated."

Bergman glanced at the police chief. His facial expression had not changed.

"Since you're currently the hero of the Berlin Police, and the press thinks you're so amazing, you're going to get a commendation, one that we will market to the media—they're going to love it, of course. We'll see if we can get the mayor behind it too."

The last thing I need, Jan thought.

"Anything else?" Bergman asked him.

"I want my own team."

"Come again?"

"My own team," Jan told him. "People who only work with me on cases. Just my team."

"This isn't fucking *CSI Berlin*," Bergman fumed. "Where did you get such an idea?"

"You asked me if there was anything else. So I'm telling you."

"It was just a rhetorical question. That's when you go, 'No thank you, Herr Bergman. I don't need a thing.'"

"If I'm to play performing seal for the media, I want some benefits. Like choosing the people who work with me."

Bergman was about to respond with an irate remark when the police chief leaned over to him and whispered something in his ear. Jan's boss calmed down, reluctantly.

"All right, fine," he grumbled. "So which officers get to join your team?"

"First off, Zoe Diek."

"The blonde from Forensics?"

"That's the one."

"She's not even a cop."

"But she's clever and learns quickly. I want her with me."

"Apparently those knockout drops destroyed some of your brain cells."

Jan sighed and looked at the clock. "I'd like to keep chatting, boss, but I'm all out of time. I have an interview to get to."

"What kind of interview?"

"A large German daily wants to know what it's like for a former murder suspect to return to his job. How his coworkers are treating him, whether things are like they used to be."

"Is that cleared with media relations?"

"Unfortunately not," Jan said. "When they called, I just had this . . . sudden inspiration."

Bergman shot up from his chair. "You trying to extort me?"

Jan scratched at his chin, thinking it over. Playing it up. "Come to think of it, yes, I am." He'd made up the story about the interview, but he'd clearly landed a direct hit. Even the police chief had winced at the mention of "a large German daily." Bergman was on the verge of charging him like a starving hyena.

"Very well. Take your forensics lady. Might there be anyone else?" Bergman asked, his voice irritated. "A pizza maker maybe?"

"Interesting suggestion, but that would be more for the cafeteria."

It was obvious Bergman did not find the comment funny.

"I would also like Chandu Bitangaro, as a paid informant. No one knows the Berlin underworld better than him."

"That bouncer and debt collector who aided you? You really have lost a few—"

"And one Maximilien Kornecker as well, a promising computer-science student who could work marvels for us. A work-study contract would make it easier to clear any bureaucratic hurdles while allowing him access to the system."

"I'm supposed to hire a hacker? I think I've heard—"

261

"Of course I'll need a budget too, so I can pay for my informants and any expenses that arise."

"Your own budget? Say one more word and I'll—"

"Fifty thousand euros would do." Jan calculated real quick. "For this year."

Bergman had no more responses left. His face had turned red. Inarticulate sounds came out of his mouth.

"We can talk about a new team vehicle and the dedicated office another time."

Bergman took a deep breath. "If you don't leave the room, and I mean now, I'll take you down right here and declare it was an accident."

Jan stood. "That would be a shame, considering I still have to finish writing my memoir. I have a tentative contract with a publisher. The working title is *From One Hell to the Next*. For the subtitle I was thinking something like *My Painful Return to Professional Life*."

Bergman planted his fists on the table and towered over Jan, ready to pounce. Then the chief of police laughed. It was an eerie sound in such a tense situation. Bergman looked over, confused.

The chief whispered something to him. Jan would have given his right hand to be able to hear it. Whatever his boss was hearing, it was not making him happy. They shared a few more whispered exchanges. Then the police chief stood up and gave Jan a terse nod as he left.

Once the door closed behind him, Jan waited for Bergman to start cursing him out. He had not lost his threatening demeanor. Jan could almost see the murder fantasies running through his head.

"All right," said Bergman, finally breaking through the silence. Jan could tell that what he was about to say wasn't coming easily. "The police chief likes your moronic idea, even though it's something only a halfwit dipshit like you could think up."

Jan fought a laugh. He'd never imagined he'd get away with it.

"You and your self-styled A-Team," Bergman snarled, looking disgusted, "will be special investigators working within Homicide. You'll receive your own cases, but once something goes wrong, I'm going to hang your ass out to dry in the front lobby." He took a deep breath, as if he himself couldn't even believe what he was saying.

"In return, you are going to play the perfect upstanding police officer for the media. You will smile at every press conference, telling Tom, Dick, and Jane Journalist how great we are and how amazing it is to be back at work. I want the teenagers to be beating themselves up in front of the police academy just to be let in."

Bergman's fingers drummed impatiently on the desk. "On Monday, at eight a.m., you will present to me your team of freaks. I'm only going to give you the really hard cases, and if the results of your investigations don't make even Batman himself green with envy, I'm going to send you down to the basement to sort the mail."

Jan nodded.

"Any of this gets leaked before Monday morning? I'll come over and I will shoot you. Got no idea how I'm going to explain this new team to your fellow cops. Maybe I'll put on some clown makeup and a red nose, you know, just to make it easier for them to laugh their asses off at me."

Jan saluted and stood up. "Till Monday." He shut the door behind him, grinning, more than satisfied. He heard yet another object hitting the wall. But by then he was already two offices down.

Epilogue

Chandu's favorite bar was hopping. The music blared too loud, drowning out all the regulars trying to talk. Up at the bar sat Chandu, Zoe, and Max. Both Jan's big friend and the medical examiner had been released from the hospital earlier that day, which had not stopped them from hitting all the bars.

The young hacker was in an equally good mood. His eyes were bright. He waved his green cocktail at Jan. As usual, Zoe ignored him as thoroughly as she did the bar's smoking ban, while Chandu refilled her glass from a whiskey bottle. His crutch was leaning against the bar. His leg wound would take weeks to heal; after that, he'd be his old self again. Zoe had weathered her injuries well too. She looked a little pale, maybe. But soon the shootout would be only a memory.

"You know, Zoe," Chandu said, slurring it a little and lifting his glass, "if you weren't such a bitch, I'd flat out ask you to marry me."

She toasted him back. "I'm a lesbian."

The disclosure made Chandu lose his train of thought. He furrowed his brow, trying to make sense of it.

"No matter," he said finally. "Sex isn't everything." He knocked back his whiskey in one gulp.

"Is to me," Zoe replied and drank hers down too.

Jan settled himself on the stool next to her.

"Janni," Zoe said, turning to him. "We've been waiting for you." She pushed a glass over and filled it from Chandu's bottle. Then she refilled hers.

She toasted Max, whose eyes were riveted on a buxom blonde, and kept her glass raised.

"To our Janni and his newly won freedom." And the three tipped back their whiskeys in one swig.

"Thanks," Jan said softly and drank as well.

Max devoted himself to watching the blonde, while Zoe and Chandu started discussing the point of marriage in the twenty-first century. Jan set down his glass on the bar and opened up his wallet. He eyed, wistfully, the photo of Betty and him. Her laughter would always be so charming and real in his memories. He still believed that she had liked him. He wasn't yet prepared for anything but that version of reality.

Then he felt the big hand of his friend on his shoulder. Chandu poured Jan a refill, while Zoe delivered a toast to the Berlin police. At some point the place got so full that the four had to press up against the bar. All around them it was just happy people, and after the third glass it felt the way it used to be. Back then. When Betty was alive.

About the Author

Alexander Hartung was born in 1970. He started writing while studying political economy and discovered his love for thrillers and historical novels. Hartung's first novel, the historical crime thriller *Die Rache des Inquisitors* (*The Inquisitor's Revenge*), was published in 2010. *Until the Debt is Paid* is set in Berlin, the city Hartung called home for a time while working as a management consultant. Hartung currently lives with his wife and child and their dog in his hometown of Mannheim, Germany.

About the Translator

Steve Anderson is a translator, a novelist, and the author of the nonfiction Kindle Singles *Double-Edged Sword* and *Sitting Ducks*. Anderson was a Fulbright Fellow in Munich, Germany. He lives in Portland, Oregon.

Made in the USA
Coppell, TX
19 May 2020